Praise for *Jezebel*

"Rich with historical detail and a fresh and convincing perspective. . . . Like so many strong women, Jezebel is loved, feared, and hated, especially by the men she rules. Megan Barnard's *Jezebel* is also strong, determined, and resourceful . . . historical fiction at its finest."

—Louisa Morgan, author of *A Secret History of Witches*

"In Megan Barnard's debut novel, *Jezebel*, the titular wicked queen of biblical lore gets a spirited makeover. . . . Redeeming the novel from well-worn tropes of female disempowerment is Barnard's subversive counternarrative. . . . This audiobook is a homage to the innate right to be heard."

—*The New York Times Book Review*

"[A] stunning first novel . . . A riveting story reinforcing the notion that there are two sides to every story. Barnard's eloquently written debut is perfect for fans of Madeline Miller's *Circe* or *The Song of Achilles*."

—*Library Journal* (starred review)

"Ambitious . . . a provocative concept."

—*Publishers Weekly*

PENGUIN BOOKS

the winter goddess

PHOTO BY ALEXANDRA PERRY

Megan Barnard is the author of novels born from an obsession with ancient myths, powerful women, and forgotten voices. When she's not writing, she's falling down rabbit holes of research and can share many a random fact, some of which occasionally even inform her writing. She lives in Maryland with her husband and her pup, Pippin.

ALSO BY MEGAN BARNARD

Jezebel

The

winter goddess

—《 》—

MEGAN BARNARD

PENGUIN BOOKS

PENGUIN BOOKS

An imprint of Penguin Random House LLC
1745 Broadway, New York, NY 10019
penguinrandomhouse.com

Set in FournierMTPro
Designed by Sabrina Bowers

LIBRARY OF CONGRESS CATALOGING-IN-PUBLICATION DATA
Names: Barnard, Megan, author.
Title: The winter goddess / Megan Barnard.
Description: New York : Penguin Books, 2025.
Identifiers: LCCN 2024037446 (print) | LCCN 2024037447 (ebook) |
ISBN 9780143137689 (paperback) | ISBN 9780593511800 (ebook)
Subjects: LCGFT: Mythological fiction. | Novels.
Classification: LCC PS3602.A83355 W56 2025 (print) |
LCC PS3602.A83355 (ebook) | DDC 813/.6—dc23/eng/20240819
LC record available at https://lccn.loc.gov/2024037446
LC ebook record available at https://lccn.loc.gov/2024037447

Printed in the United States of America
1st Printing

The authorized representative in the EU for product safety and compliance is
Penguin Random House Ireland, Morrison Chambers, 32 Nassau Street,
Dublin D02 YH68, Ireland, https://eu-contact.penguin.ie.

For Tyler (always, for everything)—

who taught me to love winter

The
winter
goddess

winter

before

In the beginning, there was darkness.

Then, Danu.

Not Danu the goddess, but Danu the mother. My mother.

Her green eyes always watched me—thoughtful, curious, and *questioning*, always questioning, as though she were waiting for me to become something—more, less. Different. Different than I was.

I had never felt this so much as I did on the day the snow fell.

I don't know how old I was, but a child still, and Danu and I had been walking through the deep parts of the forest, heading back to Tara. I was holding her hand and she was talking of this and that—Danu was always talking—when we crested the slope of a small hill, entering a clearing ringed with huge fir trees. I tilted my face up to see where they seemed to graze the sky and watched as something brushed the very tops of the branches—something white and gentle and mesmerizing. *Snow*, I somehow understood, though I had never seen it before.

I released Danu's hand as the snow began to fall faster and faster, whirling around me, clinging to my eyelashes and alighting on my outstretched arms. At first my skin stayed as it had always been—gently gold like Danu's—but as the snowflakes continued to fall, my body began to change. The blue started at the tips of my fingers, my nails turning dark as a winter's night, rivers of indigo snaking up my arms and twisting around my body until I was dappled with shades of blue from cerulean to sapphire. I was no longer simply standing in the landscape, I had somehow *become* the landscape, and when I waved my arms, my body swirled and shifted to match the striations of light and shadow around me.

I giggled, a joyous gurgle that erupted straight from my belly and whirled around to show my mother what had happened, but when I turned, I saw that Danu was not smiling as I expected, but was instead looking on me with despair, tears in her eyes. It was the first time I had ever seen my mother look so anguished.

"Don't you like it?" My voice was soft. It caught on the wind and suddenly it was everywhere; in the rustling trees, the blue shadows, the silver flakes that fell and fell, settling on my arms and shoulders, frosting my hair and eyelashes—but they shrank away from Danu's golden glow. I took a step toward her, hoping to comfort her, show her how glorious it was, but as soon as I drew near, the snow that had settled on my head began to melt, running down my face like tears, and I hesitated, taking a step back. What if her golden light melted the blue from my skin too? What if it leached away from me until I stood golden again? I knew I didn't want that, even if I wasn't exactly sure why.

There was reproach in Danu's eyes even as she said, "The blue will stay. All the gods have an . . . affinity for something. Some part of the world that calls to them. Manannán has the sea and I have the bounty of life and—" She shook her head, cutting herself off. "You will be the goddess of winter." She took a careful step toward me. "I shall give it to you, if you want it. I shall give you dominion over the ice and cold and the biting winds and soft white snow."

I felt as though my body would explode with the wanting of it, so I didn't speak, merely nodded. Danu had a strange look in her eyes—sadness, perhaps, or regret? But still, she reached out and brushed a gentle finger down my cheek. The moment she touched me I *became* winter: ice knit itself into my bones, cold north winds filled up the hollow places in my chest, and somewhere, I could feel snow begin to fall.

For a moment, I held that feeling of winter close—and then I sent it out, stretching my hands and frosting the ground at our feet, covering the trees around us with the same ice that covered my bones. I closed my eyes and called the heavy grey clouds to come close to the earth. I whispered to the cold winds in my chest, drawing them out and in, their names, *mistral, bora, levanter, buran, pampero*, like a song in my head. I laughed at their voices, at their touch, as they twined around my fingers, blowing through my hair.

Danu, though, still stood in a pool of golden light. The cold and snow did not reach her, and it did not feel right, that I should have this gift and not she. I wanted her to understand the *joy* of what she had given me, so I closed my eyes and called the winter, and when I opened them again, Danu was surrounded by snow. I beamed, expecting her to smile back, to glory in my gift, but instead she shouted my name, "Cailleach!" her voice so loud, so bright and hot with anger and indignation that the snow in the clearing vanished, turning into pools of water at my feet.

I stumbled back at the fury on her face, at the clearing suddenly bristling with hard green vines and thorns, some even snaking toward me as though they would eat me whole if they could. She had never looked at me like this before, green eyes glowing hot as fire, standing tall and straight as though she were made of stone, not soft flesh, and I realized that I was looking not at my mother but at a goddess, at *the* goddess, the first and the last, the one who had created us all, and I fell to my knees, a dog waiting for punishment.

I shivered when her hand pulled my chin up to look at her, but when I finally met her gaze I saw that the fire in her eyes was gone, her face soft. "My love. I did not mean to be— I just did not think it would be the cold that would draw you. It is so different from what I . . ." She trailed off, looked at the now-green clearing and shook her head. "It does not matter. You are my daughter, still. Now, shall we go back to Tara?"

I didn't want to leave the clearing, I wanted to stay and draw winter close again, but I did not want to make her angry either, so I took the hand she held out to me, even though it was strange now, too hot and soft. As we walked, we kept shifting and twisting our clasped hands uncomfortably, even though it had never been strange before.

The next morning when I woke, I thought only of getting back to my clearing—to the snow, the cold. I jumped from my bed and was halfway to Danu's door when I stopped. Perhaps it might be better to go on my own. Danu did not understand the cold and the cold did not understand her. If I went on my own, I could sit down in the middle of the clearing and let the white flakes fall soft around me. I could close my eyes and listen to the wind and the trees, and when I opened them, I could watch my skin shift and swirl. But I had never gone anywhere without my mother before, and the thought made my stomach twist and writhe with uncertainty, and a touch of fear. I knew who I was with her. But who was I if I walked alone?

Before I could make my decision, Danu walked out of her room. She wore her mortal face as she often did: broad cheeked, square jawed, a long brown braid. Only her green eyes remained the same. When she saw me, she smiled as she always did, though her gaze flicked to my blue skin. "Come." She held out her hand, and because I had always reached back for her before—*always*, until that night in the woods—I took it.

Tara stood on the top of a gently rising hill that was carpeted in grass and wildflowers no matter the season. Usually when we left, we went east toward the coast, but today Danu turned west, down the path that led inland.

"I want to go back to the clearing." I pointed to the north, where I could see white hills in the far distance.

Danu tugged me down the other side of the hill, her palm hot. "We have other plans today."

"But that's where the mortals live." I said the word "mortal" as she did even though I did not really understand it. I *knew* about them of course—I'd heard the other gods sigh and reminisce about the lives they'd had before Danu had given them divinity, but I had never met one for myself, had never caught more than a far-flung glimpse of them when I was out walking with Danu.

"I know." Danu's voice was light but her grip on my hand rather hard. "And it's time you walk among them."

"But why?" I whined, wishing I'd gotten up earlier and escaped to the cold blue clearing even if it would have upset my mother. "I don't want to."

Danu laughed. "We live in this world, among them. You should meet them, see how they live." Her voice grew excited in fascination, her pace quickening until I had to trot to keep up. "Mortals are not as we are. If they wave their hands, a feast won't simply appear. They must find seeds, then fashion tools for working with the earth, then dig into the soil at the right time, carefully water their plants, and hope they grow." Her voice overflowed with enthusiasm, brimming over until the words nearly ran together. "But it could rain too much or not enough, or a storm could come, or a thief might steal what they have wrought. And all for grain that they have to then harvest and pound down and bake into bread!" Danu's eyes were wide and yearning. "I *still* remember the taste of bread made from my own hands. It was sweeter than any feast I've ever conjured from the air."

She told me we were going to Mooghaun, a hill fort where many mortals lived. The people there knew her as a wise woman who brought healing potions and herbs; she'd promised them that the next time she came, she would bring her daughter.

"Why don't you tell them that you're a goddess?" I asked, looking up at her mortal face.

"They are frightened of gods," Danu said. "They know little of us, only that we are different from them, undying, and powerful—but it is enough to cause them fear. If I walked among them as a goddess, I worry that they would treat me as a stranger, as though I was not once one of them. I would rather walk among them as I once was." Danu's face grew soft, and she ran a finger over her brow. "This is what I looked like before I became a goddess."

"Won't they know that *I* am a god?" I ignored Danu's reminiscing as I looked down at my blue skin.

"I will make it so they will see you as a mortal," Danu said, and I frowned.

"But I don't want—"

"It is important, Cailleach." Danu talked over me. "You will understand why one day. You must trust me, love."

I was not satisfied, but I did not know what else to say, how to explain that even though I had only had it for one day, my blue skin was indelible, precious. A thing that should not be hidden away, not even for a moment.

Danu told me that the fort was considered a marvel by the mortals, a place of great strength and power, but as I looked up at it now, I did not think it looked mighty or marvelous. Like Tara, Mooghaun sat on top of a hill and it was surrounded by a large wooden wall. I could see mounded earth around the hill rising in concentric circles like waves. As we approached, the air filled with the noise of goats bleating and dogs barking and a murmuring of voices that echoed over and over. Painfully and suddenly, I wanted to leave, to rush back to that quiet clearing in the woods, but Danu gripped my hand firmly in her own and drew us both closer.

"Don't be afraid," she said as we approached the gates.

I wasn't afraid, I was uncomfortable; I disliked the noise and the scents that barraged my nose. The dull mortal skin Danu had forced upon me was unsettling, itchy and heavy, as though I carried a weight on my back. But before I could protest, we had reached the gates.

Danu was normally tall. She could loom dangerously over any of the other gods if she wished—reach greater heights than the trees, greater still than the mountains—but when I looked at her now, she was small, smaller than the wall, smaller even than the hard-faced men who guarded the gate.

The men—the first mortals I had ever seen—were a disappointment to my child's eyes. From the way Danu and the other gods had spoken of them, I had expected both more and less: I had thought their ruddy skin would shine with the exertion of living, that their bodies would labor under the heartbeats their mortality demanded, but I'd also pictured them wild-eyed, with leaves in their hair and blood on their teeth, carousing with the *life* that Danu said made them so different from us.

Instead, the men before us looked tired, dirty, their faces as creased and hardened as the ill-fitting leather they wore. And they looked like us. Or rather, we looked like them. I grimaced at the thought of them not seeing me as I truly was and moved to yank at Danu's arm, to demand that she remove the mist from their eyes, when suddenly they saw her, and their weary faces changed. All they did was smile at her approach, but it made them look entirely different. Their cheeks plumped, their eyes crinkled, filling with joy—a bright, shining thing that made me think of standing in that clearing, snow in my hair, and I smiled back, almost reflexively, as Danu looked down and squeezed my hand.

"Danu, it has been too long since we have seen your comely face." The man who spoke had a face that looked sweet and young, teeth flashing white.

"Ronan." Danu smiled back at the young one and patted him on the arm. "And Cormac." She turned toward the older man and there was a gentle warmth in her face as though she knew him well. "I am glad to see you safely returned." She leaned forward, as though she would reach for him, but then she seemed to remember me, pushing me in front of her. "My daughter," she said, as I stared up at the men.

"Ah, little Cailleach!" The older man kneeled in the dirt so that his face was in line with mine, and the gesture was welcoming and kind, so I nodded at him, though a small part of me was afraid to be so close to a mortal man. He glanced up at Danu quickly, as if for permission, before his gaze settled on mine again and he took my hand. "We've heard much about you, lass." I could smell his scent sharply, a mix of earth and roasted meat and leather, and this close I could see that one of his teeth was rotten, and his beard was flecked through with red. I was about to reach out, to see if it felt the same as my own hair, when he said, "I've a girl myself. Enya. Only a few years older than you. Perhaps you'll meet her today, as I think your mother is going up to see my wife." He rose, and his eyes, which had been soft when he said his daughter's name, became frightened, like a rabbit that had just heard a hawk scream. "Sorcha won't tell you herself, but the babe has been giving her trouble. She's in pain nearly all the time now and I'm . . ." The man trailed off, a flush on his face, but Danu just nodded, voice gentle.

"I'll visit her first, I'm sure I have something in my bag that will help."

Cormac's face softened again, and he pressed his hand against Danu's for a moment before opening the gate and ushering us inside the fort.

"Is that man, Cormac, a friend of yours?" I hadn't known that Danu *had* mortal friends. It was strange to consider.

Danu glanced back. "I've known him since he was a youth." Her face softened. "Before he became Sorcha's husband. He is among the best of any mortals I've ever met." She clapped her hands together. "But I've brought you to see more than just one. Look—look around us!"

I looked as Danu said, and saw an overwhelming variety of them. Even when we were all gathered together in Tara there were only six of us, but here everywhere I looked there was another mortal breathing and spitting and moving. A thousand scents filled my nose: piss and beer, roasted lamb, and animal dung. And one other specific smell I could not understand until I asked Danu. She laughed. "That is mortals themselves."

"They stink?" I made a face of disgust.

"Their bodies give off a scent," Danu said. "Like all animals. Besides, we smell too."

"No," I said. "You smell like grass because you *want* to, you like the way grass smells." I screwed up my nose. "I don't think they *want* to smell this way."

"This is why I wanted you to meet them." Danu's eyes were bright, excited. "They are so similar yet so different from us. Watch them." She pointed to the feet of the people we passed, and I saw that as they walked dust clung to their skirts, flecks of mud fell on their legs, and bits of straw blew into their hair. By contrast, Danu and I disturbed nothing with our feet, as clean and unspoiled as we'd always been.

"Here," Danu said after we'd walked up the hill, turning to a little round house that sat snugly against one of the mounded earthen walls. I followed Danu as she ducked into the dark interior. The floor was made of earth and a fire smoldered in the middle of the room, a hole in the roof letting out the smoke. It was cramped and smelly, but Danu didn't wrinkle her nose, instead exclaiming, "Sorcha! I told you to stop lifting that cauldron."

The woman lifting a black pot out of the fire turned toward us, cheeks red with heat. "Danu." The woman's smile was pinched, and I wondered if she was feeling *pain*, another thing that the gods talked about—they said it came from harming a mortal body— though I didn't understand what that meant. "I cannot let the dinner burn, and Enya has run off again to play in the forest."

Danu sighed. "That's what my girl would be doing as well if I hadn't brought her with me today," she said, prodding me forward.

The woman, Sorcha, studied me quietly. "I'd never know she was yours"—she looked at Danu then back at me—"if not for those green eyes. I've never seen eyes like yours before, but she has them too."

"She is mine, no matter how she looks." Danu's voice was firm, almost hot, as though Sorcha's words had made her angry, but before anyone could say anything else, a girl came running into the house, all out of breath and with a rosy glow on her cheeks and nose.

"I'm sorry, Ma." Her voice was fast. "I didn't mean to be gone for so long, but there was ice on the bank, and it was so—" The girl cut herself off when she saw us and blinked in confusion. She had a long black braid down her back and soft brown eyes like the guard below, Cormac. She looked a few years older than me, halfway between a child and a woman, but when she saw me, her eyes lit up.

"Cailleach, at last," she cried, as though she'd known me all her life, and she ran over to me, tugged on my hand. "You must come, before the ice melts."

I had never touched a mortal before and in that brief contact, I felt . . . *everything*: the thump of the girl's heartbeat, rushing blood under her blue-veined wrist, a constellation of lines on the tips of her fingers. Excitement rushed through me, making my head spin. Was this what it was like, to be a goddess in a mortal world? Was this why the gods sighed over their old mortality, because they missed the heat under their skin, the thumping of hearts, the rise and fall of lungs? Was this what they longed for?

I followed Enya out the door, as dazzled by her as I had been by my blue-tinged skin the day before. We ran down and out of the fort, passing her father still standing guard as we went. He gave a little laugh as he saw us run by, calling out something that was lost on the wind.

"Your ma's been talking about you for ages," Enya said as she led me west of the fort, toward a wide, dark wood. Her feet were bare, but she didn't seem to mind, even as she went crunching over twigs and kicking up swaths of leaves. "I've been hoping you'd come soon. I've no little sisters of my own anymore, not since the last three were buried, and so I've no one to show my favorite spots to. The others don't like to go out in the winter, they say the wolves'll get them. But I've never seen a wolf yet. Only heard them." Enya grinned at me and then threw up her head, howling at the sky.

Her voice, high and loose in the air, made me think of winter, of the wildness of whipping winds, and the thought made me flush with delight. Before I knew it, I too had thrown up my head and let loose a howl, and we nearly collapsed in laughter, my stomach hurting from the force of it.

After walking for a few minutes, we arrived at a frozen stream. The ice crystals had piled on top of each other, feathering over and over until the water looked like one of the cloaks I'd seen the women wearing in the fort. I reached out a finger and touched it— knew that if I wanted to, I could have gathered it up and spread it over myself. I wished I could show Enya, wished she could see the marvel of my gift, but I did not know how to undo Danu's glamour, so instead I said, "I love winter."

"I do too." Enya grinned. "My ma thinks I'm mad."

"So does mine." My fingers tingled at the similarities between us. "She prefers the spring. The warmth of the sun in summer." I lay on the cold, thick ice and looked up at the grey-clouded sky. "I like to feel cold." I rubbed my wrist against the ice. "It makes my head spin . . ."

Enya lay down on beside me. "When the snow comes and I can feel my blood pumping and heart racing and the wind howling it's like—it's like *I'm* the winter itself."

The sky above me blurred as my eyes filled with tears. What Enya had said was exactly how I'd felt in the clearing. Danu had not understood, but this mortal girl, Enya, did. Perhaps mortals *were* as special as Danu thought.

"I knew we'd be friends." Enya's voice was so assured that I nodded, though I'd never had a friend before. I wasn't even sure I'd heard the word, but I knew as soon as it left Enya's lips that she was right, we were friends. We always would be.

The first time I saw Danu afraid was the day that Sorcha gave birth to her child.

It had been my fault that we were there at all. A blizzard blew outside, and Danu had been reluctant to leave Tara, where it was unfailingly warm, with flowers blooming out of season as they always did. But since the moment the storm had started at the bottom of the hill early that morning, I'd had an itching, overwhelming desire to be out in it.

"We can go see Enya and Sorcha." My voice was wheedling, knowing that the moment we arrived, Enya and I could escape out to the forest. "It has been so long."

"Has it?" Danu blinked up at me languidly from where she sprawled in a hammock. Though I didn't actually know how long it had been since we'd last seen them, I nodded.

"Alright then my love," Danu sighed, reaching out for my hand. At the warmth of her touch I felt a shiver, as though she'd melted away a bit of the storm outside, a bit of the winter inside me, but I ignored the feeling and kept her hand in mine, and suddenly we stood outside Sorcha's front door.

I frowned because I had wanted to walk to the fort, had wanted to walk through the howling winds, but before I could object, something hit me hard in the shoulder. I spun around and was surprised to see Danu laughing, dusting snow from her hands. It was so lovely to see snow clinging to her that I laughed too, clambering to make my own ball. I threw it at her, and it broke over her long brown braid, and before she could retaliate, I danced away, calling to the flurries to hide me. My plan worked, but only for a moment. After all, I was still a child, and Danu, though she'd given me control over winter, could command me still, so she called me into her arms only too easily. She laughed, pulling me close. "I think that's enough of that. Let's go find Sorcha."

The door flew open, revealing Enya, and my heart surged with joy. Only, she looked strange, her face pinched and pale. "Danu." Her voice was heavy with relief, but it was me she looked at, who she put her hand out to. "Ma's having the baby."

The little house was crowded with women—some by the fire, some sitting at the table, and two standing at Sorcha's side. I recognized one as her sister, and the other as the village midwife. I looked at Danu, waiting for her to push her way toward Sorcha, but instead she drew back as she looked at her, sitting on a birthing stool in the middle of the room. Her face was puffy and red, her hands clenching a rope that hung from the ceiling. She cried out, but her voice, low and rough, did not sound like her own. At the animal noise of it, I shrank back toward Danu, expecting her to hold me and tell me that all would be well, but I did not find her where I thought she'd be. She had retreated to the door. I looked from Danu to Sorcha, eyes wide and confused, so afraid I did not know what to do.

Thankfully, Enya had stayed at my side. She squeezed my hand, though her voice sounded wobbly. "Ma will be fine. She's birthed many children."

"Dead children," Danu whispered quietly, so quietly that only a god—only I—could hear, and I thought of the sisters Enya had mentioned, the dead girls. I didn't *really* understand what that meant, what death meant, but I knew it could mean an end to Sorcha, and perhaps that would mean an end to our visits here, and I surged forward, my hands outstretched. I was a goddess. I would fix Sorcha, make sure she did not *end*.

"No, child." The midwife pushed me away gently. "No need to fear," she said, but she was lying because Enya had told me only the other day of the three women who had died that spring during childbirth. "It's natural," she continued. "The pain, the blood." I had not noticed the blood, but as soon as she said the word, it was all I could see, scattered over the straw on the floor—all I could smell, the scent of it rich and metallic in the air—and I was suddenly terrified, terrified of Sorcha dying like the other women had. I looked at Danu, who caught my pleading gaze and moved hesitantly forward.

"I have things, they might help." I watched as Danu pulled bottles and herbs from her bag, approaching Sorcha's side and squeezing her shoulder for a moment. I had never seen my mother's hands shake before.

Enya and I were shunted to the corner as Sorcha's labor progressed, while Danu stayed by her side. I thought as I watched her that perhaps Danu did not like blood, that perhaps it was one thing about mortality that she did not rejoice in, but though she paled when she looked at it, she did not turn away, even when it spattered on her hands, her clothes.

After hours of watching, eventually Enya and I fell asleep, curled up against each other by the fire. Our hands were clasped together, and even in sleep her hand tensed whenever her mother cried. I don't know how long we slept, but we both jumped awake at a shriek that seemed to pull all the air from the room. Sorcha was screaming, her head rolled back in pain, her body arched. Enya's hand trembled and she began to cry, not moving her eyes from her mother. "It's never taken this long before, not even with the biggest ones." She looked to Danu beseechingly, willing her to help Sorcha, but she had stepped back. I could tell Danu was doing nothing more than the other women, was not moving to heal her friend though she had the power, and I did not understand why. But she did not meet Enya's gaze, nor mine, her eyes steady on Sorcha.

Finally, Sorcha gave a gasp and something red and rotten slid from between her legs. There was a brief silence, and then the red rotten thing began to cry, and Sorcha was laughing, and Enya was running forward, flinging her arms around her mother and new brother, and a moment later Cormac came rushing into the house, his eyes bright, tears running down his cheeks as he reached for his son.

Danu and I left soon after the babe was born, walking through the village and out into the howling storm. She took a long, deep breath. I did too, letting the cold snow smell replace the blood and sweat and straw, but Danu stood for some time in the tempest before reaching for my hand. We were halfway back to Tara, walking silently side by side, when I asked, "Why didn't you help her?"

"It is not for us to interfere." Danu shook her head. "They live so briefly. Even the longest-lived ones are like a breath for us."

"But she's your friend. She's Enya's ma." My voice trembled. "And she could have *died*."

"Cailleach, my love." Danu dropped to her knees. "You have witnessed only tiny moments of mortality and all of those have been colored by your love for Enya and Sorcha. As you grow, you will understand that while mortal lives can be as beautiful as a rose, they are also as short. We cannot save them all. Not even the ones we love."

"But if she'd asked," I said. "If she'd begged you to save her, you would have?"

Danu shook her head, looking back toward the hill fort. "She is good and kind, but many of them are good and kind. How can I put her above any other? Should I heal her and let a woman in the east die?"

"Heal them both!"

Her smile was pained. "That is not what it means to be a goddess, Cailleach. You'll learn that someday."

"You could make *her* a goddess." I thought not only about Sorcha, but also of Enya. Danu could give them both godhood like she'd given Dagda and Morrígan and Lug, Manannán. If she could do it for them, why would she not for our friends?

Danu shook her head. "No," she said. "No."

"But why—"

"Everyone cannot be saved, Cailleach!" Danu's voice was suddenly hot and golden as a forge fire. "Would you have me make every mortal into a god, so as to avoid death? And how would you have me choose? If I gave Sorcha godhood and not her husband, her village, and the next—what then?"

She seemed once more like she had in the clearing when she'd given me winter, dangerous and frightening, and though a part of me wanted to shrink away from her I thought of Enya and lifted my chin bravely. "But *why* not? What do you think would happen?"

I expected Danu would be angry at the question but instead she sighed. "Changing a mortal into a god—it is not like changing a vine into a rose. Every time I give something—godhood, food, rain—a part of me is weakened. What if I kept giving and giving until I was all used up?" Her voice dropped to a whisper and she grew quiet, as if lost in thought. After a moment, she placed a hand on my cheek. "Understand, Cailleach. Even if I had healed Sorcha, she would still eventually die. And if others heard of what I'd done for her they would want the same for their mothers and husbands and sons. I would spend all my days hearing their calls."

I didn't understand. "Would that be bad?"

Her face became thoughtful. "Perhaps not. Perhaps if they offered something in exchange, something that would give some measure of power in return, perhaps then . . ." She trailed off. I did not understand her reasoning, but that did not matter because by the time we returned home she had a plan set in her mind.

She brought mortals to Tara and told them her story, how she had made other gods. She told the mortals before her that she'd chosen them to spread our stories, that they would call themselves druids and they would teach the people how to worship us. They would offer us their prayers and their voices, they would set up altars to us in their woods and fields and houses, and they would give us the choice bits of their harvest, animals, gold, and in exchange, we would listen. We would guide them and protect them and heal them.

Soon, the mortals began to call.

They asked Lug for riches and Manannán for safety on the seas, for nets full of fish. They asked Dagda for children who were hale and hearty, and Morrígan to turn the tide of battle, to make their spears sharper than their enemies'.

And they asked Danu for everything. For harvest that grew tall and golden, for the soft rains of spring, for flowers and health and safety and love. *Love us*, they said to Danu. *Great mother goddess, love us, for we love you.*

They did not often call my name, though. What did mortals want with howling winds and ice and snow? They did not long for the cold blue places as I did. But I did not mind.

I had Enya, and Sorcha and Danu. I had enough.

before

Both our mothers were besotted with the child, but neither Enya nor I cared to spend much time with it. Cathal spent his time screaming or nursing, his lips pursed greedily around Sorcha's nipple. Since he'd come, everyone was less interested in where we went; even Cormac only asked us how Cathal was doing when we went running past him into the wood.

Harvest had ended and we were laying on the frozen river. Half-asleep, I listened to the burble of the water still moving deep below the ice, until finally I pressed myself up on my elbow, yawning. I didn't *have* to yawn of course, but lately Danu and I had begun a game of mimicking different mortal behaviors; sneezes, coughs, yawns, all the things they did without conscious thought. We talked about it as we went back to Tara, laughing together about how curious it was, how peculiar *they* were.

"Cathal is getting uglier," Enya said one day when we were in the wood together.

"He *is* ugly," I agreed, thinking of his red-faced scream and the drool he'd dripped on Danu's skirt that morning.

"Ma says his teeth are coming in and that we've got to be patient with him. Even Da doesn't seem angry with him, and Da hates loud noises." Enya sighed and I made note of it, watching how her shoulders tensed slightly, her belly rounding before her body collapsed around the breath. "I hope my babies cry less."

"Babies?" I frowned and sat up fully; the ice cracked a little. "You don't have a baby."

"No, not yet. But I bled last month, so I will soon."

I pulled her hand into mine, looked down at the blue veins, but didn't see any blood.

Enya looked down at her lap. "I'm not bleeding *now*. But surely your ma's told you, all women bleed? Once we do, we can have babies."

Of course Danu had told me no such thing. Gods did not bleed.

"But you don't want babies."

"No . . ." Enya said. "I would have to spend all day in a little croft cooking and feeding them . . . listening to them scream." She shivered. "Cathal cries *all* the time. Ma barely seems to notice."

"If you have a baby, you could just give it to your ma then," I declared, feeling that this was a perfect solution. "She could have it."

"I couldn't do that!" Enya looked startled.

"Why not?"

"If I had a baby, it would be *my* baby," Enya explained. "Mothers can't just give their children away."

I frowned again, thinking of how busy Sorcha was with Cathal. Would Enya have time for me if she had a child? "Then you'll not have children at all."

Enya sighed. "Da will eventually want me to marry someone, and my husband will want children."

"But your da loves you. Tell him no."

Enya's eyes were sad. "I *can't*, Cailleach. You have no da, you don't understand."

I thought of Cormac, funny and kind. "He wouldn't force you. Danu says he is a great man."

"But everyone has children eventually."

"Not the midwife." I thought of the woman who had helped at Sorcha's birth.

"That's only because she *couldn't*." Enya half whispered the words as though they were dangerous. "Ma says everyone used to talk about it."

"You can be like her then."

"But I don't know how to . . ." Enya bit her lip. "Do *you* know how to stop a baby coming?"

"No . . ." I trailed off, wondering if Danu would know. "Then you mustn't get a husband. Not until we can figure out how to prevent babies."

"I don't *want* one." Enya's voice was vicious in a way I'd never heard before. "Ma buried all the babies except me and Cathal. I don't want to bury dead babies in the mud."

"I don't either," I said. "We won't. We'll never have babies. We'll stay together, just us, forever." Enya didn't look hopeful. "Talk to your da." I thought of Cormac's soft brown eyes. "He'll listen. He always listens to us." Enya nodded slowly. I laughed and waved my hands at the woods around us. "Tell him you want to keep coming to the forest with me."

Enya squeezed my hand and we both looked up at the sky, far away from silly mortal concerns like husbands and babies.

Three years had passed since I'd first met Enya and her family, but this was the first winter solstice we'd ever celebrated with them, and I was dazzled. A huge feast was laid and all those who lived in the hill fort arrived wearing their best clothes: cloaks trimmed in fox fur, scarlet sashes, a gold torc around the neck of their prince. The crowd laughed and smiled, kissing each other's cheeks and squeezing hands, dancing around a roaring fire twice my height. My stomach twisted with excitement as I watched them, and I ran over to Enya.

We began to dance, our feet stomping and twirling and rushing along with the beating drums, piping flutes, and sweeping fiddles. It was exhilarating to spin as we did, over and over until Enya grew so dizzy that she begged for a break, pulling me to sit by the fire.

I heard a noise beside me and saw Danu looking over us, looking at the musicians, a long tear running down her cheek. "They feel so *much*," Danu whispered to me, her voice ecstatic.

I had noticed as we'd spent time with mortals that while I had grown to love Enya and her family, Danu seemed to look on them—all mortals—as playthings. She talked to them and laughed and even wept with them, but she did so in the same way that she talked to her own great cats at Tara. She might adore them, might sigh over their pain and joy, but she did not truly look on them with gravity or respect. One of Sorcha's sisters had died the previous summer, and though Danu and I had wept with Sorcha and Enya that day, the next night I'd heard her recount the story back to Dagda, mocking the brevity of their lives, how fragile and tenuous they were. It was clear to me that Danu's tears with Sorcha had been false, as though she were only pretending to care about her sorrow.

I was glad when Enya reached for me in that moment, glad that

I could forget about Danu and turn toward the woods, but before we could leave, Cormac put a hand on Enya's shoulder and smiled at us. "We are honored that you joined our family tonight." He bowed at Danu. "You helped save the life of my Sorcha, and for that I will always be grateful." Cormac gently touched his wife's cheek, and I saw Danu's eyes fill with tears. I shifted from one foot to the other, uneasy as I watched her, wondering if, though she cried with the mortals now, she would laugh again later with the gods. "I wanted to be the first to tell you that the arrangements have been completed. Our Enya is to be wed to Aedan this very evening."

Danu's mouth dropped open in delight, and she clapped as my own body froze. I looked at Enya, her face pale as ice, and squeezed her hand tightly, showing her I was there. She didn't seem to notice me at all; she was staring up at her father in horror.

"But Da——" Enya looked across the fire to a grizzled man I'd never seen before. "I told you"—she lowered her voice, but I still heard her—"I do not want to."

"Don't be foolish, Enya. You're grown now. It's time."

"But Aedan—he has four children already and three are older than I."

"He needs a mother for the littlest." Cormac's voice was hearty but his eyes didn't meet Enya's. "And you'll have your own babies soon enough."

Enya turned to me, and I saw the terror in her eyes, remembered her talking about burying dead babies, and I straightened my shoulders, stepping in front of my friend. "She doesn't want them." I glared at Cormac.

Cormac looked down on me and gave a gentle laugh. "What a fierce lass you are."

"No!" I howled, louder than a wolf on a hunt, and the whole clearing suddenly fell silent with the sharp crack of my voice. Cormac's eyes were wide, and though his mouth opened and closed no noise came out of it. I pointed a finger at Cormac and ice began to slither up his feet. "You can't, it's not— She doesn't want—" My skin swirled and shifted, and I felt as though I were ice itself, as though I were shattering and cracking into pieces with confusion, with anger, because how could Cormac do such a thing? If he would not protect Enya, I would save her, I would save my friend from the life that she did not want, the life that threatened to take her away from me. I was reaching out, about to call down a howling storm, when Danu suddenly scooped me up, holding me against her as she loosened the ice from Cormac's legs. Then I was screaming, shrieking as she carried me away from the mortals.

Away from Enya.

They wed that night, and she fell pregnant within months.
Then Enya died, along with her cord-choked son.

After that, I no longer concerned myself with the affairs of mortals.

before

I spent the next centuries in the quiet, still places of the world, and I saw little of humans, though I knew that Danu still fawned and cooed over them, her favorite playthings. I noticed them distantly sometimes: A startled face flashing under torchlight in the woods as I hunted a deer. A woman's wide smile as she threw a ball of snow at her young son. The shadow of a boat passing over the lake I swam in.

They, in turn, rarely saw more of me than a flash of silver hair, green eyes, blue skin, and even when they did, they did not recognize me. They said I was a falling star near the horizon, a ripple of light on green leaves, the dancing colors that occasionally lit the dark sky. This was true in a way, because for them I *was* nothing more than a flicker, a moment—ephemeral and unknowable as the moon or the wind.

Danu had never reproached me for not returning to the mortals, but I knew that she still wished I would take the interest in them I once had. Each time I visited Tara, she told me of their latest exploits and inventions as if hoping to entice me back to them. She had bidden me to return to Tara for a festival she was putting on for them, as though such a thing would make me want to walk among them again. I had come, but not to please Danu. It had been some time since I'd visited my grove in the north woods, and lately I had longed to return there, to the place where my skin had become blue, where I'd first felt the true joy of winter.

Though I'd only been back at the palace for a single day I already felt caged, and so I paced the halls, walking in and out of the rooms until I saw Dagda in the courtyard. "What are you weaving?" I said, looking closely at the tapestry.

"The story of our beginning." Dagda ran a hand along his forehead, a farcical gesture of weariness that he had never given up though he had been a god for centuries. "Danu hoped I would present it to the mortals." He gestured to the tapestry.

In it, Danu was wandering, a god alone in a blue, cold world, meeting mortals here and there, but always too different, too odd for them to accept her. It showed her finally settling on the hill of Tara; building the white-walled palace, weaving pink sunsets and golden sunrises and silver moonlight into the walls; creating her beloved beehives, golden honey dripping from her hands. Dagda had managed to capture the despair on her face when she looked around at all she'd created and saw that she was still alone. The tapestry ended with her holding her hand out to a faceless mortal, light springing from her fingertips as she made him into one like her. Into a god. The weaving was beautiful—though, of course, it was not really the story of *our* beginning. It was the story of Danu. Of her, before she'd created us.

"But why are you *weaving* it?" I asked. "You don't need to. You could just wave your hand and it would appear as you imagined it."

"I like the work of it." Dagda's hands were busy as he shaded Danu's curls so they seemed to glow.

"It's a foolish impulse." I frowned, irritated by the gods' hypocrisy. They used mortal gestures and sang mortal songs, they spoke longingly of pain and heartache because they did not—or chose not to—remember the truth of mortality that I had seen as a child. They spoke of cream, warm and fresh from a cow, and did not remember how often it curdled and soured. They spoke of the sweetness of strawberries grown by their own hand and did not remember the sour disappointment of fruit rotted off the vine. They cooed over fat-bellied women and did not remember those same women's grey death faces, their dead children's blue lips.

Enya's face, white and cold, came to my mind unbidden, and I flicked my head, shaking off the thought of the long-dead girl. Enya had only been young. When mortals grew, they became cruel, selfish, betraying each other as Cormac had, with deeds both large and small. I would not be pulled into their lives again.

"You are not mortal, and you never have been, Cailleach." Dagda wiped away the flakes of snow that had swirled across his tapestry when I'd thought of Enya. "It pleases me to weave Danu's story. That is enough for me. They will be awed when they see it, as they should be. I've always said Danu should tell the tale more often."

Danu usually wore her mortal face among the humans, but as they approached us now, cresting the hill to Tara, she looked nothing like them. She stood taller than their tallest man, hair golden as the sun's rays sweeping down her back all the way to her feet. Roses twined through her hair, climbing it like a trellis, and crowning her head with pink and white buds. Her eyes were green and soft and her entire being glowed golden as though she were the sun, walking among us.

"Welcome, mortals." She swept a hand toward them, voice gentle as a summer breeze, and she smiled as if content, though I didn't understand how she could be; the moment the humans set foot in the palace I began to choke on their scent. I hadn't smelled it in so long, not since those days in Mooghaun with Danu and Enya. I remembered that I had grown used to it then, had soon stopped noticing, but now it seemed all I could smell was the sour-vinegar scent of their bodies. I wished I could escape, run to the woods once more, but I had promised Danu I would come and did not want to incite her anger, so I stood there stiffly, watching them. They looked so tired—even the children wore their mortality heavily. For all that they prayed to the gods, their lives still seemed full of hardship.

They stayed clustered together, perhaps a hundred of them, and even though they were much smaller than us, they seemed to clog the palace. A woman ran a hand through her hair and a strand floated to the pristine floor. An old man coughed, leaning a hand against the wall, and left behind a smudged handprint. A child wailed, and her voice bounced off the walls, echoing over and over. I seemed to be the only one who cared about these violations, so I did nothing, silently following Danu and the mortals into the courtyard. This was where we spent most of our time when we were all in Tara together and it looked like a clearing in a spring wood, filled with golden-barked birches, blue-green firs, rowans and alders. The ground was a mix of marble tiles interspersed with spongy moss, a spring bubbling up in the center. Tonight, the trees were hung with stars that twinkled softly—yellow, white, and blue. Danu had heaped the floor with cushions in a variety of bright and bewildering colors and laid out food on long tables. Children peeled bark from the birches, yanked flowers from their stalks, while their parents smashed the grass flat with their heavy steps, spilling wine carelessly into the spring.

I didn't want to walk into the courtyard and have all their curious eyes on me, so I waited in the doorway until Danu finally left her crowd of admirers to scoop up a goblet of wine near me.

"Why have the festival here? Wouldn't the throne room be more appropriate?"

Danu shrugged. "I did not want them to be so frightened by us that they would just stand there and babble. I want the gods and mortals to mingle as we once did." Her voice was wistful, and my stomach twisted with guilt and anger. I knew she missed my hand in hers, missed laughing together over mortal gestures as we walked back to Tara, but I was not a child anymore. And I knew it was not *me* she truly yearned for but the entertainment and adoration I'd once provided—as the mortals did now. And though I did not want to be among them again, that did not mean that I wanted to laugh at them either. I just wanted to be far away from them again, away from both their noise and their fragility.

Danu must have read my thoughts, because her face creased. "I know you still mourn Enya, but it was *so* long ago. And you could meet someone new. Find joy from another mortal as you did from her." She gestured at them, and I could tell she meant her words even as an old man scratched his nose and a child spat a gob of spit into the spring. Danu frowned. "They are more than their . . . habits. You could listen to their stories. Walk among them and learn how they live again."

"I've seen how they live." My voice was flat. "They hold nothing for me."

That night, the other gods put on quite a show for the mortals. Dagda wove their likenesses into flowers and leaves and they exclaimed with wonder. Manannán doused the room in darkness, then made the spring leap and dance, catching the starlight in the droplets so it looked like we were standing among the stars.

Danu, of course, was everywhere; holding the children, laughing with the women, throwing dice with the men. Light trailed from her, and I saw the mortals' eyes follow that golden ripple, marking where she had been, where she was going. She was the one they wanted to speak to, the one they wanted to tell their troubles to, and as the night wore on, she began performing miracles for them. She touched a woman's stomach and it swelled with a child before our eyes. She laid her hand on a man with a broken arm and the limb straightened. She turned the water of the spring to wine and back, and with each miracle she performed, her power dimmed for a moment, the golden light falling away for less than a breath. I'd never seen Danu weaken in any way, and it was disconcerting, but I wasn't sure that anyone else had noticed, not even the other gods who beamed when the mortals turned to them asking for more.

Dagda—they held their hands out in supplication—*Dagda, will you bless my nets?*

Morrígan, will you keep me safe and bloodless in battle?

Manannán, will you grant us bounty on the sea?

Lug, will you fill my purse with gold?

Finally, a woman with long black hair said my name. "Cailleach." She reached out a hand, and unconsciously I reached back, as I had for Enya, but then my hand met hers and I could feel the fine lines of her fingertips, and of course she wasn't Enya. She was just a mortal woman who was trying to ask, to *take* from me, take as Cormac had taken from Enya, as he had ripped my friend away from *me*, and I yanked my hand from hers and turned away, striding out of the palace before Danu could stop me. I should not have returned to Tara, not even to placate Danu. Mortals brought only hardship. I would have nothing more to do with them.

I walked north, away from Tara, determined to visit my clearing one last time before I left this part of the world for good.

The first thing I noticed was the smell. I was walking through a dark wood, and though there was pine and loam in the air, there was something else too; a sour dampness that I associated with mortals. I frowned and quickened my step, and soon, far too soon, the trees thinned, and I stepped out onto a huge expanse of clear land.

I stood, still as a statue, unable to fathom what I saw in front of me.

The whole section of the wood where my clearing had stood had been felled. Nothing remained but a smooth expanse of barren dirt rising to a mound. But it was not *my* mound. It was a mortal-made hill. I knew, because I could smell their hands on the smooth white stones and on the dirt and even in the air that I breathed. I choked on the overwhelming scent and fell to my knees, horror crawling up my throat.

The clearing was empty, but I could see the mortals in everything: in the tramped-grass path around the mound, in the marks on the stone where they had bit in with their sharp chisels and tools. They had taken what was mine and marked it as theirs. They had taken my clearing, the first place my skin had become blue, and they had broken it open to the sky so that my skin could not shift and twist to match the shafts of moonlight and shadow.

I numbly followed the tunnel they had made into the center of the mound. The tunnel twisted until it finally led me into a central chamber where I saw that they had further desecrated my clearing, turning it into a place of death. For in the central chamber were white bones heaped with the things mortals so longed for: golden torcs, and jeweled diadems and weapons, knives and swords and shining armor, ceramic bowls and the stone tools they had used to chip away at the stone—the tools they had used to bring down the once-mighty forest that had surrounded the mound. Tears filled my eyes as I looked at the desecration around me. They had taken my trees and my blue shadows, and they had broken the stones and churned up the earth, and for what? To fill a hole with pretty treasures for the dead?

I was suddenly overwhelmed by the smell of it, the decayed bones and strong iron and sour mortality, and I fled outside, climbing to the top of the mound. I fell to my knees and wept, remembering how I had once stood here, the earth firm and deep beneath my feet, watching my skin rim with blue and my arms gather snow before I knew about loss, before I knew of anything other than Danu and myself. And I wanted it back, I wanted it again, but I did not have Danu's power; I could not stretch out my hand and make the trees return.

So I mourned, weeping even as glittering snowflakes began to fall upon me, covering me with a soft white mantle, making me part of the landscape, and I wished that I could lie there forever, until the world turned over once again, until the mortals who ruined so much, who took and took without thought, were dead and gone, until they were as white as the bones that lay beneath me.

I could still smell them.

I lay there and let the snow fall and fall until finally, slowly, it began to push away their rancid scent; the green hills became white and the landscape became soft and formless, and their bodies grew cold, so cold, and then they could no longer take, not from the trees and not from their daughters and not from me.

I do not know how long I lay there, whether hours or days or months passed as I held winter fast, grasped it tightly in my fist so that the snow kept piling, the winds kept howling.

Eventually, though, Danu came.

"Child," she said, suddenly appearing before me. Though the snow still fell, it did not land on her. Danu reached out a hand and I let her pull me to my feet, expecting understanding. Succor, perhaps. Sorrow over what the mortals had done. Instead, she spoke sternly: "Daughter." When I looked up her expression was grave.

"It is too cold." Danu waved her arm and the mound we stood upon changed. Where a moment before there had been nothing but white, we now stood on the green hill the mortals had built. My body felt numb, as though I'd been turned to stone, and I glared at her, meeting her eyes, the only thing that marked us as kin—though hers were the spring green of new grass and mine were as dark as fir boughs. Suddenly I hated even that small similarity to her. If not for my mother's eyes, I might be able to forget that I had ever belonged to anything other than myself. How could she choose them, love *them*, the mortals who had done this to me, who had torn down those very firs? I could smell them again and I thought of the white bones below me, thought of Enya's white face, and gritted my teeth, and then we stood in a blizzard once more, the whirling snow and wind tearing away the memory and smell of death. I pulled my hand away and took a step back.

"They ruined it," I rasped. My voice was pleading and hoarse from weeping. "They stole my clearing from me. The place where I became a god. Where you gave me winter." But Danu, who had compassion for all mortals, for their toil and their burdens, their wars and weddings, looked on me without any.

"It is time for spring, Cailleach." Her voice was firm. "This winter has gone on too long, has been too deep. They have died in their thousands already. If you do not let spring come, they will all be lost. Their crops will wither. Their children will breathe their last. *More* of their children," she said, a tear running down her cheek.

"They die whether or not winter is long." My hands curled into fists, trying to bar the spring warmth that I knew Danu wanted to spread across the world.

"There will be no one left. If this winter does not end, you will bury the world and there will only be us."

Us. Only the gods. No noise and no stench.

No mortals.

"You've walked among them," Danu said. "You know what they are like—"

"It has been centuries since I walked among mortals, Danu. I was a child, and even then, I saw nothing except avarice and jealousy and death." I closed my eyes, even as other images flashed before me: Enya spinning in a circle of firelight, Sorcha's warm hands braiding my hair, the gurgling chuckle of baby Cathal. I forced them aside.

Danu sighed, and I remembered the time we had spent weeks trying to perfect their sighs. I remembered watching Enya as her body had drawn tight, then collapsed under the weight of her breaths. I remembered too her last exhale, the moment her body had fallen and did not rise again.

"If you will not end the winter yourself, then something must be done." She said the words slowly, and then she was towering over me, no longer in her mortal skin, but wearing the god form I so rarely saw, a grim determination in her eyes. Leaves spun around her head and the air crackled with the force of the light, as though the whole world was moments away from bursting into flame. "You will return to Tara." Her voice was set. "You will stand before the gods and answer for what you have done."

I had not willingly entered the throne room in centuries, but it had not changed in all that time: it was still absurdly large, with vaulted ceilings that made every footstep and voice echo as though it held a hundred of us rather than six. Its walls were made of something pink and iridescent that might have been shell and might have been flower petals and the large, narrow pool that ran down the center of the room mirrored everything in a way that was dizzying and unpleasant.

The thrones were the same too, vines twisted together into large chairs. Danu had created them, had said that she wanted them the same, as none of us was above any other god, but this was all pretense. Danu was the ultimate authority. The other gods felt they owed her everything. They gave her loyalty, devotion, love. All of them except me.

"Cailleach." Danu's voice had softened back to its usual timbre. She had changed her face, too, back to the mortal one she was so fond of. She'd told me once that she wore it to remind herself of what she had once been like, of what she had lost. "We have called you here to answer for what you have done."

"I have sent the snow. The cold. As I have ever done."

"You have buried them." Danu's voice was sad. "They have died. They *are* dying."

"I told you, Danu, it is the only way."

"The only way for *what*?" Morrígan leaned forward in her throne.

"The only to make them stop taking." My voice was quiet.

They were silent for a moment, and I wondered if they were thinking of their own mortal lives. Were they remembering that hunger of mortality, the need to consume?

"And who are you, to decide what is theirs to take or not?" Danu's voice was fierce. "We are their guardians. Their guides and friends. We do not kill them."

I laughed. "Morrígan kills them all the time, in the wars she's always fighting. She's regaled us often with stories of the men she's run through with her spear, told us about spilling their entrails onto the ground."

Morrígan shook her head, the light catching on her dark skin, on her gold-brown halo of curls. "It is not the same. I don't fight in my god form but as one of them, and only when they call. It is for mortals, and by their hand, that I kill."

"Another way we are different. All of you have a god form and a mortal form. You have two faces. I do not. I have never been anything but my true self. Perhaps this is why I can see the truth, and you cannot."

"So many have died, Cailleach." Dagda echoed Danu, his face was creased with sorrow.

"They all die eventually. What does it matter, whether they die now or in twenty years or a hundred?"

Danu looked sad. "Once you did not believe such a thing. Once you grieved over them."

I looked away from her. "I was young." My voice was hard as stone. "I understand what mortals are now." It would have been better, in the end, if I had never met Enya. Then I never would have known what it was to love a mortal. I would never have known the grief of death.

"Perhaps you are right." Danu's fingers drummed against her throne. "All of us know what it costs to kill a mortal because we once *were* mortals." Danu's face was set. "It is time for you to walk among them again."

At her words, a shiver of fear ran down my back and I thought of that moment from my youth, Danu's face hot and bright, melting the snow into rivulets of water.

Danu stood, and the light of her filled the room as it had filled the clearing that day. "You will be given a mortal form. You will live among them until you understand what it is to *be* a mortal. Why they act as they do. You will live and you will die until you understand. This is the punishment I place upon you. Do any think my judgement unjust?" She barely glanced at the other gods. She knew, as I did, that none of them would speak against her. I looked at Dagda and saw that his face was creased in sadness, but all he did was shake his head at me gently before dropping his gaze.

Danu raised her hand, and in an instant the cold that had filled my body since she had given me winter fled. The ice that ran through my veins evaporated, the frost that knit my bones together melted away, and my blue skin turned pale and white as though I were dead.

As though I were mortal.

the first life

I blinked, looking up into the sky. A moment before, I'd been standing in front of Danu, her finger pointed at me, the walls of the palace glowing with the dawn.

Now I was standing on earth, but not as I usually stood, shielded from human muck and squalor. Instead, mud covered my toes and had even spattered onto the white shift I wore. Worse still, my skin prickled and shivered from the rain falling from the sky. I looked up and began to swear. I screamed curses up at them, throwing my arms out wide in challenge. In warning. I was a god like they were, I had power, strength. I took a deep breath and grounded my feet in the earth, closed my eyes and waited—for the howling winds to sweep me up among them, for the weight of snow on my arms, for the cold to settle my breaths. For winter.

For the first time in centuries, it did not come.

A shudder ran down my body. I felt as I had the moment Enya died, as I had when I saw what the mortals had done to my clearing: grief, deep and endless, the weight of an avalanche rolling over my body. I wanted to despair, to collapse to my knees, was desperate for the comfort of snow. Instead, the rain pelted me, blowing into my eyes, nearly blinding me. The discomfort—something I'd never known before—drove me to look for shelter.

For the first time, I saw where they had exiled me. A round, decrepit hut, wide holes blooming in the thatched roof. As I stared at it, I knew they meant it to be my home. Perhaps it would at least be warm. I took a step toward it, only I was not used to mud, which had never truly touched me before, and so I slipped, landing on my back. The breath left my body, and for a long moment I thought this life was already over, that I had not made it one step before meeting death.

Except I did not die. I merely became drenched, staring up as the water continued to fall on me. I began to cough and first propped myself up on my elbow, then finally made my way to my knees. I feared that if I stood, I would fall again, so instead I crawled to the hut—only to find it had no door. Just a length of tattered cloth that would keep out nothing, not cold, animals, or mortals. In a fit of fury, I stood and wrenched the cloth down, throwing it aside and leaving the shelter open to the sheeting silver rain.

There were few things in the shelter: a hearth, a black cauldron, a pallet with a blanket, and a round table with no chair, only a broken, three-legged stool. On the table sat a loaf of bread, brown and hard, and a large, yellow candle. It looked like one of Danu's, made from her honeyed golden hives. I flicked a hand at it as I normally would, but of course it did not light. Mortals did not keep fire in their fingertips as gods did. I pictured Sorcha bending over her fire and doing . . . what had she done? Shifted the coals around with a stick? Added logs? It was so long ago now, and since Enya's death, I had barely allowed myself to remember them at all. Did Danu truly think that I could survive as a mortal because I had spent a few short years among them? I curled my hands into fists and

stared at the hearth. How could Danu be so cruel? I found myself
wishing that Sorcha were here, that *some* mortal were here to show
me what to do, and resented the thought. So what if I had a mortal
body? I was still a god. If a mortal could create fire so could I.

There was some kindling nearby, and I threw it on the coals, but
the fire did not flare. I recalled suddenly Sorcha blowing on them
before they turned to flame, and so I did the same, but still no flame
grew. In anger, I shoved another stick into the mess, and finally, finally, saw a gleam of red. I moved closer, prodding the coals again,
and they all began to gleam. I blew on them gently, foreign heart
thumping in my foreign chest, and a tiny lick of flame burst up
from the coals. I held my breath as it wavered, worried it would go
out, but then it caught on the kindling and grew until I could feel
the warmth of it. I sat back on my heels, triumphant, a small smile
on my face.

The triumph died, though, as I thought of how Danu's face
would *shine* if she saw me smile over the small flame. This was
what she'd always wanted. Ever since Enya's death she had tried to
entice me back to the mortal world, and when that had not worked,
she had simply used her power to send me back anyway, this time
in the humiliation of a mortal body. But why? What did she think I
would learn from this? I *had* spent time among mortals. I knew
what they were like, understood how they thought, without needing to become one of them. I had watched Sorcha give birth to
Cathal, still remembered her pain; had seen Enya dream and bleed
and die; had heard Cormac struggle, fight, and laugh, even as he
betrayed her; had walked through their markets; had learned their
habits; had eaten their food. What more could she expect me to
learn from them?

But, I thought suddenly, *Danu's mind is as changeable as the wind*. If I pretended to go along with her punishment, if I practiced mortality as she wished, there was a chance she would release me from this mortal body in a few days. The fire popped as I considered this, and I jumped when an ember bit at my hands.

My hands, pale and white instead of blue.

It had been centuries since my skin had first turned in that glade, and my chest ached as I looked at those hands. Since the moment I had gained that glorious blue, I had *become* winter. Cold and hard and howling as the wind and soft and quiet and gentle as the snow. Who was I without it? What would I do now?

Tears gathered in my eyes, but I didn't let them fall. If Danu was watching me, I didn't want her to gain the satisfaction of my grief. I lifted my head and looked around the hut. If I was going to practice mortality I might as well begin now.

Night was drawing closer as I went out into the rain to try to find some more kindling. Thankfully, I didn't have to go far because the forest was nearly at my door. I tripped several times, falling in the mud, but finally managed to strip a branch from a squat tree. I dragged the kindling into the hut and swore, seeing that the fire had burned down to coals again. I rushed to stir it with one of the branches I'd gathered, thrusting it into the fire. Nothing happened. It had been long ago, but I knew this was how Sorcha had always brought her family's fire to life. Why was it not working for me now? I held the branch closer, closer, until my fingers began to scorch, but the wet wood would not light. I did not know what else to do but wait and was relieved when it finally caught. But then so did my sleeve. I dropped the twig and frantically patted my arm until the sparks fell away, leaving the scent of char in my nostrils and blisters on my wrist. I touched one and felt a spike of *something*— like ice cracking sudden and sharp under your feet.

Pain, I thought. I had just felt *pain* for the first time.

I had seen pain before, in the set of Sorcha's jaw when she'd lifted a heavy pot off the fire, in the sweat on Cormac's creased brow when he'd broken a leg, and in the blood that covered the floor after Enya died. But I had never known it myself. Not until this moment.

Were the gods laughing or sympathetic? Were they arguing over whether to help me, to light my candle, heal my wrist? The thought of them watching made me clench my teeth in anger. I stood, yanked the candle off the table, and held it over the fire even as golden wax began to drip down my fingers. I did not move, until the wick was finally alight. I placed it back on the table, but the scent of it, of bees and clover and syrupy-sweet drops of honeysuckle did not make me feel better. It just made me think of Tara and my immortal body, a place with no pain.

Even lit, the candle barely gave light, only enough to fill the corners with shadows and make the darkness seem closer, so I took the loaf of bread from the table and crawled onto the pallet, pulling the blanket around me. For the first time in my life, I fell asleep not from the pleasure of drink or food, but from a deep weariness that filled my bones and pulled me quickly down into darkness.

When I woke the next morning, the first thing I noticed was that even more pain filled my body. In my blistered wrist, and the place between my shoulders where they met my spine, and even the balls of my feet—feet that had so recently run with ease and swiftness over any surface, stone or grass or broken shells, and never once grown weary or ached.

At least it had stopped raining. From the open door I could see a pale blue sky. Nothing like the sky that soared above Tara, but at least it would not make me damp if I had to go out in it. Slowly, I clambered to my feet and surveyed what the gods had given me in the pale morning light. It looked worse. At least with the rain and cold I'd been grateful for a roof to cover me, coals to light my candle. My *one* candle. I was suddenly sure that it was not a gift, but a cruel prod. One thing of beauty in the heart of such squalor, to remind me of what I'd lost.

I limped to the door because of the stiffness in my limbs and tried not to think of my immortal self, lithe and supple. The hut was set on the crest of a hill with a valley spread out beneath it, the sea to the right and a stream to the left. I could see other similar structures in the valley and realized they'd placed me so I was never far from mortals. This too was a punishment: no matter where I went, I would be able to see and hear them, even if it was at a distance.

I managed to gather an egg from where a chicken had laid it in the nearby meadow and brought it back to the hut, but I hesitated before placing it in the black cauldron that swung over the coals. I stirred it and waited for something to happen to the egg. I wished again that I had paid more attention to Sorcha's cooking, but my time with her family had been so long ago . . . and when I'd been there, I'd been consumed with Enya, not with watching Sorcha sweep or cook or feed her baby. Why should I have cared, when food could appear at the flick of my wrist?

The egg's shell was a lovely color, blue speckled; it reminded me of my own changeable skin. Well. The skin I used to have. My hands were now dull and pale and clumsy besides, because when I picked up the egg I held it too tightly and crushed it. Slime ran down my hands. It had not cooked at all, not like the eggs I had seen when Sorcha served her eggs, had merely been scorched in its shell. Still, I was desperate for food, so I crouched, sucking what was left from the smashed shell, licking yellow remnants of yolk from my hand.

That was how they found me.

I grew aware of them only because someone cursed, making me jump. I'd never once been startled by a mortal before, but now I leapt to standing even though the ones in the doorway had not made a move toward me. There were four of them, two men and two women. I rolled my shoulders back, trying to lengthen my spine and appear lethal and graceful as I had been, like a cat before it strikes. Rather than intimidating them, my movements seemed to make them think I was frightened.

"We're not going to harm you." The woman who spoke had a young face and thick, red hair. "We saw smoke in the air this morning and realized that you must be Fianna's niece, come to work the land."

I huffed out a breath. Apparently Danu had meddled with these people, made them think I belonged when I did not.

"You're hungry?" Their eyes were wide, and it was obvious they thought I was mad as they took in my yolk-stained hands, the ring of yellow around my mouth. One of the men backed away a pace, but the woman who had spoken took a step toward me, pity in her eyes. "Fianna was in a bad way before she died. She didn't leave much." The woman proffered a basket covered in a cloth. I did not take it from her, so she set it on the table. "We'll gladly help you get things in better order." Her eyes swept the room. "The garden looks fallow, but the land up here will reward your hard work. You'd not believe the size of the strawberries she used to grow."

Strawberries. That was why they'd sent me to this horrifying place. To grow strawberries. The thought made me angry, so angry that I seethed, "I do not need your help. Leave me." I held the gaze of the mortals until they began to move uneasily, to twist their hands and twitch their feet. They whispered to each other, and for a moment I was afraid they might try to restrain me or drag me to one of their druids. "I've not got time to worry about a mad woman," I heard one of the men whisper to his companion. "I came only because of Fianna. If she doesn't want our help, we'll leave her." The others nodded and backed out of the room. The woman who had looked on me with pity lingered only for a moment longer before sighing and leaving too.

That was fine; I preferred it. I did not want their help, nor to accept anything from them—but I could smell something, and my stomach twisted in hunger. I tore the cloth off the basket to find bread, glorious and golden. I ate the loaf so quickly I began to cough, and my mouth felt suddenly hot and burnt like my blistered wrist. I spat out the half-chewed piece on the ground, gasping. How did mortals *live* as long as they did? How did they survive with throats that could be choked so easily by *bread*, with mouths that could be burned so quickly?

After I ate, I did not know what to do. As a god, I had done whatever I wanted at the very moment I thought of it. If I wanted to eat, I waved my hand and a feast appeared. If I was thirsty, I would summon whatever it was I wanted to drink: icy water from a mountain stream, wine in a golden goblet, morning dew from the petals of violets. If I wanted to run, I ran. If I wanted to sleep, I slept. Nothing could bore me; time was meaningless. And now that life had been taken from me.

I could have stood there a long time, mourning what I had lost, but I was too restless to stay indoors, so I went back outside. Danu had sent me here in early spring, and while the air smelled of it, of wet earth and new green buds, it was still cold. I shivered and shivered, but I managed to find my way to the nearby stream. It was large, nearly as large as a river, and I could tell the current was swift, but I wanted more than anything to be clean—to wipe away the mud that had dried on my feet from the night before, to clean the remains of the egg from my hands and mouth—and so I dove into the stream, just as I had a thousand others before.

The river was wide but deeper than I'd thought, and when I tried to push off the bottom, I couldn't find it: the current was too strong, tumbling me over and over until I no longer knew which way was up and down. I knew how to swim of course, but had only done it lazily, easily, all water parting before me as though I were a sleek seal. This river paid no attention to me, no matter how much my legs and arms tried to push me to the surface, and I inhaled water and began to choke. I would have drowned there and then if I had not managed to grab onto a sapling that grew there in stubborn defiance of the stream's might. I clung to it, choking, sobbing, coughing up the river, my heart still racing.

I had nearly died.

I had never been so frightened before. Had perhaps never been *truly* afraid, if this was what fear was. Had Enya felt this way? The same overwhelming . . . *eternity* of fear. I clung to that sapling and wondered if I should have held her hand tighter, if I should have whispered—

I shook my head violently. I could not obsess over Enya again. She had been gone for centuries.

I finally climbed up the bank and made my way to my hut, grateful to find dry, clean clothes in a chest at the bottom of the pallet. They were simple and scratched at my skin, but the skirt was warm and thick, and I even managed to knot a yellow shawl around my shoulders. I had a sense of satisfaction when I tied it, just as I had when I'd finally made the hearth flame, but even as I felt it, I pictured the gods watching me and laughing. Had Danu seen everything too? Had she looked on with delight as I nearly drowned, as I slipped in muck the night before?

I walked out of the hut to try to find another egg, and I was not surprised to see the hill was now covered in bluebells. They had not been there the day before, and I did not know if they had opened simply because it was spring or because Danu had sent them. I wanted to cover them in frost, but I had no power left in my veins, nothing but weary resignation as I crushed them underfoot, their sweet scent unable to mask the stench of the birds, of my rough-wool clothes, of my own foolish mortal body.

the first life

It took me days to hunt down a rabbit, even though the hill was full of them. I'd watched them go in and out of their burrows, and at first I'd thought it would be easy—all I needed to do was throw out my hand and grab one—but my hands were slow and all the rabbits escaped me. Thankfully, I found an old snare in the wood, and after much trial and error was able to re-create it; before long, I'd caught several. Their meat was tough and fairly tasteless, but the hens did not lay enough eggs for me to depend entirely on them.

I was chopping through a rabbit heart when the knife I was using slipped, scoring a line through my thumb. One moment, my skin was whole and smooth, and the next it was as bloody as the creature I'd just put into the stewpot. I was startled by the blood's brightness, could only stare at the gash as red trickled down my finger.

I had never bled before; gods did not bleed. And even if we did . . . I could not imagine Danu dripping red. *Her blood would be sap green, slow, and sticky and sweet, and mine should have been silver, silver as ice, and Lug's would be*—I would have stood there stupidly coloring all the gods' blood had my thumb not begun to throb. I hissed at the pain, setting down the knife I still gripped, wrapping a cloth around my thumb tightly until the bleeding stopped. After that, I gently dunked my hand in the bucket of water I'd brought from the stream, cleaning the blood away, but when I held it up, I still saw a slender red slash where the knife had bit. Enya had once shown me a thin white scar on her knee, and I remembered now that I had not been able to understand how her skin could hold such a mark. But now I understood; now I remembered that mortal bodies *changed*. They grew thinner, fatter, greyer. They grew lined from smiling and from weeping alike, scarred from war, marked by falls and brambles—and knives.

After that, I was more careful and finished the stew slowly, pleased with the scent it threw into the air. I had not had a real meal since I'd been forced into this body, and I decided to enjoy it outside in the cooling spring air on the hill, which sloped down a long way until it met a green wash of sea. It was pleasant to sit there with nothing but the frogs croaking while swifts flew overhead, rising and falling, their bellies gleaming, catching the last light of the sun.

I stayed out there for a long time, my face softening as I watched the birds, filled with a quiet peace I had not known since Danu had sent me down here. I would have stayed longer if my stomach had not started to pinch with pain. Had the stew made me ill? I didn't want to go in, but sitting out there in pain made me feel small and fragile as though I were no stronger than the tiny birds above, so I went inside and fell into a blurry sleep.

I woke just a few hours later to a prickling feeling between my legs. I reached down, and when I pulled my fingers up, they were tipped with blood. I heard Enya's voice echoing down through the centuries, *Surely your ma's told you, all women bleed? Once we do, we can have babies.*

I shivered and wiped my fingers on the pallet. Enya had bled

and then she had died. I knew that she had died because of the babe
in her belly, but I found myself wondering if, because I had bled, I
too would die. Worse, a shiver of fear ran down my back at the
thought. How strange it was, to have a body that knew instinctually, in some animal way, that death came for all. But was this just
the fate of all women? To bleed and be marked as ready, then to
bear children for their husbands until they died?

I tried to make the idea a shape I could understand, but I must
have fallen asleep because I suddenly jumped awake at a knock. I'd
rehung the curtain over the doorframe, so I could not see who was
banging on the hut. At first I thought it must be Danu, that she had
watched me bleed into the pallet through the night and decided I
had suffered enough and could now be allowed to return home. I
flung the curtain away from the door, but when I saw a red-haired
woman standing there, all welcome slid from my face. It was the
same woman who'd come that first morning. I had seen her down
in the village below me, could pick her out by her bright hair, but
neither she nor anyone else had even glanced at my hut on the hill
after their first attempt at welcome.

"Thought you'd be more settled by now and wanting a bit of
company." The woman pushed past me and into the hut. "I'm Siobhan. And you're Fianna's niece, are you? The others thought I
should just leave you alone," she continued without waiting for my
response, her eyes darting penetratingly around the cabin, "but my
mother made me promise to always aid strangers when I can."

I frowned, about to tell her I did not need her pity, when a
cramp roiled through my belly and I grimaced, pressing my hand
against it.

The woman narrowed her eyes at me, looking me up and down
before her gaze flicked to the pallet. When she saw the bloody

stain, her face softened. "Did you not feel it coming, is that why you bled through the pallet?" I shook my head. "But surely it's not your first time? You're much too old for that. You're of an age with me, and I've just reached my thirtieth year."

I stifled the urge to laugh. I was older than her oldest relation and could have told her so, but of course she wouldn't have believed me, would have just thought I was even more mad than they had first assumed.

"Did your mother not tell you what to do?"

The thought of Danu teaching me about blood was ludicrous; she cared only about pleasant things. I opened my mouth to tell the woman as much, but my stomach twisted again and I winced, shaking my head.

"Well, I've no liking for you, but I can't leave you alone here, bleeding freely," the woman said. "The wolves will smell you."

I had never thought of wolves as dangerous. Even the greatest of them frolicked around me like puppies when I stepped in their midst, recognizing me for what I was. I'd heard howling a few nights before, and I hadn't been frightened—indeed, I'd smiled when I'd heard them lift their voices to the air—but now just remembering the sound made my skin prickle with fear.

"It was a long winter. They don't come down to the village, not after we drove them farther out into the forest some years back, but they've been known to come to the hill. And now they have pups to feed. I don't think they'll pause just because you've not got the weight of me." She stoked up the fire then glanced at me. "Well, at least you've water," she said, peeking into the pot that sat over the fire. "You can clean those"—she pointed at my soiled undergarments—"while I show you what to do." She reached as if to take them off me herself, but I backed away, not letting her touch me. She raised an eyebrow but just said, "You can take them off on your own." She turned away and I slipped the bloodied things off, throwing them into the pot. After I pulled on my other pair, she tied her shawl around my waist like it was a skirt, pushing me out the door. "My ma said that some women who don't get enough to eat never bleed. Maybe your bleeding never came because of how thin you are." She strode into the forest. "But if it's started now, you'd best know how to attend to it." She turned to see that I had not followed her and gave me a long, hard look. "I'm offering you my help. And I'm not asking anything in return."

I looked away from her. I did not *want* to learn, to be among mortals, but it was true that she was offering me something kind, something I desperately needed. It was foolish, absurd, to need her help, but what choice did I have? So when she began to walk toward the wood, I followed her. Reluctantly I asked, "Is there something that might help the pain?"

"There are some plants and herbs we can gather in the forest that will help," she said. "But first we need to fix it so you're not bleeding down your legs and walking around without anything decent on."

Siobhan and I walked through the forest quietly, until we came to a large mossy clearing. She reached over, peeled a large piece of moss off a tree, and held it up. "This absorbs the blood. And it's soft besides. Go on now, gather it yourself. Pull it gently so you don't have any bark come off with it." It was easier said than done, but eventually I managed to fill a pocket.

"The other too," Siobhan said when I showed her all I'd gathered. "Even then, probably won't be enough. You'll bleed for several days at least. You'll need to come back."

Days, I thought in disbelief. Mortal women bled for days?

Siobhan must have read my face because she said, "Did you truly grow up around no women?"

I thought of my brief days with Sorcha, with Enya. They had been the only mortal women I'd ever known, but it had been so long ago. So I said, "No. We did not live near any others."

The woman looked sad. "That must have been lonely."

I shook my head. "I liked it." I tilted my head up to the green trees, let my eyes linger on them for a moment. "It was peaceful."

Siobhan didn't respond, though I waited, and I wasn't sure why I felt a twinge of distress at her silence. She was just helping me because her ma had once told her she must. And why was I searching for anything more? It didn't matter. I did not need a friend.

"You'll need shoes," Siobhan said after several long minutes of silence. "Not during spring and summer, but the winter here is cold."

"Is it?" My voice was tight with longing, remembering the soft, quiet world I'd walked through so recently, my feet bare in the snow.

"Sometimes it is unbearable." Siobhan's voice was quiet. "I . . . I lost a child to the winter. I've never known a winter like that." Her eyes were distant, remembering. "It happened the first year after I was married. Snow up to my waist, cold that stole breath. My babe was just a wee thing, and she began to cough. I'd heard of it before, babies that could not draw breath in the cold, and all that winter I waited, holding her close to me, until spring came. Only that year . . . it never did." Siobhan sighed softly and turned her back to me. I thought she might be wiping her eyes.

I remembered how I'd grieved for the mound they had dese-crated, letting the world turn white around me in my anger and loss, but I felt more than sorrow at the memory. I felt . . . shame, my cheeks flushing red. She did not know that it had been because of me, my fault that she had lost her child. Had we wept together— me over what the mortals had taken from me, and she over what *I* had taken from her? I looked down at my pale white hands and knew that as I would mourn my clearing forever so too would she mourn her child.

Shame, I thought triumphantly the next moment. I had felt *shame* that I had caused her child to die. Surely now Danu would end this punishment? She would know that I understood what she was trying to teach me.

I looked up into the sky, but nothing happened. Danu did not come down and release me. "I'm sorry," I said finally, hoping that Danu needed me to speak the words aloud, to *hear* me express my sorrow to this woman, but nothing happened. Siobhan just kept gathering moss. "I'm sorry!" I repeated, louder, and Siobhan turned.

"I heard you. But your sorrow won't bring back my little girl, will it?" Her eyes were hard. "All of them say 'I'm sorry.' They say it as though it will be the same as having my girl in my arms again, as though their words can ease me." Siobhan ran a hand through her hair, and suddenly she looked very young.

"Brigid." A familiar voice spoke. "Her girl's name was Brigid." Danu stepped through the trees, close enough to Siobhan that she could touch her cheek, though the woman did not move or give any indication she knew Danu was there.

"Danu." Relief flooded me, making my hands tremble. Danu had come to take away my punishment. "I'm sorry." I pointed at Siobhan. "I am truly sorry that her daughter died because of the cold."

Danu didn't say anything, just looked around the clearing, touched the moss that bulged from Siobhan's pockets. "They are fascinating, aren't they? They bleed between their legs every single moon. But they find a way to stopper it up with the simplest of things. Moss." She looked down at her own legs. "I don't remember bleeding as a mortal woman. I wish I did."

"You don't." My voice was pinched as another wave of pain ran through me. "It's horrible."

"You've bled?" Danu's voice held a note of wonder, almost of avarice.

I nodded. "I had to get something to stop it up so the wolves wouldn't smell it on me." I hoped Danu would pity me. "It hurts."

Danu's eyes lit up. "You get to *feel*, Cailleach. Do you understand the gift I—we have given you?"

If I had been in my immortal form, I would have bounded away from her foolish questions. I would have gone somewhere quiet and cold, a place with snow so thick it muffled all sounds. But I was not in that form and would not be without her consent, so I nodded. "I understand." My voice was quiet. "And I am sorry. Did you hear me tell Siobhan I was sorry?"

She shook her head. "No." Her voice was distant. "I merely thought to see how you were doing after so long away."

"It has only been six days."

Danu blinked. "Only six? I thought it had been . . . months at least. Years, perhaps."

In a way I understood. Time passed differently as a god. We did not mark the passing of it, not as mortals did. But . . . I'd thought they would all be watching me. To see how I fared. I found that I was angry that they had not been. "It has been six days." I tried to keep my voice soft. I needed Danu's pity, her desire to make me happy again. "Six. Surely, Danu, you will not doom me to stay for years. That will be thousands of days. Tens of thousands."

Danu's eyes sharpened. "Six days is nothing, Cailleach. Six days does not atone for those you killed. You must stay until you learn what you did. Until you understand what it is to be one of them."

"But I had *remorse* for this mortal, that her child died. I've bled. I've known pain. Is that not enough?"

Danu glanced at Siobhan, who was still motionless. "Her child did not die; she was killed, Cailleach. By the winter you brought."

I caught her arm in desperation. "You were right." My voice was pleading. "I understand mortals now. I understand their pain and fear. I understand blood. I was wrong to do what I did. Please, Danu, give me back the winter."

Danu looked at me for a long moment. "You understand mortals now," she said dreamily, smiling, and a deep relief filled my body, making me sag like I'd suddenly dropped a great weight. She believed me. She saw I had changed.

Then her smile vanished like the sun behind a cloud. "In all of six days? I am not a fool, daughter. You will not end this punishment with sweet words," she snapped, before she disappeared into a slant of sunlight that blinded me before being doused by the shadow of the trees. I wanted to run after her, to scream now instead of beg, to say that this punishment was cruel, unjust, but without my true form I could not follow, could only feel my heart thudding in my chest, a swirl of emotions that I could not interpret.

I decided then that I would not pretend or playact for Danu anymore. Even though I wore a mortal body, I was still a god. And I would act as one.

"Thank you for your sorrow," Siobhan said, turning back to me as though she had not just been frozen and mute. I did not respond as she shoved one final handful of moss into her pocket and began

walking back toward the hut. "My daughter's name was Brigid."
Her quiet voice carried through the forest. "Brigid."

Spring and summer passed slowly, but not easily. Never easily. I
fought with weeds in my garden, with small animals that ate my
carrots and onions before I'd harvested them. Each day I walked to
the stream multiple times to fill my pail with water, my back aching
at the end of each evening.

At first I thought I would be able to live with what I had at the
hut, but some days I did not catch a rabbit or the hens didn't lay,
and I went to bed hungry. Worse even than the hunger was the
endless repetition of the same food day after day: tough, gamy rabbit cooked inexpertly; eggs without salt; berries sour from the
bush. One day after I'd eaten yet another breakfast of the like, I decided that I could no longer stand it and would go down to the village to trade for something else.

Siobhan had told me a little about the village that day in the
wood, had said it was small and unimportant, ignored by the local
king who cared only about the fertile inland and not the sea-
hardened coast. The little sickle-shaped clearing of land encom-
passed the hill my hut sat on and the village below it—no walls, no
defenses, just a squalid collection of round huts with thatched
roofs. What likely protected it most was that it was surrounded by
a dense forest on one side and by a roiling sea on the other.

As I walked through the village, the people I passed did not look
terribly friendly. I assumed Siobhan had told them of me, so they

did not pull out knives when they saw me, but it was clear that they did not trust strangers—made more obvious when I tried to trade the rabbits for milk and cheese. I had cleaned them well and they were fat, but none of the villagers wanted them. I was about to trudge back up the hill when I saw Siobhan. Several children trailed behind her, all with her red hair, and when she saw me, she raised a hand. "You've finally come down," she said when she reached me.

"I was trying to trade for some cheese and milk." I contorted my face into a tight smile. This was one thing I remembered quite well from my time among the mortals; they smiled at each other even when there was no true joy in their hearts.

"What have you got to trade?" Siobhan lifted an eyebrow, and I opened the sack to show her the rabbits. She held one up, stroked the soft fur. "I can use them." Her voice was soft. "I want to make sure my children have fur-lined boots this winter."

She gestured for me to follow her, and we walked to her hut in the center of the village. She didn't invite me inside but came out with a jug full of creamy milk and a large piece of yellow cheese. My mouth watered at the smell, and I threw the rabbits down, grabbing both from her before she had the chance to change her mind. I paused before turning away to walk back up the hill. "Why are you trading with me? No one else will. They say they can't spare it." I was uncomfortable with her generosity toward me and I needed to know what she wanted. What I owed her for it.

Siobhan wiped a hand across her brow and looked out toward the sea. "My mother was very devout; she prayed every day and she hung on every word that the druids said. She believed that sometimes the gods walked among us in mortal skin." I laughed then, bitterly and without mirth, but Siobhan didn't seem to take offense, just continued her story. "I prayed, as a child prays, but I didn't believe her." Then she pointed out toward the harbor where the fishermen bobbed in their little hide-covered coracles. "I loved to swim, you know, just there. One day, I was swimming in my usual place when I was pulled out to sea by a wave. It was too deep, and I could barely move against the strength of the tide. I was drowning. I was certain I'd taken my last breath—but then I was pulled from the waves. I felt arms around me, carrying me back to shore. They laid me on the beach . . ." Her face grew soft, almost dreamy. "Their face was like a mortal—the most beautiful of mortals. Too beautiful to be one. And their blue eyes that shimmered like fish scales." As she spoke, I realized that she was describing Manannán. God of the sea. "I was certain in that moment that my mother was right. That gods walked in the earth in disguise, and I had just been spared by the god of death. Since that day I've treated all outsiders as though they might be gods." Siobhan sighed and looked at the ground. "I felt that same god's presence on the night that my—that Brigid died. It was the only way I could let her go. Knowing that she would go to be with the god who had saved me."

I had opened my mouth to say no, that it was not Manannán who had sat by her. Manannán might have rescued her from the sea, but they did not care about death. If there had been a god with her, it would have been Danu. *With her great compassion for mortals*, I thought sourly. *And wherever your child went, it was not to the gods*. I nearly spoke the thought but kept silent. Siobhan was willing to trade with me. I did not want to give her reason to stop. If I had a twinge of guilt at allowing her to have faith in such falsehoods, I ignored it.

But perhaps Siobhan could see some kind of conflict on my face. "Do you believe in the gods?" she asked.

I didn't know what to say. I didn't need to *believe* in the gods. But

I knew that some mortals were so devout that they grew angry when they found someone who wasn't. "I don't believe the gods *need* worship like the druids claim," I said carefully. "I think it would be better if mortals and gods left each other alone."

Siobhan blinked at me, surprised by my words. "But the gods require worship." Her voice was insistent. "They require our prayers and sacrifice in order to listen to us. That is as it always has been."

"The gods must have had their beginning, once. As everything begins." I thought of Danu deciding that the gods could not give their gifts for nothing in return. She had been the one who had wanted burnt offerings and gifts of gold to make Tara shine all the brighter.

"You don't worship them?" Siobhan looked concerned. "Not even our mother, Danu?"

I laughed, short and bitter, at the irony of her question. "I suppose I *do* speak to Danu. But often I find she does not listen."

Siobhan sighed, as if there was relief in my answer. That was another thing I did not understand about mortals and their worship. Was their belief, their faith, so faint that the absence of it in another could cause them such worry? Was that faith at all? A part of me wanted to stand there, to argue about it with Siobhan, but I didn't want to press her; I needed her if I wanted to trade again and upsetting her wouldn't do any good. I had already said too much. So instead I thanked her for the milk and cheese and walked back up my hill alone, wondering if Danu had been listening.

After that, I walked to the village every few days to trade with Siobhan. I brought rabbits and birds in exchange for milk and cheese from her cow. She smiled when she saw me and sometimes invited me to sit with her, even once to eat with her family—a boy and two little girls. Sometimes I even *wanted* her company, wanted to stay and talk with her awhile, wanted to play with her children, but I worried that Danu would see a friendship between us as me softening, as her being *right* to take away my godhood, and so I always shook my head when Siobhan asked me to stay.

The weeks went on. I had enough to survive but little else, and the little I had needed my constant care and attention. When the trees began to lose their leaves, I finally had some degree of comfort. I had never liked spring and summer—these were Danu's domain. I mistrusted their warmth, their sweetness. I was more clearheaded when cool wind blew on my face, when my feet crunched against the ground. Sometimes that winter, when evening had finally fallen and there was less to do, I would lie down in the frosted grass and look up at stars. Even when my fingers and nose froze, I resisted returning to my dank hut, preferring the clear night. I could pretend I was as I had been—that I, Cailleach the goddess, was in a clearing in a dark wood, gazing up at the stars. Those times were the closest I ever felt to my winter self and were some small measure of happiness, and so I stayed out as long as I could—until my whole body began to shake with cold.

When it grew colder, I traded with Siobhan for boots. Though the shoes were soft, lined with rabbit fur, I hated wearing them— they pinched and constrained my feet with every step. But after the first snow I had realized it was not possible to gather wood or check snares without them or I would injure myself.

However, my boots did nothing to warm my hut when the wind battered it—so hard I thought it might fall down on top of me. I wore all the clothing I had each night, but this did not fully protect me from the drafts that blew down the chimney or from the fire going out in the night.

I spent long hours gathering wood, going deeper and deeper into the forest to try to find more when I'd gathered all near me. I was watchful as I walked, listening for what might be around—for bears, yes, but mostly for wolves, as I had to go into their territory to gather kindling for my fire. Because of this, I carefully checked each clearing before I entered. I had thought this one I entered was safe, that I was alone, but while crouching to grab a piece of wood, I saw a pair yellow eyes just through the bush. The wolf was crouched as well, and so close I could have brushed its ears with my sleeve. I would have in my immortal body—would have run through the forest and hunted deer with it, but now as I caught its eye, my heart began to race.

The wolf was white with flecks of grey, melding perfectly into the snow-covered forest. It was fat and round, with ears that flicked forward then back, but it didn't snarl. I wondered where its pack was. I rarely saw a lone wolf; more often they hunted together in order to bring down their prey. I wanted to race away but I could not seem to stop staring into its eyes. There was something I understood when I looked at him. Some quiet coldness that promised an end to this mortal life. And for a moment, a brief moment, I considered it. I knew, though, that if I took that death there would be pain and blood—things I now knew to fear—so instead, I slowly let go of the stick and backed out of the clearing until I could no longer see the wolf. Then I turned and did run, as fast as I could—past my hut and all the way into the village, toward the yellow light coming from the crofts. Siobhan was standing outside her door when I approached. "Have you come to celebrate the solstice with us after all?" She held a burning torch out to me, but I did not take it.

"A wolf," I gasped. "I saw a wolf in the forest."

"Already?" Siobhan sighed. "It's early for them to be out. A bad sign of the cold to come." She looked for her children. They were bundled up and obviously warm, their cheeks flushed, but I saw the fear on Siobhan's face, that the frost would take them from her. She turned back to me and held out the torch once more. "But here. We can still celebrate the light."

I had forgotten that tonight was the longest night of the year and that the villagers gathered together to celebrate. Siobhan had told me a few days before that they would light a bonfire and dance around a sacred oak, singing and praying all night, staying up until dawn when light returned. She had invited me to come, but I had turned down her invitation. Now, I was so frightened from seeing the wolf that for a moment I considered staying. Some part of me longed for the light, for the warmth of their fire and songs, the comfort of company—something I had not felt in so many years, so long that I had forgotten I once enjoyed it.

But then I remembered with whom I had shared those nights. How Enya's future had been ripped from her on one of them. How her face had paled when she'd looked at the old man she was to marry, at the father who had promised he wouldn't force any such thing upon her. I remembered how Danu had carried me away shrieking—remembered Enya's lifeless body. I had to bite my cheek to keep tears from filling my eyes. I turned away from Siobhan and said, "No. I have to return home."

I trudged slowly back up the hill and lit my fire. I'd forgotten that I had not actually gathered any wood that day, but I couldn't go now. I kept thinking about those yellow eyes and was too frightened. Again I wished for my goddess self, who would have never feared such a creature—but in my god form, I wouldn't have needed a fire at all, and frustration coiled tightly in my bones. I decided there was nothing to do but go to sleep and hope for warmth. I lay there with all my clothes on, my blanket pulled tight as it could be around me, and, unbidden, I thought of Enya with a ferocity I had not in years; the village and their celebrations had awoken something in me. Or maybe it was the cold of the night. I found myself wishing that she were here, that she were still alive, that we could fall asleep curled around each other as we had so many times as children. I missed her so much then that I began to cry. I did not bother wiping away my tears. After all, who was here to see them? I was alone, not even the winter to give me solace. So I lay there and sobbed for a long time until finally, I fell asleep.

When I woke in the dark some hours later, I realized it was still night. The longest night. My fire had gone out, and I knew I needed to stand, to go and stir it up, to go out to the forest to gather wood, but my body was too stiff, too cold. I couldn't uncurl my fingers from around my blanket, couldn't get my legs to swing out into the open air. I was frozen with the same panic that I'd had the day I'd nearly drowned in the stream—a swirling, gasping terror—but this time, I could not respond to it, could not make my limbs move, could not make them fight. I could only lie there, knowing that I was about to die.

My last thought before blackness took me was that I had never before been afraid of the cold.

the first death

Death was louder than I thought it would be.

I could hear the gods murmuring—about me, I was sure, though I could not make out the words. My eyes were closed, but I knew I was back in my god form, could feel the litheness in my limbs, the strength in my body, which could once again bound across mountains, swim to the darkest part of the sea. The only thing that was missing was what I'd longed for most—winter. And as I realized that I opened my eyes and jumped to my feet, letting loose a string of curses so violent that Manannán blushed and Dagda covered his ears.

I thought Danu might reproach me, but she said nothing, just waited until I'd stopped seething and then gestured toward the other gods looking down at me from their thrones. "Ask her what questions you have." She smiled as though this were a pleasant little game.

"How did it feel?" Morrígan leaned forward, eyes glittering. "To die?"

"I don't know." I was not sure how to explain the paralysis of my limbs, the creeping darkness, the sense of my heart slowing.

"You must have *felt* something." Dagda flicked a tear out of his eye. "*I* did and I was just watching—"

"I wish *I* could have tried it," Lug interrupted, clapping his hands together and grinning. "I think I—"

"You don't know for what you *wish*," I said viciously. "You watch and you play with me as though—as though I'm *one* of them—as though I would be eager to come back and give you a report on every moment of pain, every time darkness floods my vision, every time—"

The gods erupted in a clamor of voices at my words, but before I could make sense of their speech, Danu swept her hand and they fell silent. "Do you not see? You live as we once did, as we can no longer. These lives can be a gift, if you would let them." She looked at me, her gaze steady. "Tell us, what did you feel before you died?"

I looked down at my blue hands and felt a cold but weary anger. There was no point in trying to fight against Danu's will. There never had been. "I was cold. And confused." *And alone*, I did not say.

"Were you frightened?" Danu did not meet my eyes.

"Yes," I said stiffly, hoping that if I was truthful this would all end.

"If you'd stayed with the villagers, celebrated their festival with them, you would have survived. They would have kept you warm through the night."

"I would change nothing." My voice was loud. "I vowed long ago I would not attend one of their solstices again."

"I don't know why," Danu sighed. "They're wonderful, full of dancing and revelry and . . ." She trailed off as she met my furious gaze. She had forgotten the solstice we'd spent together. She'd forgotten what happened. She must have, for her to say such a thing.

Her eyes darted away from me, and when she turned back, her voice was formal, as though she were giving a speech. "What have you learned about mortals? What has your punishment taught you?"

"I have learned," I spat, "that they are foolish and slow. They bleed and they hurt, and their flesh is weaker than a just-opened bud in spring." I thought for a moment of Siobhan's daughter, of the sorrow I'd felt at learning of her death, but Danu already knew about that. She knew and did not care.

She waited but I said no more, and she shook her head, weary. "Well, I can see you have really learned nothing. Perhaps in your next life." She pointed her finger at me.

For a long moment there was nothing—

No sound.

No smell.

No touch.

No feel.

Then, light.

the second life

At least Danu hadn't sent me down in the rain again.

When I woke, I found I was lying on something soft. I could hear bees droning nearby, could smell something sweet. I opened my eyes and when I saw where I was, I laughed, short and bitter. Danu must have thought herself very clever. I hadn't thought she'd been watching when I trampled the bluebells in the garden, but she must have been, because I lay in a field of them. They stretched as far as I could see, reaching up toward the cluster of birch trees that let in the gentle golden light that hit my face, but it wasn't warm; I could see my breath in front of me when I lifted my head, and the bluebells were lightly covered in snow, so it must have been early spring.

I stood, and while my body wasn't as strong as it had been in my god form at least it didn't seem as slow as it had the first time. I swung my arms once and then set off toward the break in the trees. I had no idea where she'd sent me, but when I walked out of the clearing, I saw my hut. Only it was not as it had been. It was built of stone now, not flimsy wood, and the roof that covered it looked as though it might actually keep out the rain. The land around it was different too. I could hear a beehive somewhere nearby, and I could see many viny bushes that I thought would hold flowers when the spring came, but right now the land was bare. It was obvious to me that some long years had passed since I'd died.

So Danu had taken away all my sources of food and left me only with flowers. Did she mean to starve me in this life? *No*, I thought, looking down onto the village below me. She meant to force me to interact with the villagers. I squinted, shading my eyes with my hands, and saw that my hut was not the only thing that had changed. The village had grown too, creeping out across the finger of land that swept out to the sea.

I did not turn toward it as I knew Danu wanted me to, but instead walked toward the forest. It had used to be almost on my doorstep, so close that a long stride could bring me to it, but now I had to walk across a little meadow to reach it. I realized that I could likewise see the village more clearly than I'd been able to before.

The villagers had been cutting down trees.

Taking, I thought bitterly. Always taking. But of course, I had to take too, now that I was back in this body—if I meant to survive. I looked at my little hut in the distance and could feel, almost like it was a physical thing, the weight of mortality falling back onto my shoulders again.

I thought of how death had taken me in my first life and decided that I would gather wood. I would ensure that I would never run out of it, that my hearth was heaped high each night. I could worry about food after. I walked a little farther into the clearing and froze as I reached for a piece of dead wood when I once more saw a pair of eyes staring at me. Had I returned only to be killed by a wolf my first day? Then I heard a whimper. I drew closer and saw not a wolf but a dog, caught in the thorny brambles. It mewled again and tried to flee as I drew closer, but it only backed into more thorns and gave a yelp of pain before crouching and looking up at me, terrified.

I pulled my hand back. I had been sent back in thicker clothes than in my first life, but I knew I could ill afford to tear them. If I'd had warmer clothes last time, I might not have succumbed to the winter. I did not want to die like that again. I went to take another step back but stopped as the dog began to shake. I remembered how I had shivered just like that the night I had died. I had been cold, but more, I had been *frightened* of the cold. Afraid to die, just like the little dog in front of me was. I did not want this creature to die as I had, afraid of what should be beautiful. Suddenly, instinctually, my arm was shoving its way through the branches, pushing through the brambles even when they tore through my sleeve, catching my skin and drawing blood, until I'd firmly pulled the dog free. He was white and black, with a slim face almost like a fox's, and though he had a long, matted coat I could still see how thin he was. He began to shiver again as I stared at him, then curled himself into a tiny ball as though trying to hide from me. He was nothing but skin and bones. Would he survive even though I'd freed him? I was going to leave him to continue gathering wood for my fire when he licked my hand. He did it tentatively, just a quick swipe, but in that brief contact I felt his gratitude, and I picked him up gently, swinging him under my arm and taking him to the hut with me.

I placed him carefully on the pallet where I slept. It was the first time I had entered my home in this life. The bed was made up but was covered in a layer of dust; I thought I could even see the stain where I'd bled through my bedclothes that first life. The dog curled up on the blanket while I lit a fire, and I found it strangely comforting.

I started small, with a few sticks of kindling from the basket and the fabric from the edge of my sleeve; it was torn beyond repair from the thorns anyway. When I struck the stone against the flint, a line of sparks flew out and immediately caught on the cloth. I thought of how long it had taken in my first life, how I had sat for hours striking the stones together, and a small smile spread across my face as the yellow fire gave warmth to my cold skin. I jumped slightly when I felt something against my side but saw it was only the dog who had crept down beside me. He gave a little sigh and lay down, putting his head on his paws. "I guess I'll need to feed you now." I looked around the hut, though it could barely be called that anymore. Before it had been nothing more than a round building with a dirt floor. It had been expanded, with a floor of pale wooden planks and a stone exterior, so that though I could hear the wind whistling around us, I could no longer feel it blowing through cracks in the walls. There were shelves full of a variety of things: yarn, a needle and thread, and rows and rows of fat yellow candles. What could I *do* with so many candles? Then the realization hit me: I was to use them to trade with the villagers. Of course. And when they ran out . . . I thought of the buzzing hive outside. I sighed. This, too, was another one of Danu's cruel games. She had candles exactly like this all over Tara, candles she'd made herself from beehives that she tended lovingly each day. She'd always wanted me to learn to make them, to help her with them, and I had never agreed. Now she was forcing me to, whether I wanted to or not. I had not understood her love of the work, the joy she'd found in the intricacies of a piece of honeycomb then. Now I understood her even less. I had spent my time chopping wood and cooking stews and stirring up the fire because it was the only way to survive—not because I enjoyed the work. It only highlighted the foolishness of Danu, of the other gods, of myself when I'd walked with Danu among the mortals as a child. When we'd spent those years in Mooghaun, we had worked alongside Sorcha and Enya, but only as we wished. We did none of the difficult tasks, did not carry water from the stream or tan leather in great, stinking pits. All we did was push our hands once or twice through soft, already-worked dough or add a twist of wood to a fire that burned because of the logs they had chopped down, not because of our paltry offerings. The gods longed for work only because they could not remember what it was like to go to bed with an aching back and frostbitten hands, could not remember the desperation of survival—they did not truly wish to spend their days in such drudgery.

Still, it did not matter how annoyed I was at Danu. I had to eat, as did the little dog who sat on the bed looking up at me. So I gathered a few of the candles and put on my shawl, ready to descend to the village.

I was going to leave the dog in the hut, but he jumped up when I opened the door and ran outside with me, following me down the hill.

When I'd last been to the village it had been small and shabby like my hut, but I could see as I drew closer that the years that had passed had been kind to it. There were more houses, built out of slabs of stone—roofs covered in thick thatch. Sloping down toward the sea, I could see tilled fields waiting to be seeded, and the group of children that I passed were plump and hearty They did not look at me suspiciously, and I wondered if the villagers were more used to strangers than they had been during my first life. Perhaps bards and other travelers had made their way here.

As I walked, I looked out for Siobhan or her children, and

though I saw several women with red hair, none had the particular shine of hers. There was a hollowness in my chest at the thought of never again seeing her smile, never watching her eyes roll toward the heavens when I was rude to her or ignored her instructions. Siobhan and her kindness had been what had kept me alive that first life, and I was ashamed that I'd never thanked her. And as I looked around at faces I did not recognize, it dawned on me that I had no idea who would trade with me, who would even speak to me, and at the loneliness of the thought I realized that I'd been wrong about Siobhan. I had not considered her a friend, but she had spoken to me, hadn't she? She had helped me when she didn't need to—I *had* had a friend. Now I no longer did. And I would never be able to see her again, never thank her for that friendship, and it made me sad. The loss of her was not like the loss of Enya— I had not known her well enough for that—but it touched me in the same place: a tiny grief that seemed to lodge in the hollow of my throat, a sensation so surprising that I stumbled a moment and had to catch my breath before continuing into the market.

It was near the harbor, and at the scent of fish the dog began to sniff the air, trotting faster. The closer we drew, the more his body shivered, and my own stomach growled in answer.

I walked over to a woman selling fish from a little cart and held out one of the candles. "Will you trade?" I said. "A candle for a fish?"

The woman squinted at me. "You're Cailleach, then," she said, startling me so much with my name that I nearly dropped the candle. "Heard from a bard that a widow, cousin to Fianna, was coming to live in her little house up the hill."

I wondered if this "Fianna" was a little trick Danu was playing and wanted to ask more about it. Just then, the dog tried to take a fish from the woman's cart. She growled and would have kicked out at him had I not grabbed her wrist. "I will pay," I said quickly. "With candles. For all the fish he wants." I looked down at him; he had gone down on his belly again, ears back, afraid, ashamed. "He's my dog."

The woman grunted but agreed. "What do you call him?"

"Failinis." I didn't quite know where the word had come from, but something about meeting him had felt . . . fated. Right, in some way that I could not quite put into words.

The woman squinted at him. "He doesn't look like any destiny I've ever seen, but I've never been fond of the word myself. The only destiny we have is what the gods give us."

"I do not have much use for the gods."

It was a small thing to say, harmless, but the woman's eyes grew wide, almost frightened. "You'd do well to speak with the druid, otherwise your soul could be in peril." I looked up to see a man with golden hair standing in the sunlight and speaking to one of the fishermen. I'd never met a druid before myself, but I'd thought that they would seem . . . grander, somehow. This one didn't look particularly impressive, with a young face and brown robe that marked him as the least of his order.

I gave Failinis a small fish as we walked back toward my hut, and he ate it quickly, nervously, as though worried I would take it away. Where had he come from? Many of the villagers before had dogs, but they'd looked more like the wolves in the forest. None had this dog's coloring or long coat.

When I got back to the hut, I gave the dog another fish to eat, then began to turn the rest into a stew. There was still a large black pot swinging over the fire, and I wondered if it was the same one

I'd used before. I did not know how many years it had been, but I thought it must have been at least the length of two generations, with how the village had changed in that time.

I threw the fish into the pot and then blinked at it, realizing I had nothing else to add. Learning to cook had been another hardship, but Siobhan had taught me some basic things; how to roast birds and rabbits, how to cook carrots and onions without scorching them, the places to find herbs that would add flavor to my meals. Small things, things that all mortal women knew how to do. Now, I had nothing for flavoring. I scowled at the fire, then went out to get water. I was at least glad to see a round, stone well in the yard—I no longer had to go to the stream. It would be a relief not to have to haul the water back and forth every day.

I found a long rope attached to the end of a bucket. I threw the bucket down and then pulled it back up, taking a long sip. The water was cold and sweet, better than that of the stream. That water had tasted of too many things—of the mountains it had come from, the silt that had lined its streambed, sometimes even like salt.

I set the bucket down at Failinis's feet, and he drank from it thirstily and for so long that I realized he must have been desperate for water. I sighed and patted him gently. *I* had not even survived winter in my previous life; what was I thinking, trying to take care of a dog too? But I doubted any of the villagers wanted a puppy from a woman they didn't know. No doubt they would kick stones at him if he tried to steal their food or drown him if they saw him getting too close to their chickens. "I will do my best," I said softly, as Failinis finally lifted his head from the bucket and gave me a sloppy grin, water running down his chin.

With some grim effort I managed to dig up some early wild

onions, even though the ground was still half-frozen, and I threw them in the pot with water and fish. I'd not collected the wood I'd meant to earlier but noticed a stack of it sitting neatly against the side of the hut that I'd not seen before and relaxed a little; it might be warm now, but it was still early spring by the sea and it would get cold at night.

As the sun began to set and the stew bubbled, I walked toward the beehives. There were actually two large, conically shaped hives, nestled inside large upright jars made of golden stone. I could hear a gentle buzzing from inside and even saw one or two of the bees flying around nearby, perhaps returning from the bluebell wood. I sighed, frustrated. I knew nothing about keeping bees, knew only that Danu gathered the honey and wax three times a year: after Beltane, at the height of summer, and then early after harvest, before Samhain. I had enough candles that I thought I could survive until Beltane . . . but *how* exactly was I supposed to learn to keep bees? How was I to keep them alive till then? Danu had her eternal patience . . . but I had neither eternity nor patience.

"Danu," I said loudly, startling the dog, who had followed me to the hives. "Danu!" I shouted. Failinis watched me, tail wagging energetically, then let out a sharp, high-pitched howl that made me jump. He looked so surprised at my reaction, barking in response, that I could not help but laugh.

"It is good to see you happy." Danu appeared suddenly at my side. "What a lovely dog." She gestured to Failinis, then held out her hand to him. Failinis sniffed it, sneezed, then backed away from her into my legs.

Disappointed, Danu stood and threw her long hair over her shoulder. She looked very young, barely more than a child. Certainly nothing like an immortal goddess. She looked around the hill with interest. "I wanted to see the hives for myself." She reached out a finger and touched the top of one gently.

"I don't know how to keep bees." My voice was stiff. "Did you give me these only so that I had to beg for your help?"

"Oh, child. Mortals give great thanks for bees. They're a source of sweetness, of wax. I have given you a gift." She smelled of summer, of wild hay and sharp green grass and roses. She took a step forward as though expecting an embrace, but I moved out of her reach. Her mouth suddenly firmed, and she no longer looked like a young girl. "No. Even if you asked, I would not help you with them. I gave you many chances in Tara. You are a mortal now, as they are. You will have to learn as they do." She did not touch me again but gave Failinis a farewell pat before fading away into the sunset.

"You commune with the goddess herself." I whirled around to see the druid from the village speaking, eyes wide.

I was not sure how to respond. Should I try to refute his words, say that he'd seen nothing but a strange trick of the light? Something in his clear eyes made me uncertain of whether he would believe me, so I said nothing.

"I am Dagda, the druid," he said finally. "I've lived in Daingean Uí Chúis for several seasons now. Liam told me that you are a widow here to work Fianna's croft."

"Did you become a druid because you are named after one of the gods?" I asked, thinking he looked nothing like the Dagda I knew—he had neither his thick green beard nor his height. This man was shorter than I, had brown eyes, and, unlike the god, his golden hair was his only claim to beauty.

"I was named after an uncle," the druid said. "My parents did not worship any gods. They lived in the mountains far to the east of here, in a valley surrounded by tall peaks. Few left, and when they did, they did not return. We knew nothing about the world outside. I was half-grown when a druid came to our village and began to teach us about the gods. About Danu and Dagda and Lug. But I'll confess, I have not seen one until today." His eyes flicked back to the space where Danu had stood so recently. There was nothing there now but a dark blue sky on the edge of night.

I sighed. It was clear that I would not be able to convince him that he'd not seen Danu. "I have spoken to the goddess on occasion," I admitted.

"She must favor you greatly." Dagda spoke with longing. "I've known only one druid who once glimpsed a goddess. And even then, they did not see Danu herself but another goddess, one with silver hair and blue skin whose steps crackled with ice, leaving a trail of frost wherever she walked."

I swallowed at his description of me, wanted to fall to my knees with despair. I *longed* with sudden and acute desperation to be back in my immortal body, in my own skin. To walk under the snow-covered firs, skate over icy rivers, vanish from mortal sight.

"Perhaps it is because of your silver hair that Danu shows herself to you," Dagda mused, yanking me from my cold memories and returning me to my human squalor, the hut on the hill, hands that used to feel as sweet as a kiss now cracked and chaffed red from cold. "Were you grey even as a child?"

"I was born like this." I shoved my hands into my shawl and stamped my cold feet. "And Danu does not favor me. If anything, she torments me."

The druid looked surprised. "The gods do not torment us," he chided gently, "they take our offerings and listen to our prayers. Whatever we suffer comes from within."

I scoffed, looking at his young face. What he would do if I told him the truth, that I was one of the gods he worshipped, that I had been punished with a mortal body? I thought he might actually believe me . . . but what would telling him do? I had no need of his sympathy, and he could give me no help. "Believe me, druid. My torment was specifically designed by the gods." I turned away from the thought and from him, back toward the hives.

"I came to invite you to worship with us in the forest." He appeared at my elbow.

"I do not worship the gods," I responded, leaning an ear against the hive. I did not know what I was listening for, I just knew that Danu often listened to her hives. I'd expected a drumming, like a mortal's heartbeat, but the sound was slower and more sinuous than that. It rushed and ribboned back and forth, constant as the tide. I was moving to press my ear against the other hive when I knocked heads with the druid. He winced, then chuckled. "I'm sorry. I did not mean to get so close." He pointed to the hive. "They are strong and healthy. Otherwise you would not be able to hear them so loudly."

At his words, I knew, suddenly, why Danu had sent me this man. "Did you keep bees in your village?" I asked, voice resigned.

He nodded. "Before I left with the druid."

My first instinct was to send him back down the hill, try to keep the bees on my own—but the reason I had died in that first life was because I had not asked for help when I needed it. I knew Danu was testing me, to see if I would learn from my previous mistake . . . and I did not *want* to. I did not want to please her. But neither did I want to starve myself or Failinis. Perhaps I could trade with this druid just as I'd traded with Siobhan. "I will ask Danu to show herself to you," I said slowly. "If you teach me how to keep bees properly."

The druid hesitated, but I saw the longing in his eyes. He wanted Danu to appear for him as much as he'd ever wanted anything in his life. He wanted, like all humans, to be chosen by her. For a moment I wondered if I should tell him the truth of her, tell him that no matter how she loved mortals, no matter how she loved *him*, she would forget him soon enough in her pursuit of the adoration of another. As I looked at his face, though, I knew no matter what I told him, he would not listen. Mortals grew up on stories of Danu's goodness, her love for them; my voice would do little to convince him. Maybe he even hoped that if he was good enough, brave enough—or whatever it was that Danu sought—he might become a god himself, as the other gods had.

"I will help you." His voice was eager. Then he did something I did not expect. He took a deep breath, and I *saw* him push down the burning desire in his eyes. "But you must worship with us. The gods will it. They ask that every mortal brings them sacrifice."

I was surprised that the man's avarice had not been enough to sway him, even with thoughts of the great goddess Danu before him. I was impressed, so I nodded, even though I did not intend to worship his gods at all.

Danu's control over winter was quite different from mine. I let it linger, swelling and receding like a wave on the shore, but my mother displayed no such care: one day there was snow on the ground and the next day it was a morass of mud and spiky green grass, the trees flooded with flowers. Her spring was startling, too heavy with scent and blossom, and she'd brought it on two whole months before Beltane, but there was nothing I could do about it except keep a wet rag by the door to clean Failinis's feet before he tracked muddy footprints all over the house.

I spent my first few weeks in that second life gathering kindling from the forest and chopping down a dead oak that stood near its border. Failinis hated the wood and never set foot in it, instead standing at its edge whimpering until I came back. He rarely barked, but he whined often to tell me when he was hungry or wanted to go out. I had to get up to let him out multiple times a night in those first few weeks and was amazed again that any mortal creature, human or animal, survived with such requirements. It reminded me of how Enya had complained that her brother Cathal took all her mother's time with his need to eat and sleep and be changed, but I had never seen it in practice until I had Failinis. When I wasn't busy running after him, I spent my time learning how to keep the bees, Dagda at my side.

"The wind and warmth keep them dull and docile," he said on one particularly hot day he had come up the hill to show me how to find the queen. He'd pushed his sleeves up and was bent over the hive. Failinis, who'd been standing at our heels, jumped away when Dagda moved the lid off the hive. Failinis was as skittish as a young horse, panicking at strange noises, sudden movements, and even the trees blowing too hard in the wind. One day he'd tripped and fallen partway down the hill when scrambling to get away from my *laundry*. His eyes had been wide with terror as if my dress were a demon.

"We're looking for the queen—we won't be disturbing them much." Dagda beckoned me and I came closer, looking down into the golden-walled hive. The bees seemed frantic, and I couldn't make any sense of them until Dagda pointed to one in particular

that was sitting quietly, circled by other bees. Dagda need have
said nothing; I knew immediately that was the queen. The others
looked as though they were bowing to her, and Danu looked much
the same when she made some great pronouncement—serene, ut-
terly sure of herself, the other gods hanging on her every word.

"It's good they're still alive," Dagda said after we'd checked
the second hive for its queen and found her as well. "Sometimes the
queen does not survive this long. Then you have to collect the
honey and wax immediately before the rest of them die, and you
can't collect any more until you get a new hive the next spring."

"How does one keep them alive during the winter?" I dangled a
finger into the hive, almost grazing the drowsy bees.

Dagda frowned. "You don't. Before Samhain, you destroy the
hive entirely to get the last of the honey and wax. Then you find
another swarm the next spring. Isn't that how you got these bees?"
He pointed to the hives.

I shook my head. "They were here when I came. But I'm sure a
hive can last even through the cold. I've seen—" I was about to say
Danu, but I didn't like to mention her name around Dagda, so I just
said, "I've seen it before."

Dagda shrugged. "Perhaps there is another way. But not one
I've learned."

"It doesn't seem right." I thought about how busy those bees
had been, their lulling hum. "They create the honey and the wax
for us, and they're killed for it at the end." Even as I said *us*, I bit my
tongue. I'd never referred to myself in the same group as mortals
before. I shifted uncomfortably, a tightness in my chest—a spark
of fear, that I had counted myself among them.

"They would die anyway," Dagda said. "Only queens live longer than a season."

"But it's not—"

Dagda held up a hand, smiling gently. "I commend you for your tender heart, Cailleach," he said, ignoring my bitter look at his words, "but I don't have time to argue further. Tonight, we worship." Dagda glanced at the darkening sky. "We're meeting in the clearing near the large oak. You know it?" He continued once I nodded. "I'll see you there once the moon rises?"

I wanted to protest, to say that I was too busy to come, but I had made a bargain with Dagda and I was no *mortal* who would go back on my word, no matter how much reluctance I felt, so I agreed.

I shut Failinis in the hut an hour later, heading toward the wood. He gave a long, lonely howl, and my eyes filled ridiculously with tears that I rapidly blinked away. It was absurd to feel such sorrow over leaving him for a few hours. He would not go into the wood with me, and he was safer shut up than standing on the edge of the forest where a wolf might see him as an unexpected dinner.

I entered the wood expecting the ease I usually felt under the trees, but as I walked I jumped at each branch breaking, every time something unseen rustled in the underbrush. I wished for Failinis, wished the moon wasn't huge and red. When I finally saw a glow of light from between the trees and heard the murmuring of the villagers, I was more relieved than I wanted to admit. I smiled, or tried to smile, when I entered the clearing, but then someone gasped and the whole crowd of them turned, staring at me, their eyes gleaming under the torches they held.

"It is only the widow who has taken over Fianna's croft," Dagda reassured the villagers. "Welcome, Cailleach." He held his hand out to me. "You looked like a goddess when you stepped out of the wood like that, with your shining hair," he said to me quietly.

For a *moment* I had looked like a goddess. But Dagda—

everyone—had now decided that it had been nothing more than a trick of the eye, a confluence of light and shadow that had made me look strange and otherworldly. They were just like the those who had glimpsed me long ago, the ones that excused away what they saw. Of course, these mortals were right to excuse it away. I was *not* a goddess.

Dagda moved to the center of the clearing where a huge oak stood. It was a beautiful tree, large and strong, with limbs that spread out as if embracing those around it. Siobhan had once told me that this oak was the reason mortals had settled nearby—and I'd learned then that they'd long believed that oaks were sacred to the gods, and that their prayers would be granted if they worshipped near the tree. Where had such beliefs come from? Perhaps Danu had proclaimed this or perhaps their ancestors had simply considered it a convenient place to worship, and this had then been folded over time into the people's conceptions of what the gods did or did not want.

Dagda lifted his hands and began to pray. I didn't listen to his words, instead letting my eyes wander around the clearing at the villagers, heads bowed in supplication. Perhaps Dagda had overstated the importance of the worship, because it was obvious to me that the entire village was not gathered here. A number of the women from the market stood there with their children and some old men, but I saw few young men and none of the fishermen. Perhaps they had stayed out on the harbor late into the night, fishing with the full moon.

Dagda finished praying and those around him lifted their heads, looking at him with eyes shining with faith. It was obvious they believed in what he told them. He cut mistletoe from the oak and passed it around, asking each person there to touch it, to imbue it with some of their strength. I did not recognize what rite he was performing, but I touched the mistletoe, if only so he would not chide me later. For a moment, I wondered if even in a mortal form I would imbue it with some kind of power—light, frost, ice—but when I looked down at it, it had not changed at all. It was nothing more than a bit of leaf, a white berry. My cheeks heated with shame, and my hands shook as I passed it to the woman to my left. I bent my head, digging a nail into my wrist so that the pain distracted me from the overwhelming desire for my winter power, and by the time I looked up again, the ceremony was over.

I was about to leave when I heard someone say "My granny Siobhan—" and I whirled back around to face a tall woman with dark hair.

She looked nothing like the woman I'd once known, but still I put a hand on her wrist. "You knew Siobhan? The Siobhan who lived in this village two generations ago?"

The woman looked startled, but she nodded. "Did you know her?"

I hesitated; I knew I didn't look old enough. "Fianna did," I lied. "I am Cailleach."

"I'm Niamh."

"I work Fianna's croft now," I said. "She'd asked before she passed that I speak to Siobhan for her, give her thanks for her help, if she still lived. Does she? Is she still here?" I looked around the crowd, could I have missed her? Of course, if she had seen me, she would not have recognized me. That was part of this punishment, Danu had told me, to walk among mortals but never be remembered from life to life. Still, I wanted to see Siobhan again, take her hand and thank her as I hadn't then.

"She passed on long ago." Niamh's eyes were sad. "Far away from here."

"Oh . . ." I drew in a deep breath. For a moment I had hoped that she might still be alive. But she was gone now, to a realm even a goddess could not follow her to. For a moment I thought I might cry, but then I shook myself. I did not deserve to weep over her; I had returned her kindness with nothing.

"Where did she go?" I was surprised that Siobhan had left Daingean Uí Chúis. She had seemed so firmly rooted here.

"She went south to warmer winds. She found someone else who had died of the cold. A woman, a friend. It was one more loss to winter than she could bear. She was tired of the death, so she and her family left the town and went to live with her sister."

A friend. I turned my head for a moment as though I were looking at the oak, but I was just trying to blink the tears out of my eyes. I swallowed against the lump in my throat and looked back toward the woman. "I am sure she was a wonderful granny. She was—that is, Fianna told me that she was a good friend too. Did she know you came back?"

"Oh no." Niamh shook her head. "No, she died when I was a girl. But I follow the druid wherever he goes"—she gave Dagda a tender glance, blushing—"I am devoted to him."

"You're a druid too?" I was surprised because she wore no robes.

"No," Niamh said, "I am too old to learn. I came here when Dagda did, and I felt . . ." She hesitated. "You'll think me odd. But I felt that this was my home. It was where I was meant to be. Now I help with the babies, like Siobhan taught me. She had eight of her own after she lost her first child and became a midwife after she was done having children. Speaking of"—she looked to a young woman on the other side of the clearing juggling two babies in her arms—"I told Meghan that I'd help her bring the children back to the village." She gave me a small smile then walked away, and I went back into the forest, ready to go home.

I was walking quietly through the wood thinking about what Niamh had told me when I heard someone approach. I knew it was a mortal—no animal was so loud—and after a moment Dagda appeared out of the darkness. I did not know why he had followed me, but I didn't want to disturb the night with words, so I said nothing to him. When we reached my hut, I opened the door and was almost bowled over by Failinis, who threw himself into my arms. He licked my face and I held him close against me, happy to hear his heart beat in time with mine. He let me hold him for a moment, then wriggled until I put him down, and he began to jump at Dagda, barking with excitement, until he turned to me again, dancing under my feet and knocking me over.

Dagda grinned and reached out a hand to pull me to my feet, but got twisted up again by Failinis himself, joining me in a heap on the ground. There was something so foolish, so absurd about the moment that I laughed, exciting Failinis enough that he licked my face again before prancing off to get a drink from the stream. Instead of getting up, I cushioned my head on my neck and looked up at the stars.

Dagda didn't rise either, closing his eyes and inclining his head as if listening for something. I heard only the forest swaying in the breeze, a frog croaking from near the stream . . . and . . . singing. I lifted myself onto my elbow and realized it was coming from the fishermen on the harbor. I could not make out the words, but I could hear the melody, sharp and cold and lonely. The song reminded me of winter, the bright coldness of ice singing through my body, crackling frost in my fingertips, the winds waiting for me to beckon. *I would do anything*, I thought. *Anything. To stride through the world like that again.*

I turned away from the sound and found Dagda staring at me. His face was close to mine, so close I could smell the sweat of him.

"I would bed you, Cailleach," he murmured. "Right here, out under the stars."

As he spoke, his eyelids fluttered shut and his lips drew together, and I realized he was trying to kiss me. I was startled by his desire, surprised by how close he was to me, and I pulled away, then jumped to my feet, until I stood over him like a parent over a child. Like a god over a mortal. My first impulse was to rebuke him harshly, to slap him even, but as I looked down at him, I softened. In the moonlight he looked so young, so *earnest* in that way that mortals could seem, faces unsullied as new snow. "I am not interested in bedding you—or anyone else," I added when his face fell. "I am sure there are others who would. Go and ask one of your devotees for such a thing." I thought of Niamh's face, how her eyes had tracked him around the clearing.

"Cailleach— I thought— I thought we felt the same." He reached out a hand, perhaps in supplication, or sorrow.

"I do not feel as you do," I said gently. "We have an agreement. I will ask that Danu speak to you, and you can continue to teach me how to work with the bees. We can be friends," I said, thinking about Siobhan. "But no more than that." He blinked and turned away, and I thought he might weep. It was foolish for a man to cry because a woman wouldn't bed him, but men had wept for less.

"You truly looked like a goddess when you stepped into the clearing tonight. Your hair shone silver as the moon, and in the torchlight your skin looked blue. I thought for a moment that it was a sign, from Danu perhaps. A sign that we should be together."

I drew in a breath at his description. Had some part of my immortality shone through at that moment? Or had it only been a trick of the light?

Dagda sighed. "As the druid, a leader of the community, I often . . ." He hesitated, and as he paused, the song drifted between us again, clear and cold. "I am alone," he finally said. "They look at me as though *I* am a god. But I am not. I'm just a mortal man, doing what I was taught by other mortal men. The only times I ever felt anything approaching divinity was when I saw Danu there"—he pointed to the place where she'd faded into the light—"and tonight, when I saw you step into the clearing."

"It is good to be alone," I said. "When you are alone, you can hear all the thoughts that the noise of this world tries to crowd out. Now—" I gestured him down the hill. "It is time to return to your bed—alone."

He gave a small smile and squeezed my hand for a moment. At first, I thought he would plead with me again to bed him, but then he dropped it, and I realized he had only meant it as a kind gesture.

I lay in bed that night, Failinis snoring beside me, and thought of Dagda's hand on mine. It was true, I did not want him or anyone to bed me. I had never had a lover, man or woman, even as a goddess. I had never wanted another body so close to mine, had never wanted to someone's breath in my face or their hands on my skin. The other gods took lovers, both mortals and each other, but I had always been able to please myself with my own hands and that had been enough. It was still enough. But as I thought of Dagda's hand on mine, I found that I did not mind that he had touched me. He had done it gently, without asking for anything in payment. He was my friend, like Siobhan had been. And though I had not been able to return her friendship in that life, perhaps I could try to return Dagda's in this one.

A comfort in this wearying world, like Failinis, I thought, as his paws began to twitch in a dream. I patted his side, and he rolled over onto his back, all four legs sticking straight into the air, and gave a little grunt of pleasure, still deeply asleep. Perhaps once I returned to my immortal form, I would keep dogs as Morrígan did. It might be pleasant to stride through winter with a dog at my side.

Failinis loved the snow.

I had thought he might retreat from it as he did from many things, but he bound into the first snowfall that we got that year— early, before Samhain—with enthusiasm, tongue lolling, jumping at the flakes that swirled in the air above him.

I stood still and silent, my head tilted toward the sky. I did not have a shawl for my arms, and they prickled with cold, but I didn't care. It felt as though it had been centuries since I'd woken to snow, since I'd been able to lift my head and feel it on my face—cold and soft as the touch of a feather. I looked down toward the village and saw smoke rising from their fires, the harbor white. It was not entirely frozen, but the edges of it were, and the sound of the ice cracking against the shore gave me a shiver of pleasure. I loved the crackle of winter, how it muffled all other sound. I saw no boats in the harbor and no children in the streets, and I assumed the villag-

ers were inside, perhaps taking the storm as an opportunity to pre-
pare the food they would eat at Samhain, two nights from now.

I wanted to stride out into that quick-falling snow barefoot,
naked, as I once had, but instead I turned to the ablutions that my
mortal body required. I returned to my hut, gave Failinis water
and food, shoved a heel of bread into my skirt, and put on a shawl.
I knew my feet would freeze if I walked out barefoot as I wished to,
so instead I put on the sturdy boots I'd traded for a few weeks ago
and stepped out.

The moment my feet touched the ground I inhaled, and my
chest expanded with the sharp, cold smell. I grinned, giddy as a
child; I wanted to dash out into the snow, to throw myself down
and make shapes in it, to taste it on my tongue and crunch it under
my feet—and so I turned to the forest. I could walk and play there
alone, with no one to judge me or think I was mad. I could walk
under the firs and not worry about chores, could simply walk and
walk until I was tired.

I was about to enter the wood when I heard a whine. I looked
down and cursed. I hadn't realized that Failinis had followed me.
He usually played around the hut when I went into the wood and
had not yet entered it since he'd been trapped there.

"Go." I extended my arm. "Go back."

He looked back toward the hut, where spirals of grey-blue
smoke rose from my still-hot fire, then he looked back at me. He
wagged his tail at me tentatively and looked deeply hurt when I
tried to gently push him back toward the house. "I'm going for a
walk." I took another half step into the forest. I could smell the firs,
their fragrance always sharper in the winter, and was desperate to
enter the trees. I turned my back to Failinis and took another few

steps. I wanted to be alone, without any companion, mortal or animal. I closed my eyes and I could hear only the almost imperceptible sound of the falling snow hitting the branches above.

I took a step into the shadows of the trees and my heart began to beat fast, my breathing intensifying, waiting, waiting . . . *For what?* I thought. *For my blue skin? For the winds to come at my bidding?* Nothing happened, of course nothing happened—it was only my body remembering what it once had been, reminding me, with the very tremble it now sent through me, that I was mortal, pale and fragile.

I was suddenly weary, bone-tired at the weight of having to *remember*, again and again, that I was not as I had been.

I would have lingered in that disappointment if Failinis had not rushed forward and licked my hand gently, tail waving with pride at his courage in braving the wood. I could not help but laugh, even though he made an absurd racket and ruined the quiet, the loneliness of the wood.

"Well then." I patted his head. "Shall we walk?"

I should have been more wary under those trees. There were still wolves about, and I knew that Failinis would be less than helpful if one approached, but we did not see any wolves during that long walk. Instead we wandered alone and uninterrupted under the twilight that the heavy snow cast. The shadows were blue and purple, and though I did not find the solitude I had longed for, I did not miss it as I might have. It was diverting, watching Failinis run and play in the wood, and it made me think of Enya and me playing together on the frozen river and through snow-covered trees. For the first time, I thought of Enya not with pain but only pleasure, knowing she would have loved my little dog.

Failinis kept leaping at snow-heavy branches, startling himself when the bounty fell on top of him. He blinked up at me with white-frosted whiskers and shook himself, spraying the snow on me, which he seemed to take as a game. He ran back and forth, trying to catch branches, even ones that were much too high for him. He leapt and barked and growled, his tail wagging constantly, and when he finally tired of his game, he panted beside me, occasionally pushing his cold nose into my hand.

We were about to enter a large clearing when Failinis stopped, his ears pricking up. Failinis had one ear that always stood straight up and one that flopped down, giving him a comical appearance, but now both ears were alert, his body still as he looked into the clearing.

A doe stood there, snuffling at the white ground, no doubt trying to get at the grass that lay beneath. She was small and looked old, with a swayed back and sagging belly. Most dogs would have run at her, but Failinis seemed content to sit there, entranced. The doe lifted her head and looked at us but did not run. She and Failinis stared at each other for a long time until Failinis sank down onto his belly, his head on his paws. Then the doe flicked her tail as though some agreement had been made and continued to dig into the snow. I sank down beside Failinis and watched the doe with him until a nearby branch fell, startling her. She bounded away, swift and surefooted as I had once been, disappearing into the darkening wood.

I would have walked for many more hours, but I could see Failinis was tiring, so instead we headed back toward my hut. When we saw light spilling out from the door, Failinis yipped with excitement and raced ahead toward it. I too quickened my steps as I approached home, happy to see my own light shining at me from the wood, pleased at the thought of the soup that I'd left bubbling in the pot before setting out.

I had just reached the door when Dagda appeared over the crest of the hill. He clutched his side, panting, though it was not a steep slope; he had grown soft and slow from staying in the village for so long. I watched his chest rise and fall, almost mesmerized by the motion. Mortals moved *so* endlessly, fidgeting and twitching all the time, even in sleep. Danu had been the one to point that out to me one day when she'd held Sorcha's boy Cathal asleep on her chest. She noted how he smacked his lips and scratched his nose, his chest always rising and falling. Danu had told me that she missed it, the breath thrumming through her. I, though, missed the *stillness* of my immortal body, a body that obeyed my every wish.

"I thought we could harvest the rest of the honey today," Dagda said, once he'd caught his breath. "The bees will be dull with the cold, and we'll be stung less."

Reluctantly, I nodded. I'd known this was coming, that Failinis and I needed the honey and wax to help us survive the winter, but I did not want to destroy the hive.

Dagda and I gathered several large buckets. I hesitated before drawing near, closing my eyes and listening one last time to the sound of the bees, but Dagda wasted no time on sentiment. He slowly waved a smoky torch near the hive, telling me that it would dull them further. Then, he carefully opened the top of the hive. A bee flew out, and I was foolishly pleased when it stung Dagda. I expected him to jump, but all he did was grimace.

"Cailleach"—he motioned me forward—"you must do this with me." I gritted my teeth but walked toward him, knowing he spoke the truth. I peered down into the hive and saw the swarm of bees clustered around their queen. Their wings beat slowly, and Dagda gestured at them. "They keep her warm," he said, "even if it exhausts them. Even if they die of it, another will instantly take their place." The other gods, I thought, would do the same thing for Danu. They would give her everything without a moment's consideration. The sudden understanding made me uncomfortable. I'd always *known* that, of course, but had never really *seen* it for its truth until I looked at the bees in front of me. Danu always claimed that we lived above such human structures as hierarchies, but I knew that she expected each of the gods to give their all to her. And they all would have, instantly, gladly, to keep their queen alive.

Dagda dipped his hand into one of the buckets and began sprinkling water into the hive. "I've mixed it with a bitter herb." He gestured at me to do the same with the other hives. "They'll leave and we'll be able to gather the rest of the honeycomb." I scattered the water, and the bees began to rise from the hives like black smoke. A few landed on Dagda's hands and several flew right at me, stinging my bent face. I flinched from the pain, cursing, but I didn't stop sprinkling the water, and soon the swarm had flown away, leaving us with two empty hives. Dagda and I carried them together into the hut, placing them on the floor. Dagda lifted my soup cauldron from where it swung over the fire and set it on the table, then pulled a stout knife from his belt and held it over the hot coals. After a long moment, he walked toward the first hive and began scraping the sides so that the soft yellow wax and honey cleaved away from the walls. "I always liked this part best," Dagda said, directing me to heat another knife and begin on the other hive.

"The destruction?" My voice was sharp with disappointment. Of course he liked that best, he was mortal, all they wanted was to—

"No." Dagda interrupted my thoughts and tipped the hive toward me so that I could see inside. "Everything falls to the bottom, ready for me to find, like a pool of sunlight. It makes me feel godlike"—he blushed and looked away from me—"as though I'm creating something special—with my own two hands. It is . . . tangible in a way that leading worship is not."

"You're right, of course." Danu appeared suddenly in the doorway. Failinis howled and ran for me, hiding behind my legs as Dagda spun around, knife dripping with honey.

She was in her goddess form. Her hair was long and golden and fell in waves to her feet. Her lips were pink, her hips and breasts pronounced. She even wore a golden robe that glimmered with jewels, and her skin gave off a gentle light, as though it were woven through with rays from the sun.

"Goddess." Dagda knelt before her, head bowed, knife shining under her light. Drops of honey fell from it to the floor, and I watched them instead of meeting Danu's gaze. I did not want her here, in my house. I did not want her to see how I lived, to look at the pallet where I slept, to smell the soup that I'd made, to see the jars of honey that lined the shelves. She would approve of all of it, of course. She would see it and think she was right, wise, that she had done the right thing by punishing me.

"Rise, mortal." Her voice was different than usual, too—deep, and rich, resonant as a bell. She touched Dagda's cheek and he rose, though I saw his knees tremble. He glanced back at me, eyes wide with fear and excitement, and grabbed my hand, lacing his fingers through mine, tugging me toward him, toward Danu.

She grinned at me, and I knew it was because of Dagda's hand in mine, but as she did her mantle of godhood seemed to fall away, the golden light around her dimming, her vastness receding until she stood no taller than I was. "Thank you for showing Cailleach how to keep the bees." Her voice was light, no longer echoing around the hut. "She has found a good friend in you." She smiled again and suddenly her golden hair was gone, replaced by a long brown braid and wide, broad cheeks. "I often wear my old form." Her voice was soft, trying to reassure him, but seeing her transform from goddess to mortal seemed to frighten him more than anything else had, because he only blinked in response. When I went to pull my hand away, he held on so tightly my knuckles turned white. Warmth rose in my chest at the thought that he wanted me, needed me—his friend—by his side, but as I looked down at our twined hands, I thought about how frightened he would be if he knew that the hand he held had once been blue and hard, commanding the winds, the snow. And I was certain, with a sudden rush of sadness, that if he'd known the truth of me—of what I'd done—he would have cowered behind Danu to hide from *me*.

The thought made my cheeks flush with shame, and suddenly I wanted nothing more than for both of them to go, so I said, "My promise is fulfilled. Now leave us in peace."

I heard Dagda suck in a breath, perhaps terrified that we would be struck down for speaking so to a goddess, but Danu merely shook her head. "I have come to learn," she said. "I keep bees myself. Perhaps you can teach me something new, Dagda." She gave him another brilliant smile.

As darkness fell around us, Dagda showed us how to separate the wax from the honey, how to break apart the hives. I saw Dagda watch Danu carefully whenever she wasn't looking, especially at one moment when she had her sleeves rolled up to her elbows and was arm-deep in the hive, humming to herself, a splatter of honey shining on her cheek. I thought I knew what he was thinking: Danu was not like the goddess he'd imagined. In a way, I was sorry for him. For the illusions that she must be shattering. Would he still pray to her in the same way? Would he gaze into the heavens and imagine her immortal face? Or would he see her only as she was now, as mortal-looking as him or me?

I thought he would pepper her with questions—about her immortality, about Tara, the other gods—but he spoke little that night. He only gave instructions on how we were to work with the wax and honey, how to purify the honey, how to create the candles that I would sell in the market, then said, "I must leave now, goddess. I promised a sick woman that I would look in on her before she slept."

Danu nodded. "It is good to see that mortals still keep their promises." She reached into her robes and held out a small vial. It was full of a green liquid the color of her eyes. "Perhaps you would offer Máiréad this tonic? It will greatly ease her cough."

Dagda's eyes widened slightly, but he nodded and reached for it—carefully, though, not touching even the smallest part of her skin. "Goodnight, goddess." He inclined his head toward Danu, then looked at me. "Cailleach." His voice steadied as he spoke my name, as though it were a comfort, a talisman.

"I'll walk out with you to get more wood for the fire," I said. He was quiet as he walked to the woodpile with me. "I am sorry if she was not what you wanted, what you thought. Danu is—"

"She is *more*," Dagda breathed, his voice trembling. "She is more than I ever thought. She is at once goddess and mortal; she holds up the world in her palm, but she hears Máiréad coughing and wants to ease her. She is . . ." He trailed off. "It is difficult to remain in her presence, to look on her, even in her mortal form. I do not know how you sat by her so comfortably." He squeezed my hand. "Thank you," he said. "Thank you for letting me see her . . .

I . . . I am dazzled by her kindness. She need take no notice of us, but she does. She *does* love us, just as we have been told."

He squeezed my hand once more and went down the hill solemnly while I stood staring at his back. I wanted to be angry at him, at his adoration for Danu, but what could I do? She *did* love mortals. She didn't respect them, but she loved them, and it was wonderful to be loved by Danu. In my earliest years before my skin turned blue Danu had loved me like that, unreservedly and wholly, her hand always in mine, the brightness of her pouring into me and over me—until she'd given me the power over winter and seemed to . . . to step back in some way, seemed to look at me and see a lack that she had never noticed before.

I wished . . . I did not know what I wished, and so I just turned and went back to my hut. I expected to find it empty, but Danu was still there, bent over a length of wax she was breaking into pieces.

I stopped for a moment in the doorway, unsure if I wanted her to leave and let me be alone with my thoughts, or if I wanted her to stay. It had been a long time since we had been alone together; once she had been my whole world. I couldn't decide, so I settled on saying nothing and began to cut wicks, then dip them over and over in the hot wax, as I tried to contain the swirl of emotions within me. Failinis crept onto the pallet, and though he tried to keep a watchful eye on Danu, he eventually fell asleep, his snores filling the room.

We worked silently for a long time, and when I finally got up to light a candle, I looked down at its yellow sides and remembered the load of candles we'd brought to Sorcha and Enya once, remembered too how we laughed returning to Tara that night, at the thought of mortals needing candles to light their way. I looked at

Danu working beside me and thought of all the mortals who had her love but not her respect, and it suddenly made me angry that she sat beside me like this, completing a chore because she thought of it as a child's game, not because I needed the light.

"You left me a candle, during that first life." Danu blinked, looking up as though I'd woken her from a spell. "You left that candle to spite me"—I snipped off the ends of the wicks so violently that I knocked several of the candles together—"to remind me what I had lost, not because you knew I needed the light."

She shook her head, her eyes pools of hurt. "Cailleach, no. I only wished to give you something of Tara . . ." She trailed off, letting the silence build for so long I thought she had stopped speaking, but then she turned toward me, her eyes wide, almost pleading. "Something of me."

Before I could speak, she faded away with a sound like wind through long grass.

the second life

Dagda's skill and knowledge of bees helped me survive that winter and the next. I became more and more adept at keeping them myself too, able to tell on my own when a hive was sick or had lost its queen.

Failinis was my constant companion as the years passed. Though the villagers had once thought him nothing more than a nuisance, they grew to adore him, calling him when we walked through the main road, holding out bones they'd saved and letting him take them gently from their hands. Several children took their first steps with his help, a fistful of his long hair tangled between their fingers. Sometimes the fishermen from the harbor would even whistle for him when they'd had an especially good catch, and they'd laugh and laugh as they watched him race down the long hill toward them. It made me glad to see how they loved him, and with their love for him their wariness of me decreased. I would not say I was friends with any of them, not like Dagda, but people liked me at least well enough to give me small smiles or nods when they saw me.

I had not seen Danu since the night she'd shown herself to
Dagda, and I was glad. I certainly lived better now than I had my
first life, but I still did not want her to see my mistakes: the afternoon I dropped the well lid on my foot, badly bruising it, or the
days I spent in bed after eating rotten fish, or even smaller mis-
steps, like the time Failinis ate half a jar of honey when my back
was turned. I also didn't want her to see my triumphs. She did not
need to know that the villagers loved my honey, saying it was
sweeter than any they'd known. She did not need to see that my
candles always shone gold and true down to their very dregs, or
that my friendship with Dagda had become strong and sturdy as a
deeply rooted tree. If she saw any of these things, she would take it
as proof that I liked the life she'd given me—or worse, that I was
grateful to her for it. And while there were things I did appreciate
about this life—Failinis, talking with Dagda, the satisfaction of
selling all my candles during a single market day—I did not like
mortality. I still longed for the freedom to do whatever I wanted, to
eat and drink as I wished, to spend my days in more than endless
chores. I missed the easy power of godhood—a wave of a hand to
light candles, a blink of an eye to bring water to my lips, a thought
from Danu that I could answer even if I was on the other side of the
world. Mostly, though, I missed winter. It had been heady to send
wind sweeping over the mountains, to release the weight of snow
from my shoulders, to send that weight over the hills and watch as
they turned from green to white. The days I'd sent winter had
made me feel complete, as though I were giving the ever-moving
world a small rest, a moment when it could close its eyes and sleep
for a while, a bear in its den.

Now, when my longing for godhood grew too strong, Failinis
and I would walk through the wood as far as my dog's little paws

would allow, or into as much cold as my fingers could stand, before we turned back for home and the warmth of our own fire.

We were coming home from one such walk when I noticed that Failinis was trailing behind me. He'd been a bit slow all day, but I thought he'd just spent too long dozing by the fire. Usually a walk invigorated him as it did me.

"Come"—I clucked my tongue at him. We had stayed out longer than we should have. I could hear wolves' cries in the air; the moon was rising above us. He lumbered toward me and kept up for a few paces, but quickly fell back again. "Failinis, come," I called again impatiently. He could not be so slow when there was so far left to go; I still could not see the light from my hut. He tried to bound to me, but his head was low to the ground and his ear that usually stood up so jauntily was flat against his head. He looked exhausted, as though he could barely stand, and gave a little whine as I hurried back toward him, chest tight in worry.

"I'm sorry. I'm sorry." I stroked his head gently before picking him up and cradling him against my chest. He licked my neck, then buried his head in my shoulder. It was a struggle to walk through the snow with him, but I marched grimly on until we finally reached our hut. I set him down on the pallet and examined him closely, but I didn't see any wound or obvious problem. "Did we go too far?" I murmured, sitting beside him. He gave a little sigh and stretched his head across my stomach. "He just needs rest," I said to the hut, to the coals that had burned low. "He'll sleep and wake better in the morning."

Failinis usually slept against my leg, but that night he sprawled across my chest. When I woke the next morning and tried to get up to feed him, he whimpered softly until I returned to bed and let him curl up against me again. I gave him a few sips of water, but he refused to eat, and fear rose in my throat like a great black snake. Failinis had been young when I'd found him, and even now he couldn't be older than seven or eight. I'd only recently begun to see grey hairs on his muzzle.

He refused to move for the rest of the day. Evening drew on, and I knew I had to get him to eat. I went to retrieve the large bone that Dagda had given me a few days before; I'd meant to use it for soup, but now I offered it to Failinis, hoping the smell of it would tempt him to get out of bed. He climbed wearily from the pallet and took the bone from me, and my worry retreated slightly. He would be fine. He was just sick. But he gnawed at the bone only for a moment before dropping it with a soft *flump* on the floor. I sat back on the pallet and put my head in my hands, all my fears returning. What could I do for him? He crawled back into my lap, setting his head on my knee with another sigh, and I lay back onto the pallet, holding him against my chest. We would sleep again. Then I would get up early the next morning and go to the village to see what remedy they might have.

When I woke, Failinis was still asleep on my chest. I eased him off me to lay him gently down on the pallet. I did not even bother to tie my shawl around my head and ran out the door, barefoot and bareheaded as I'd once run through the world. I banged on Dagda's door until he appeared, bleary-eyed. I told him about Failinis and begged him to ask around the village to see what might be done for him. Dagda, who loved Failinis too, nodded gravely and set out with an urgency that made my heart ache. Then I ran back up the hill to my dog.

Failinis rested in my lap all day as the villagers came, bringing what remedies they could. They offered him tinctures and tonics, bones still thick with meat, cream, and honey, but he refused them all. Several of the children who loved him best tried to get him to chase them as he always did, but they had to be taken wailing from the room when he only watched them with dull eyes.

Dagda and I finally managed to get him to swallow one of the tinctures that Niamh had brought, saying that it was her granny Siobhan's recipe to cure ailing livestock. After he drank it, Failinis's eyes brightened and the tightness around my chest loosened. Siobhan would save me again, save my little dog.

Dagda would have stayed with me all night, but I told him to return to the village, saying that I wanted to sleep. He gave Failinis a kiss right between his eyes, and Failinis licked his cheek. I laughed, and then surprised both of us by kissing the same spot on Dagda's forehead. "Thank you"—emotion welled in my chest—"for helping us." I could have been alone in this life, but I wasn't. I had Dagda, and just knowing that I could turn to him when I needed to filled me with relief in the same way that the scent of snow in the air did.

Failinis fell asleep cradled on my chest, and finally I did too, holding my little dog tightly against me.

It was Dagda who found us early the next morning. "Cailleach," he said, tears in his eyes, shaking my shoulder. "Cailleach."

I did not need to open my eyes to know that he was dead. There is a peculiar lightness to mortal beings that leaves them as soon as their souls do. Failinis, my little dog, was heavy against my chest, his body already growing hard as a stone. Tears welled in my eyes, but I didn't let them fall; I was brittle as glass. If I moved, if I even tried to, I would shatter with the despair of losing him—but if I stayed still, if I stayed perfectly still, I could keep him against me a little longer, long enough that perhaps I would turn to stone too, and then we would be two stones together and I could follow him to where he had gone. So he would not be alone. And neither would I.

When Enya died, I had instantly felt her absence in the world. I had known as soon as I saw her chest stop rising that she was gone and would not be coming back.

Though I knew that Failinis too was now gone, I could not understand it. I did not believe it. I could not fathom that he would not come padding up to me, rest his head on my lap, and beg to go out to the stream for a drink as he'd wanted to each morning. Why was he not begging? I stood, unsteady on my feet, needing to go out there myself. Perhaps he was already there. Perhaps I would find him, bring him home to me.

I stumbled over rocks and twigs, my feet cold on the hard ground, but I did not care. I was numb to the pain. I needed to find Failinis, I needed to get water for my dog. The stream was frozen over when I got there, but I did not care. Failinis wasn't there. I needed to find him. I needed to get him water. I walked out onto the stream, the ice clinging to my warm feet. The water rushed by beneath me. I needed to reach it. I took another step, searching for a stone I could use to carve a hole in the ice, when I heard it. A *crack*, like the sound of a great tree groaning under a strong wind— or of thin ice breaking under mortal feet. *I have to get water for Failinis. I have to get water for my dog*, I thought, as I fell into the icy river.

the second death

"Danu, please."

I knelt on the green moss floor of the throne room and bowed my head, weeping. "Please bring him back."

"She's hysterical." Lug's voice was heavy with derision.

Danu put a soft hand on my cheek. I looked up at her. Tears were falling down her cheeks. "I can't bring him back, child, you know that."

"I will never harm another mortal—never again—if only you'll let him stay at my side. Please." My voice trembled and I barely managed to say the words. "Please, Mother."

Someone gasped. It had been a long time since I'd made any claim to the kinship between us.

"Mortal beings die," Danu said. "If they did not . . ." She trailed off.

"I didn't think he would die. I would have called you. I would have asked you to heal him."

"Even if you'd called, I would not have been able to help." Danu's voice was solemn but firm. "It is one of the prohibitions of your punishment. That we would not interfere with your life."

I wrapped my arms around myself, hugging my knees to my chest, and began to shudder. I wept and shook for too long there on the warm stone of Tara, but Failinis did not nose his way to my side, did not lick my cheek. No one moved to comfort me.

"I must ask you again"—Danu finally spoke—"what has your punishment taught you? What have you learned about mortals?"

"I have learned only what I always *knew*," I said bitterly. "Their lives are short and miserable and end in death. I *knew* this already, Danu. I watched Enya die. Now I have watched Failinis die. What do you wish for me to say? That I am sorry? That I am grateful? I am not. All you have caused me is more pain. All you have taught me is that I was right to leave the mortal world alone."

A tear tracked down her cheek, but Danu did not look sad; rather, she looked angry. "But you had so much in this life. So much that you did not have before. I saw you take pleasure in the bees, in your friendship with Dagda. You loved that dog more than you have loved anything since—"

"Since Enya!" I cried. "I have not loved like that since Enya, and it *still* is not worth it. Her friendship does not erase the memory of her dead face or her son's dead face. And with Failinis—my memories of him do not take away this *feeling* of loss—of the breath in my body rising and falling when he breathes no longer." I sobbed, holding myself closer, turning away from her, from them all. "I do not want to remember any longer. It would be better, *better* if I had not known their love at all."

Danu shook her head, her gaze filled with pity as she pointed her finger at me once again. I was glad when it hurt, glad when *pain* filled me as pieces of my skin—cerulean and indigo and slate—peeled away and I could do nothing but scream—not for my own suffering, but for my little dog. For Failinis.

spring

Listen.

Listen, and I will tell you a story.

The story of a girl who stood against the gods.

And from them gained her heart's desire.

Her name was Fia, and she was a mortal girl.

And she was hungry.

Fia spent her days working in the fields for little, and had little to spare. She had no jewels to light her hair except the yellow sun, no mother left to hold her close, no warrior to go before her and clear her path.

Fia was alone in the world but for her brother: the story-teller, she called him, because at night when they lay in their croft he would tell her tales of the great gods, the Tuatha Dé Danann. She would listen and long for more, for the gods to come down and offer them a new path, one different from the wood and saws and aching backs that made up their days.

And at night Fia dreamed of full, groaning tables. Of hot fat glistening on plump birds and round, golden loaves of bread, still steaming. She would stand over the food in her dreams, her eyes full of yearning, but never be able to taste it. No matter how close she got, how far she stretched her hand, she could not eat a single crumb of the feast laid before her.

Every morning she woke up hungry.

Then one day, the storyteller found a berry—and everything changed.

Such a small thing, to cause such a shift.

He found the berry—glistening bright and sweet-sharp— when he was hurrying through the woods one day. He was not supposed to be there—to pass there was forbidden, too near Síd in Broga, a burial ground sacred to the gods. But the boy was late and trying to avoid a beating from the carpenter he worked with, so he took a path he should not have—and there they were, so many berries, a purple red that stained his feet as he ran through the clearing.

He had a gift of telling stories, it's true—and yet when he found himself at the start of one, he did not notice it at all. All he saw were bushes fat with food, food that would ease his sister's hunger.

When he told Fia about the bushes, he described at great length the way the berries weighed down the branches so that they nearly touched the ground, the sticky-sweetness of the air, the gentle hum of the bees that filled the clearing, stumbling, nectar-drunk.

Before her brother's tale had reached its end, Fia was already running: to the woods, to the berries. To the edge of Síd in Broga.

She ran there every morning when her hunger was at its sharpest and for a time was satisfied. But Fia always wanted more. And when those bushes grew empty, she went even farther into the wood than her brother had, closer each day to the forbidden burial ground.

I see how you frown, how your lips draw down. Foolish

*girl! you want to say. **Does she not see the danger she's in? To
you I say—remember.** Remember the times when your own
belly groaned and pinched with hunger—remember how little
you cared about anything but filling it. What lengths would
you have gone to to make the hunger go away?*

Fia would have done anything.

*And one day, in search of her precious berries, she finally
tread on the sacred ground of Síd in Broga.*

*She climbed to the top of the burial mound, seeking that
which would sate her hunger. Finding nothing there but a
smooth expanse of grass, Fia sat and wept, the gnawing in her
stomach only growing.*

"Why do you cry, child?"

*Fia lifted her tear-streaked face and looked up at the most
glorious woman she had ever seen. She had golden skin and
golden hair that hung to her feet, eyes green as spring, and a
voice that echoed like a song. Before the woman spoke another
word, Fia knew she must be a goddess.*

*"Aren't mortals taught not to tread here?" the goddess asked,
though she didn't sound angry.*

"I'm so hungry," Fia whispered.

*The goddess's face softened. "Ah, little daughter." The
goddess waved her hand, and just like that the mound was
covered in food. Steaming loaves of bread, tureens of stew,
and platters piled high with roasted meats and cheese and
nuts—it was a feast that would make kings weep, but Fia
didn't waste any more time with tears. Her eyes gleaming, she
reached for the nearest drumstick and sunk her teeth into it,
drinking and feasting until even **her** belly was full.*

Only then did she turn back to the goddess. "Who are

you?" she finally asked, her voice sounding thin and small in the air.

The goddess smiled. "I am Danu, the mother, the creator of life."

Fia was a mortal girl, yes, yet not one like you or me. She was quick and bold and brave. She had not been scared when the goddess appeared, had not shied away from the feast that had appeared before her, and she was not afraid now when she leaned toward the goddess and asked a second question.

"Are gods ever hungry?"

The goddess laughed, placing a hand on Fia's head. "Dear child. Of course not," she said, before fading into the dawn light.

the third life

I did not return to my hut when Danu sent me down once more to the field just outside it. When I rose and looked at it, my stomach roiled with nausea at the thought of returning there alone, lying on the pallet where Failinis had taken his last breath.

Instead, I sat on the bench that overlooked the sea. Dagda and I had often sat there after working with the bees. Sometimes we'd talked, but mostly we'd just watched the boats come into the harbor as evening drew on. I had not realized how much his presence beside me had meant until I found myself sitting there alone—no friend beside me, no dog at my feet. Watching the boats come in now only sharpened the sense of isolation. All those fishermen had families to welcome them, people who would see them home from the sea and be glad. No one in the village below knew me. None would remember me even if they *had* known me in my previous life. I was alone again, and it didn't bring me the pleasure it once had.

When I could not stand to watch the boats any more than I could handle going into the hut, I decided to venture down to the village. Perhaps if I sat for a time in the tavern, the noise and warmth around me would grate once more and remind me that I preferred my solitude.

Perhaps it would remind me *how* to be alone again.

I was halfway down the hill when I heard something behind me.

"Failinis?" I spun around, sure that Danu had sent my dog back to me. I saw a pair of glowing eyes and joy leapt to life within me like a sudden fire. I took a step toward him, then another—to see nothing but a fox, crouched on its belly, watching me approach. The joy left as quickly as it had come, and I let out a cry, kicking a stone at the fox so that it would flee.

Danu had not brought Failinis back.

In whatever time I was in, Failinis's bones were dust.

I quickly made my way down the hill to village, and no one noticed when I entered the old tavern. I had never sat in it before, had never done more than stick my head in looking for Dagda, who liked to sit on one of the polished stools and drink mead with his friends. I stood in the crowd for a moment, looking around for him out of habit, until I remembered once again that even if I found him, even if he were still alive, he would not remember me. I knew that should upset me—knew that somewhere deep down, it did— but I was . . . dazed. Dazed with grief, with longing for my dog, and for the life I had been leading.

"Are you Fianna's granddaughter, then?" I turned to see a woman approaching me. She had long black hair and bright blue eyes that reminded me of the ice in the far north. She smiled at me, but her eyes were wary; perhaps the village had grown cautious of strangers once more.

I sighed and nodded. I had been Fianna's niece, her cousin, why not her granddaughter?

"I'm Áine." The woman held out her hand. Her fingers were long and delicate, and her skin was warm, though calloused.

"Cailleach," I said, in no mood to talk. I wanted only to sink onto one of the stools, was overwhelmed at the thought of having to make conversation, at having to be subjected once more to such pleasantries and gestures. I had been in Tara for such a short time yet felt once again torn between my god and mortal selves, unsure of how to be in either world.

A man behind the bar set a tall glass of golden liquid in front of me, and I finally sat down, taking a long swallow even as tears burned my eyes. I'd never drunk alcohol before, had never understood why mortals liked it so much. Why would they dull their already dull senses further? But I understood now the need for dullness. The need to close one's eyes and forget for a moment life's hardships.

"Do you like Daingean Uí Chúis?" the woman—Áine—said, sliding onto the stool beside me.

"I've only just arrived, haven't I?" I said, voice rough.

The woman's suspicious look returned. "I thought you were Fianna's granddaughter. Did you not know her?"

I closed my eyes and took a long swallow of my drink. "When I was a child. I came and saw the bees."

"And do you have family here?"

"No."

"Well," the woman finally said, looking a little surprised by my short answers, "I shall leave you." She hesitated, as if waiting for me to ask her to stay, but I didn't and eventually she left. I watched her for a while and could tell she was well-liked by everyone. She flitted like a butterfly from one table to another and whenever people saw her approach their eyes lit up. What would it be like to have that easy way with people, to be so effortlessly liked? Few had ever liked me—mortals and gods alike—and only my friendship with Enya had truly been effortless.

I drank for a long time, silence filling up the tavern as it slowly emptied. At the end of the night, a fisherman approached me. He was drunk, but by then so was I, so when he put his hand on my knee, I let him leave it there and later I let him come home with me so I would not have to be alone in the dark.

He was my first lover.

I was not impressed.

His back was sweat-slicked, and his hair smelled of fish and salt. Still, his hands were gentle. He stayed until dawn, then he rose, grunting and sighing in the loud way that mortals have, before clothing himself. He hesitated and turned back toward me, opening his mouth to say something, but I merely pointed a finger out the door. I did not want his mumbled excuses, or worse, pleas for love. I had brought him back with me for no other reason than I had been unable to enter my hut when I knew that there would be no Failinis to greet me.

I stayed in my pallet after the man left, trying to sleep a little longer, but I soon grew cold and my mind flashed again to Failinis, always curled up around me keeping me warm. At the thought, my eyes began to water, and I climbed wearily to my feet. I needed to get up, to do something other than think of him.

I went to the door and threw it open so I might better see what had happened to my home since I'd died. The sun had only just risen, but it was already warm out, warm enough that I realized Danu must have sent me back in late spring. It was one of her favorite seasons, everything in full bloom; wherever she walked, flowers blossomed at her feet, ripe fruit dropping into her waiting hands. It was the season I hated most, with its slick sweetness, its warm breezes—as far from winter as a season could ever be.

Even as I thought this, I brushed against a flower that was curling around the lintel of my house. I turned and saw a yellow rose, Danu's favorite flower. I realized there was not just one, but hundreds: my hut, which had been a plain stone building, was now *covered* in golden roses. They twined over the doorway and crawled up the sides and almost entirely hid the stone. The roses reminded me of the lone golden candle that had been left for me in my first life. They must be another way for Danu to jab at me, to try to *make* me see the beauty in the mortal world around me. Perhaps she had forgotten that I didn't like roses, or perhaps that was why she had done it. Either way, I ignored them to look over the rest of the hut.

It had not changed much. The pallet was larger, enclosed by itself in a tiny room that had no door, only a length of fabric hanging from the doorframe. I thought of the cloth that had stood in the place of the hut's entrance the first time I'd arrived, how I'd torn it down in fury and watched the silver rain sheet down. Then, I might have been grateful for the extra room, but now I only thought of how far I would be from the fire, alone and enclosed in the dark like in a tomb. I went back into the main room and saw with some relief that the shelves were covered with jars of honey, salted fish, and grain; at least Danu had not sent me back only to starve me again.

Sitting in the middle of the hearth was a black cauldron. I picked it up, swinging it slightly by its handle, and realized it was *my* old pot, the same one I'd had in my first and second life. I knew its weight as well as I knew the weight of my own body. I had spent so much time bending over it trying to keep food from burning, swinging it onto the table, holding it in one hand as Failinis wove between my feet, waiting for his share of dinner . . . I shuddered at the memory and nearly dropped the pot before forcing the vision as far away as I could.

When I saw the golden hives behind the hut—four now instead of two—my body sagged with relief. I would not have to learn new things again; I could get back to my bees. I rested my forehead against one of the hives and did not move, even when some curious bees flew out and landed on my fingers. They walked over my hand so gently that I might have begun to weep had I not heard a voice behind me.

"You do not fear them."

It had been a quiet statement, not meant to startle me, but I still jumped and three of the bees that had been clinging to my fingers flew away, one stinging my thumb hard and sharp. I turned angrily, ready to confront whoever had interrupted me.

"I didn't mean to frighten you," Áine, the woman I'd met the night before, said, stepping toward me.

I wanted to bare my teeth at her, to growl and bite like one of Danu's cats, but I had seen the way those in the tavern the night before had spoken to her. She was clearly widely respected, and I knew how difficult it was to live by villagers who didn't trust me. I did not want to lose her favor and thereby make enemies, so I forced myself to speak calmly. "You should have announced yourself earlier. That bee will die now."

"You *do* know about bees." Áine looked surprised. "Most don't know that they die after they sting. And if they do, they rejoice in it."

"I do not rejoice in death," I said quietly, realizing that my words were entirely true. Not only did I not rejoice in it, I hated it. I did not want to cause it for anyone, even an insect.

A soft breeze blew in my face, and for a moment I thought it was Danu, there to tell me that I had learned enough and could return to my former self. But no matter where I looked for her, I could not find her. Either she wasn't listening or I had still not understood whatever it was she wanted me to.

Áine pushed her sleeves up and moved toward me, but I threw out my arm and she stopped. "Why are you here?" I did not want her scaring my bees again. "Have you come for honey?"

"I thought Fianna would have told you?" she said. "I'm the village midwife, but since there's only so much need for me, I also help with the bees. Four hives is too much for one woman alone."

She was right, of course. The two hives I used to have had almost been too much for me, even with Dagda's help. I bit down on my tongue at the thought of my friend. At least he had not died in front of me. At least he had lived a long, full life.

"You know how to care for them?" I did not move my arm but swung my gaze back toward her.

She laughed, pushing a dark curl out of her face. "I should. I've been caring for these hives as long as I can remember. My granddad taught me how. He used to help the woman who lived here before Fianna."

My throat tightened, and I looked at the woman more closely but I could not see any sign of Dagda in her face. Her eyes gleamed bright; she was much lovelier than he had ever been. She ran a hand through her hair again, and I realized she had his hands. His long, beautiful fingers. "Dagda," I said in amazement. "Your grandfather was Dagda?"

The woman nodded and looked at me curiously. "You knew him? But you're of an age with me."

I laughed then, hard and short. I was older than her oldest ancestor.

"He taught me how to care for bees too. The summer I visited Fianna."

"I don't remember you." Áine frowned.

"I stayed close to Fianna that summer. I did not go down to the village."

Áine cocked her head as she studied me, but only shrugged. "Granddad loved it here." She gently pulled a rose vine away from the hive and tucked it around the low stone fence instead. "He used to tell me about the woman who lived here before Fianna. I don't remember her name"—she frowned again—"I'm not sure Granddad ever told me. His mind grew soft as he got older. Sometimes he claimed he'd met the goddess Danu." She laughed. "And he told me about the woman's dog, Failinis—did you know him? Granddad loved that dog, even long after he died. He buried him on the hill there." She pointed. "The dog liked to sit there and watch the boats come in."

I looked at the spot on the hill, fighting the tears in my eyes. It had been Failinis's favorite spot. I should have known that Dagda—gentle, kind Dagda—would lay my dog to rest in a place he loved. *Thank you*, I thought to my old friend, as I placed a wandering bee back into the hive just as he had taught me.

The woman continued to chatter on, but I did not truly listen. I paid her no real attention, letting her noise fill the silence and wash over me like the buzzing of the bees as we worked on the hives, until she remarked, "I passed Ruaidhrí as I walked up here."

I had just found the queen of the colony, and I did not look up until I assured myself that she was healthy. Then I set the little ceramic lid back and looked at Áine. Was she trying to rebuke me? Perhaps Ruaidhrí was her husband or her brother. I had not thought, had not cared, about who he might be attached to when I'd pulled him into my bed.

"A handsome lad, but a bad lover from what I've heard." Áine's lips quirked.

I laughed, pleasantly surprised. I'd been warned early on in my first life that mortals did not speak openly about whose bed they were in and what they did there. I'd once said something to Siobhan about a woman who I knew was bedding a man other than her husband, and Siobhan had hushed me fiercely, telling me that it was no one's concern but theirs. Áine's frankness was welcome.

"For someone who catches fish all day, his hands were slow," I responded, and Áine chuckled, a loud, bright sound that filled the air around us.

We worked together in silence the rest of the morning until we were both wet with sweat. Why could Danu never send me back in the middle of winter? I was curious too if the village still worshipped her and the other gods and asked as much.

Áine shrugged. "Most still do"—she wiped at her brow—"but I never liked the stories my grandfather told of Danu. If she is a goddess, the true mother of all, why does she let children die of fever? Why do the seas rise suddenly and swallow sailors who only wanted to feed their families? She seems careless to me, in the way that a true mother would never be."

I didn't respond, but I hoped that Danu was listening to this mortal woman speak ill of her.

We worked until the sun was lowering; then Áine stretched and wiped her hands on her dress. "I hate when the sun is this hot." She shaded her eyes and looked down toward the sea. "I'm going to the stream."

She didn't ask me to follow her, but I did anyway, thinking that the cool water would be pleasant against my thumb, which still itched from the early morning sting.

I did not remember until I saw the stream that this was where I'd last died.

It had been winter then, and the river was almost unrecognizable now, lush with greenery, lazily flowing toward the sea. It did not look like it could ever be stoppered by ice, could ever crack under the weight of a woman trying to get water for a dog. My stomach tautened in fear as I looked at it. How many more times would Danu have me die before she was satisfied?

I would have turned from the spot altogether had Áine not pulled off her dress and thrown it onto the bank, then ducked under the water. When she surfaced, she blew out a great breath and laughed, her black hair sleek and shining like a seal's.

As I watched her, I felt an ache at her simple joy. It had been so long since I'd been so free, so effortless, and I wanted to share in it, so I took a deep breath and jumped in beside Áine. The water pulled at me, but not hard, and the gentleness of it, cold against my skin, made my fear dissipate. I could not lose this. No matter what happened I would *not* lose the love I had for the cold. I would not lose the faith in my own body, because eventually I would return to godhood. Eventually Danu would let me.

Áine smiled even as she shivered, goosebumps cascading down her shoulders. "This stream is still cold with snow melt." She raised a hand and let a couple drops of water fall back into the river. "The sea is too warm right now." She wrinkled her nose. "I prefer it in the winter. Everyone thinks I'm touched, but I like it best when ice is cracking at its edges."

I could picture that easily, her long, lean body cutting through the ice like an axe. I wondered why I'd never thought about swimming in the sea myself. I so rarely left my hut on the hill, and when I did go for walks they were through the forest, not along the beach. Perhaps I should try the sea when the cold came.

Áine blew bubbles in the stream and let her hair swirl around her. She was as lovely a woman as I'd ever seen, with her clear eyes and lithe body. Eventually she stood and climbed from the stream, wringing out her hair. "I must go." Her cheeks were flushed pink as she pulled her dress over her head. "Granddad will be looking for me."

I jerked my head so violently my whole body flinched. "Dagda? Dagda is still alive?"

Áine looked at me curiously and laughed. "Well, he wasn't yet gone when I left this morning."

I clambered out of the stream and yanked on my own clothes, my fingers trembling. "Can I come with you? To see him? He was—he was very kind to me when I was a girl." There was something in my trembling, wide-eyed pleading that my immortal self hated, but I ignored that part of me. I knew he would not know me, but . . . but I would know *him*. I could recall, still, how he came panting over the hill, clutching his side; how gentle he was with my bees, the first time his hand had touched mine as a friend.

Áine smiled. "I'm sure Granddad will be pleased to see you. Come on, then."

As we walked down the hill, Áine continued to chatter, and I learned that Dagda had married Niamh, the devotee who had so loved him. Together they'd had one daughter called Ciara—Áine's mother, who had died when she was three. Áine had been raised by Niamh and Dagda, and she still lived in their house to take care of Dagda after Niamh died.

"Granddad hasn't been the same since she passed," Áine sighed as we entered the village. It did not look like it had grown much, but the houses looked more prosperous, and I could see that the farmed fields stretched much farther than they had in my previous life. We passed a group of women chattering together as they spread seaweed out to dry in the sun, preparing it to enrich the soil for the crops.

The women too looked more prosperous. In my first life, most had worn whatever clothes they could cobble together, scraps that were worn and faded. Many had been thin, just this side of starving, but now the women were plump, with soft faces and cheerful smiles, not worn down by poverty and loss.

"He gets confused." Áine stopped in front of a grey stone house. "I'm sorry if he doesn't remember you."

I wanted to laugh, but only because I already knew he would not and that it did not matter. I was going to see him again, my old friend, and my hands trembled with excitement as we entered the house. I would remember for the both of us.

Dagda was sitting outside in his little garden. Áine walked out first, and I hesitated in the dark doorway before finally stepping outside. The sun shone so brightly in my eyes that I could not see anything for a long moment. When my eyes finally adjusted, I saw an old man bowing before me.

"Goddess." His forehead was almost on the ground. "Goddess," he repeated, and I felt a burst of pleasure. Danu had failed. He did know me. Slowly he raised his head and looked me full in the face. His expression changed. He looked confused, and as Áine helped him to his feet, I realized that of course he did not recognize me. He had never known me as a goddess, only as a mortal woman called Cailleach. "Danu?" he said, voice feeble, reaching a hand toward my face, toward my green eyes. I felt as if a hand squeezed my heart; the idea that he saw my mother in me was even worse.

"No, Granddad." Áine was gentle but not patronizing, matter-of-fact. "This is Cailleach. She's Fianna's granddaughter come to work the bees at her croft. She said you taught her how to work with the bees one summer."

I watched him carefully, searching despite myself for a flicker of recognition in my old friend's face, but I found nothing. It was more discomfiting than I'd expected, seeing him like this. When I'd last seen him, only two days ago for me, he'd been young and hale. Now his golden hair had gone grey, and his face was creased with wrinkles. I'd always hated the sight of wrinkles on mortals—they made them appear weak and aged, like the sagging belly of an old doe—but now, looking at Dagda, I found I did not mind them. Rather than weakening him, they seemed to lend him strength, carving something beautiful where there had once been a face as plain and unadorned as a stone.

Áine helped him sit back down on the bench where he'd been a moment before and then went back into the house, and I tentatively sat next to him. I remembered again the first time he'd touched me, his hand reaching out in the darkness.

"With the light streaming behind you, I thought you were her. The goddess Danu," Dagda said. "Your eyes are green like hers. Though now that I see them closely, they're much darker, like a fir in winter. Did my Áine say that I taught you about bees?" He peered at me closely again, then smiled wistfully. "I'm sorry, but I don't remember you. My mind is not what it was. What is your name, my dear?"

"Cailleach," I said. "You taught me how to work at the hives at my—at Fianna's croft. How to gather the honey and wax and make it into candles."

"That croft is a sacred place," he said slowly. "It was there that I saw the goddess Danu. I was— I had made a bargain—" He frowned, and I knew it was the clouding that Danu had placed over his mind. He could not remember our bargain because he could not remember me. "There was a woman who lived there before Fianna . . ." I looked up with hope, but he just shook his head. "I've forgotten her in the years since." My throat ached with sudden pain and my excitement fell away. I had not thought it would matter, him not remembering me . . . but it *did*. It hurt me to think that all we had done together was lost to him. Perhaps in the end, it would have been better if he were dead. It was near impossible to look at him and know him, only to have him look at me with nothing more than the kindness he would show a stranger. "She had a little dog." He turned toward me. "A little black and white dog with one ear that stood straight up and one that fell down flat. Failinis. I loved that dog. The whole village did. But he got sick, so sick." Dagda brushed a tear away from his cheek. "He died and then she—the woman who lived there—disappeared. We never knew if she died or just left . . ." He sighed quietly. "The whole town gathered to bury him. All of us, up on the hill."

"He must have been remarkable." Áine appeared in the doorway with a loaf of brown bread and a jar of honey. "Some have dogs, of course, but I think most would sooner attend their enemy's funeral than one for a dog. They'd think it would show that they'd grown soft."

"He *was* a remarkable dog." Dagda took a bite of bread. His lips shone with honey before he licked them clean. "He was the gentlest soul I ever met. The children would pull his ears, his tail, but I never once saw him snap at them. Everyone he met was a friend."

I took a bite of my own bread, trying to mask the tears that had gathered in my eyes. The memory was bittersweet. I was glad that Dagda remembered Failinis so well, even though it must have been more than fifty years since he'd seen him last.

I sat with Dagda and Áine for a long while, longer than I'd planned, and by the time I noticed how close the shadows had drawn, the sun was already near to setting. Finally I stood, saying that I must be home soon. Áine walked me to the door, promising that she would be back early the next morning to help with the bees, but she did not offer to walk me back up the hill.

Of course she wouldn't, I chided myself as I strode back toward my hut. I was not a child. Until Failinis, I had always walked around alone, even in the dark. I would simply have to learn to be alone again.

"Perhaps I should show myself to your druid again, before he dies." Danu suddenly appeared at my side as though she'd been there the whole time.

"He's not *my* druid." I noticed that where she walked, green grass sprang up beneath her feet. I stopped and looked out to the sea where the sun was just a glimmer of red on the horizon. "He was my . . . my friend. And now he doesn't remember me at all." I turned away from the sea and continued back up the hill.

"He remembers your dog." Danu's voice was resonant in the darkness. "You know it's not possible for him to remember you," she said after a few quiet moments. "It's part of—"

"My punishment." I snapped the words out so fast my teeth

clacked together. "I *know* the terms of my punishment, Danu. With each prick of pain, each monthly bleed, each time my muscles groan after lifting water from my well, I remember them. I do not need you to remind me."

Danu sighed but didn't say anything else until we reached my hut. I stopped. I did not want to enter it in the dark, to fumble around alone until I had lit the fire and made whatever measly meal I could. "I thought the roses were a nice touch." Danu's voice was heavy with satisfaction. "Though I can't see them properly now." She waved a hand and suddenly my house was ablaze with light, as though she'd lit every candle inside. The light made the roses gleam like coins, and when Danu reached out a hand to them, the ones that had been buds burst into full flower. She walked into the hut without asking for an invitation and surveyed it with pleasure. "It's such a pleasant spot." She patted a hand on the round table, waved at the roaring fire she'd conjured with nothing but a thought. She looked up at the ceiling and frowned. "Though that's a bit dull"—she pointed at the thatched roof and suddenly green tendrils started curling through it, bursting into yellow blooms when they drew near her. My floor was soon covered in yellow rose petals, and Danu took a few dancing steps in them, laughing.

"Now when it rains it will drip on me," I sighed, stalking toward the shelves to see what I might eat for dinner.

"Can't you just enjoy the flowers"—she waved a hand, stirring the scent of roses through the house—"without worrying about the rain?"

"I'm mortal, Danu," I said sharply. "That means I have to worry about whether rain will drip through my roof or if I have enough wood or if my dog—"

"Why don't we eat together?" she interrupted me, waving a

hand. My table became full of food: a fat bird with golden skin, purple grapes round with juice, a creamy white cheese drizzled with honey. I'd not had a feast like this since I'd left Tara, and I wanted to refuse it, wanted to push her from my house, but my mouth was watering at the smell. Danu must have noticed because she smiled widely. "Come now, don't be foolish. No mortal has ever refused a feast I set before them."

I knew she was testing me, seeing if I would rebuff a perfectly good meal out of pride—but I was not so *foolish*. I swallowed the bitterness in my throat and sat at the table with a hard *thump*, eating everything in front of me while Danu hummed and only drank wine. It was clear as glass but tasted spicy and strong; it reminded me of a fir tree, of a cold, cold winter's night.

I'd never had an immortal drink in my mortal state, and within minutes my eyes started to blur and my head lolled to the table. I would have stayed there all night, but I felt—while on the very edge of deep sleep—Danu pick me up as though I were a child and gently place me on my pallet. She stroked my face and sang something that made me picture hay swaying under a golden sun. For once I did not turn away.

When I woke the next morning, the darkness was gone from the house and so was she.

the third life

After that, I rarely spent a night alone.

During the day, Áine and I worked together to maintain the hives, to bottle honey and make candles, and at night, I always had someone in my bed. Mostly men, but some women; whoever was lonely at the end of a night at the tavern. Most of them were fumble-handed, too rough or too quick, but it was not really their caresses I wished for. All I wanted was someone to keep me company until dawn rose.

Usually, they left before anyone else in the town awoke, but occasionally one of them would pass Áine if she came up the hill early. Áine did not mention this until one day she passed a woman called Bride, the sweet, empty-headed sister of the village baker who was surprisingly good with her hands. "Women too?" Áine raised an eyebrow, watching Bride's cheeks turn pink as she hurried down the hill to cover herself in flour and pretend she'd had her hands in the dough all night.

I shrugged. "They weep less than the men. Pine less too. Men are always wanting something *else*. Hands to knead their backs, honey to sweeten their lips, reassuring whispers that they make

love as well as a god. Women don't ask for more than they themselves would give. And they leave quickly. Then I can be alone
again."

"Do you want so badly to be alone?" Áine asked curiously,
pouring a long measure of honey into a small jar then sealing it
with golden wax. A few drops spilled onto her skin, but she didn't
flinch or peel it away, just let it harden against her fingers.

"I've always been alone." My voice was husky from the smoke
I'd used earlier to soothe a fractious hive.

"Not as a child, surely." Áine frowned. "You must have had parents. Siblings. Friends."

I thought of Enya for a moment, then shook my head. "My
mother had no other children."

"That sounds lonely," Áine said after a long moment.

"I enjoy my own company," I said, thinking about those long,
sweet days walking under a cold blue sky.

"I hate being alone. I don't understand what there is to like
about it."

"It's peaceful," I tried to explain. But how could I capture how it
felt to stand alone on the edge of the world, to smell the sharp scent
of snow and broken firs in the air, to fill your mouth with water
from a stream still crusted with ice, no soul around but your own.
"The noise of the world retreats." I thought of Failinis then, looking up at me with his brown eyes. I had not minded him joining
me, in those moments, no matter how he ran and barked and disturbed the silence—and suddenly I missed him so much that I had
to turn my head so Áine wouldn't see the tears. To be alone meant
no little dog waiting for you each night.

But it also meant that your heart would not break when that dog
left you.

"And when you're by yourself," I added, "you're not beholden to anyone. To anything."

It was better, safer, to be alone.

The air smelled like smoke, and even though the sun had barely risen, I could smell cold on the wind. We needed to gather the rest of the honey and wax from the hives before the bees died, and I was impatiently waiting for Áine. When I saw her finally crest the hill, she wasn't alone; she was holding Dagda's arm.

"Granddad said that he could smell snow," Áine explained when they reached me. "He insisted on coming to help gather the rest of the honey and wax, even though I told him it was too early for it."

"He's right." I looked toward the sky. "I can smell it too."

Áine lifted her nose and sniffed the air delicately, like a rabbit trying to scent a fox, and shrugged. "I can't smell anything. But if you agree with Granddad, I'm sure you must be right."

We set to working at the hives together and even though Dagda's hands trembled slightly, he was careful and gentle, never spilling a drop of honey. After a few hours Áine went back into the hut to get some food for us while Dagda and I continued to work, our hands moving in perfect harmony as they had in my previous life. For a few moments, it was as if we were both young and strong again and I had my friend back at my side. Dagda began to hum, and I joined him just as I used to, but then he stopped and looked at me, his eyes wide. As the last notes fell away, I realized we had been humming the song that we'd heard the night we'd watched the stars and listened to the fishermen singing on the harbor. He blinked, and for one brief moment, I thought I saw recognition in his eyes. He reached out a hand, but before I could do anything, say anything, he dropped it and took a step back, looking confused. Bitter disappointment coiled in my stomach, but I ignored the gesture as though it had not happened, bowing my head and continuing with my task until he said, "The woman who lived here with Failinis—she hated this part of keeping bees. That we take the honey and wax from them and kill the hive. Not even a child would complain about killing insects, but she did." He smiled fondly.

Áine and Dagda stayed with me for dinner and long after, telling stories of Áine's childhood, of her mother Ciara and of Niamh. Dagda talked long and Áine laughed easily; I was happy to have them beside me. Áine was halfway through a story when I realized that Dagda had fallen asleep in his chair. His head had fallen onto his chest, and he'd begun to gently snore—a peaceful, quiet sound like the droning of the bees. "He gets tired easily these days." Áine sighed and bent toward him. The firelight shone golden on her face and in her long dark hair and for a moment I wanted to lean forward and run my hands through it. My cheeks colored at the thought, and I jumped to my feet, turning to the fire so that I might have some excuse for the blush. Áine had become my friend. More, she was a leader in the community. Getting involved with her would not be simple; I could not risk the ease I had finally found in this life. We sat in a comfortable, lingering silence. Once the moon was clear in the sky, Áine put a gentle hand on Dagda's shoulder and woke him, calling a quiet goodnight to me before she helped him back down the hill.

Dagda faded from life slowly that winter. He had no pain and no nameable illness, but anyone who saw him knew he was not long for this world. His energy slowly waned; at first he kept making his way up the hill but worked slower than he had before. Then he came up, but no longer worked, only watched as Áine and I tended to the bees. Eventually, he stopped coming at all.

After that, each time I saw Áine I held my breath, wondering if she would tell me he had gone, but he lingered for a long time, though he spent most of his days sleeping. As his health dwindled and his need for her increased, Áine too stopped coming up the hill, unwilling to leave his side—not knowing which breath might be his last.

I missed her company more than I was willing to admit.

On the coldest day we'd had so far, a few flakes of snow blowing through the air, I had gone down to the village to trade for fish when I saw Áine hurrying toward me. She was pale and looked as though she hadn't slept in days.

"Cailleach"—her voice was tired, the whites of her eyes shot through with red—"I was going to come and find you. Roisin's husband is begging me to attend her. She's having a difficult birth, and their farm is halfway down the road." Áine glanced back at her croft. "But I can't leave Dagda for so long. Would you stay with him? He gets so confused with everyone else but always seems to find comfort with you. I wouldn't leave him, but Dagda would never forgive me if a child died because I chose to stay, and there is no one else to help—" Her voice trembled and I reached out a hand, clasping hers in mine.

"Of course I will stay with him. I will not let him be alone in case—" I did not have to say it. Áine squeezed my hand tightly for a moment, then turned in a swirl of skirts, leading me back to her house.

She gathered her things and said goodbye to Dagda, kissing his thin cheeks and holding his hand for a long moment. "Granddad, Cailleach is going to stay with you tonight. Roisin is having trouble with her baby. I have to go help." Her voice didn't tremble, and she wore a bright smile, but I saw the way her eyes traced his face, as though trying to memorize his features.

Dagda patted her hand. "We'll be grand, love." Áine kissed his cheek, then left the house.

Dagda barely had the energy to eat the dinner Áine had left, but he managed a few bites before I helped him back to bed. I sat at his side, watching the candlelight flicker on his old face.

"Dagda."

I jumped, startled by the voice at my elbow, and Dagda's eyes flew open, staring at Danu, who had appeared at his side. She was not in her god form—had no hair of gold, no shining robes, just pink cheeks and a soft smile on her face. Only her eyes were the same spring green. Still, Dagda clearly recognized her, and when she reached out a hand, he grasped it tightly, his face glowing with the golden light that poured from her. "My lady." He struggled to rise from the bed, but Danu put a hand on his shoulder and sat beside him.

"I thought, perhaps, you might like to see spring again. One last time." Her voice was gentle, and as she spoke, I knew these were the last moments Dagda would have. He knew it too, but it was not sorrow I saw on his face. Only serenity.

I knew that seeing her again would be the crowning pleasure of Dagda's life, but I was angry that she'd intruded once more. We'd been sitting together peacefully, and he could have gone quietly, gently—but instead my mother had to interfere, to make his end a spectacle. It was not fair. She did not know Dagda, not as I or as Áine did. I had seen how careful his hands were around bees but how clumsy when holding glass. I had watched him cry for my little dog, had watched his face glow with reflected glory as he'd conducted his rites under the oak in the forest. Danu knew him only as another acolyte of hers whose life was no longer for her than an indrawn breath. Still, even if I didn't like it, I thought I understood why he cared so much about Danu. At almost every moment, mortals stood on the knife edge between death and life, and the idea that there was something, *someone*, greater than themselves, who could pull them back from that edge or give it meaning, was comforting. It was Danu, not I, who could offer Dagda that comfort.

When Danu waved her hand, transforming Dagda's small room into a garden bower, I could not prevent the gasp that escaped me. The room suddenly seemed as though it sat in a forest glade, glowing with light like that of the setting sun. Bees droned back and forth, and one fat bumblebee landed on Dagda's outstretched hand, making him laugh as it bobbed about for a moment before flying off again. The air was soft, warm, even though the village was covered in a fine layer of snow. Dagda still lay in his bed, but now moss pillowed his head, the blankets on his legs covered with a mass of fallen flower petals. Roses twined over the wooden bed frame in yellow and white, and honeysuckle hung from the ceiling. Dagda sucked in a deep breath. "Thank you, great goddess. You have given me so much more than I, a mere mortal, deserve."

Danu's face was a rosy glow as she bent toward Dagda. "I will sit here and talk with you." She did not need to add *till the end*, although we all knew it would come soon.

He did not speak, as I'd expected, about Niamh, Ciara, or even Áine. Instead he spoke to Danu about *herself*—about his faith and devotion toward her, how he had always felt her presence in the forest come spring. He told her that from the time he'd been a child and heard the stories of her goodness, he had sought to worship her and do it well. He'd had such a large life and many who had loved him better and longer than Danu . . .

But at the end of it, it was still her approbation he was reaching for. His adoration, when in truth he knew so little of her, made my stomach roil. But what could I say? These were his last moments. He had a right to do with them as he wanted.

Finally, his voice began to grow hoarse and his breathing slowed. After a while he sat silent, hand in hand with Danu, bright eyes wandering through the enchanted bower she'd created for him. Just before dawn, his eyes caught mine and I smiled at him.

"Cailleach." He looked directly at me, but before I could discern whether he'd said my name because he remembered me or because, in his final moments, he recognized the truth of my godhood, his eyes closed. I watched him for a long time, but his chest did not rise again.

Danu squeezed his hand one last time and then gently laid it on his chest, but she did not get up as I thought she would. "He looks so peaceful," she said, peering into his face.

I wondered as I looked at him where my old friend was. Was he with his wife and daughter in some other veiled realm? Had my Failinis come running up to him, tail wagging? I realized that even though I did not know the truth, did not know where he was, I believed, in some way, that he was happy still. An unexpected peace filled my chest, and I thought that perhaps this was what Dagda's worship really was. Belief, even without knowing—and in that faith, a sense of ease and tranquility.

Danu moved as if to close his unseeing eyes, but I caught her wrist in my hand.

"I will do it," I said. "I was his friend." She had given him a garden. But I would be the last one to touch him. I turned away from her, facing Dagda's body. I wanted to thank him for all the kindness he'd shown me, shown Failinis, but I suspected that he'd known even more than I how much I'd needed him, how much I'd cared about him, so instead of saying anything I just kissed his cheek, then closed his eyes. When I turned around again, the garden bower had disappeared and so had Danu, and so I sat alone there for a long time until the blue light of dawn brushed against my old friend's still face.

Áine returned home later that morning, dropping her bag at the sight of Dagda's unmoving form. She let out a half-choked sob. "I have to tell them. The rest of the village," she said, and ran from the room.

Dagda had been beloved, and before long the house was full of people. Some wept, but most seemed pleased that he was finally at rest. They talked about how Dagda would be happy to be finally with his gods, and I said nothing to challenge their beliefs. Wherever Dagda was, he was not with Danu or the others. That was the one thing that I knew.

I stayed with Áine that day and the next, helping her put out food and drink, even washing Dagda's body for her. She had tried to, had lifted a dripping rag over his pale chest, but her hand had begun to tremble and she'd run from the room. I even heard her retching, which surprised me. I would not have thought she'd be squeamish about such things, but perhaps it was different when it was your own kin. I tried to imagine seeing Danu laid out like Dagda, her body stiff and blue, but I could not picture it. The moon could fall into the sea and still Danu would be filled with life, the green-sap blood in her veins rushing quick and strong, flowers blooming in her hair.

We buried him under the sacred oak in the forest on the third day.

We walked in a procession through the wood, several men carrying Dagda's body on a smooth board. They'd covered it with a green sheet, and I thought again of Danu's eyes. Perhaps Dagda himself had laid the cloth aside, thinking of the goddess he so loved. As we walked, Áine asked the gods to gather Dagda in their embrace. It was foolish, and it made me angry—not at Áine, but at the gods and their encouragement of such worship. They had grown, like Danu, to love hearing their names on mortal lips. They felt it was their due—the sweet smoke of sacrifice and the blood spilled for them. I alone knew how senseless and false they were, and watching the villagers worship them in front of me, listening to them talk about Dagda at peace with the gods, was wrong—a perverse lie.

It was bitter cold when we entered the clearing where the sacred oak stood. Even leafless at the height of winter, the tree was impressive, with limbs that stretched wide and high and a trunk that three men could not wrap their arms around. The ground had already been prepared. They had lined the pit with stones to keep out animals, and as the men slowly lowered Dagda into it, I turned away, not wanting anyone else to see my tears. They would think I was absurd, think I was grieving a man who in their eyes I had barely known.

Normally they would have sung and danced around the grave, would have brought out food and wine, but a bitter wind was blowing, the cheeks of all were red, and some of the children's lips had turned blue. I heard murmuring, a decision that they would gather instead at the tavern.

I closed my eyes, waiting for them to leave, and I thought they had until I heard a quiet sob and saw Áine standing beside the grave.

"He was like my father," she said when I went to stand by her side.

"He was my friend." I took her hand and thought about all the times he'd crested the hill clutching his side and smiling widely. The thought of seeing him no more made me cry too.

For a long time, Áine and I stood there, growing colder and colder. I was about to suggest we head back to the village when Áine suddenly turned and kissed me, lips cold and smelling of snow. Surprised but grateful, I kissed her back, hard and urgent.

We did not go back to the village but instead stumbled our way back to my house and into my bed. My hands were rough and quick, and her long hair fell over her breasts as I made her cry out. Then she began to weep, and I gathered her close to me while her tears fell hot down my skin.

the third life

No one asked why Áine moved into my hut.

I don't know if they thought we were living as lovers or as sisters, but the villagers did not seem to care; if anything, they seemed pleased, glad to see that Áine would not have to suffer alone in the house where Dagda had died.

We had lived together for a few months before I learned about Áine's nightmares. Spring had turned to a long, hot summer, and that night I had not been able to fall asleep, tossing and turning. I lay there in the dark, wishing I still had the ability to send ice crackling down my arms. My days were so full that I had not thought of my immortal self in a long time, and my stomach writhed with guilt—as though the desire itself meant I did not want Áine anymore.

Áine was usually a still, quiet sleeper, but that night her body began to shake, and when I bent over her, I could see her eyes fluttering wildly behind her closed eyelids. She cried out then, so loudly that my heart jumped—still she didn't wake up, just continued screaming. I wrapped my arms around her as her hands grasped for something invisible in the air. I called her name over and over, trying to soothe her, until finally her eyes flew open. She looked at me, but it was obvious she didn't truly see me because she pushed me away and hunched over, hands in front of her face as though I would hurt her.

"Áine." She had her knees pulled up to her chest, and I crouched down as one would to a frightened child. "It's Cailleach. I'm here, Áine, I'm here." After a few gasping breaths, she finally lowered her arms. When she looked at me again, I could tell she knew my face.

"I'm sorry." Her voice was trembling and weak, as though she'd just been ill. She raked her fingers through her hair and looked away from me, but I could see tears in her eyes.

"I don't know why you call us 'mortals' so often," she said suddenly, breathless, as though she'd been running. "You're a mortal too, you know." The look she gave me was almost suspicious, but before I had time to say anything she sighed. "I'm sorry. The dreams," she whispered. "They're terrible." She twisted her braid around and around in her hands. "I dreamt about Dagda—that he was alive again, reaching out to me, but . . . but then his face . . . it changed." She shuddered.

"Changed into what?"

Áine didn't answer me immediately, instead moving to stand by the cold hearth. "You know that Dagda and Niamh raised me. I adored Dagda, but he was often away, sometimes on the road with other druids, sometimes worshipping on his own, so most often I was with Niamh. She taught me how to heal, how to bring babies into the world. I loved being with her, but she had . . . moods. One day she would be so happy she would tell me to forget our chores and would instead take me for a swim. On other days . . . well, she did not get out of bed, and I would have to take care of everything on my own. On the good days she told me stories about her own grandmother, Siobhan."

I forgot sometimes that Áine was related to Siobhan. They looked nothing alike; Áine had a light, laughing quality about her that I had never seen on Siobhan's face. I was glad that Áine had never known her troubles, that the hard lines that had been on Siobhan's face had not marked her own in the same way.

"Niamh would tell me that we must be kind to all strangers, because they might be gods in disguise."

She told me the same story Siobhan had once relayed to me, of when Manannán saved her from drowning, and though it had been many long years, I could still hear the echo of her voice in the words that Áine spoke.

"I loved that story." Áine gave a small smile. "To me, the gods Dagda worshipped were always . . . distant. But Niamh made them seem real, as though I might meet them at any time. But on the bad days . . ." Her smiled dropped. "On the bad days, Niamh told me much darker stories. Things that used to terrify me, about demons, evil spirits. About things that watched from the forest. And I began to wonder, if a god could inhabit the body of a mortal . . . could those . . . *things* do the same?" Áine stirred the hearth with the iron poker as though expecting a shower of sparks, but it remained as dead as it had been a moment before. "I began to have nightmares. About Niamh and Dagda, about my mother. They would reach for me, but their eyes would be empty and their smiles . . . their lips would twist, their teeth would begin to rot, and their faces—" Áine cut herself off, shuddering. "Dagda said that I had nothing to fear, that only gods could walk among mortals. That they would protect us. But Niamh never did. She would hold me tight when I woke screaming, she would kiss my forehead, but she never told me that I was wrong."

Her gaze moved to the open window. "Any time I meet strangers, I am so . . . torn. I want to treat them as Siobhan wanted, as gods in disguise, but I'm also *frightened* of what they might be, what might be hidden behind their face. I wanted to go to the druids as Dagda did, learn to heal with great skill, but when the time came . . . I couldn't leave Daingean Uí Chúis. It would have been too much, to be surrounded by strangers all the time."

Áine turned toward me then expectantly, as if I could offer her reassurance, perhaps, or comfort, but I did not know what to say. I was ashamed, as though she had seen the truth of me. But I knew that to be foolish—I wasn't an evil spirit, a demon. I could tell her who I truly was—but was what I had been as a god so different from what she feared? So though I wanted to reassure her, had opened my lips with that very intention, I held back. Instead, I asked, "Why did you talk to me, then? In the tavern that first night we met?"

Áine sat on the floor, put her head on my knee. "I don't know. You were sitting there all alone. And when I looked at you, I felt as though somehow I knew you. As though I'd always known you." She blushed and reached out, caressing the side of my face. "Besides, you're not really a stranger. You're Fianna's kin. You knew Dagda as a child." She smiled at me, so widely and so sweetly that I put away all thoughts of telling her the truth about what I was. We were together now, in this life. That was what mattered. I was no longer the goddess Cailleach, no longer blue-skinned and powerful. Now, I was the same as Áine. Mortal.

With only the memory of once having been more.

I liked having Áine in my bed at night, liked that I no longer woke up cold and alone in the dark, but I did not care for the number of people who now flooded my house. Before the sun had even risen, they would come trickling up the hill, wanting her prayers, her touch, her thoughts. They lingered even after she'd eased whatever worry they had: they liked to stay and have a drink with her, and while they chatted, the villagers would let their children wander in my garden and splash in my stream. Áine never seemed to mind or to long for quiet. Indeed, in the few moments she would have been alone, like when I had to go trade for fish or wanted a walk, she would twitch and fidget and usually accompany me anyway.

At first I did not mind because when we were together I did not think about Failinis as much. Did not listen for his feet padding across the floor or look up to see if he was asleep by the fire. We passed our first winter together like this, and it wasn't until late spring that I began to wake with a tightness in my chest, craning my neck as I listened to the sounds of people in my house, longing for their absence.

I woke one morning later than usual, and when I stumbled from our small sleeping chamber, I found that we were, once more, not alone. Áine sat at the table, a fat baby bouncing on her knee, chattering away with Saoirse, a woman from the village who had always rankled me; being around her was like having the sun constantly shining in my eyes. No matter where I went I could hear her laughter, her jests, her voice—always pitched too loud.

"You must have been sleeping like the dead." Saoirse clucked her tongue at me when I entered the room. "We've not been able to keep the children quiet." She pointed out the door to where three children were playing a game that seemed to involve shrieking at the top of their lungs. I winced and went back to the little room, dressing quickly and yanking my hair into a long braid. Áine usually brushed it for me each morning, twisting it into a pretty knot that kept it out of my face, but I'd never allow her to do something so intimate with so many people around. "There's porridge in the pot."

I stiffened with annoyance as Saoirse addressed me so casually, as though she had some claim over my hut, over the food in my old black pot.

Áine flicked a glance at me, frowning in warning, so I grit my teeth and held my tongue, walking outside without any breakfast. It was a cool, breezy spring day where the air smelled of wet earth and green, growing things. The scent irritated me; it smelled like Danu.

I walked to the hives and peered in at the bees. The smallest hive had been troubling me lately, and I was worried that the queen was ill, but I found her easily, and she was alive still, surrounded by a clutch of followers. She looked like Áine, I thought—always surrounded by a buzzing, clamoring crowd.

I walked to the stream to dangle my feet in, trying to cool my irritation, but Saoirse's noisy children followed me and began splashing each other, shrieking. I moved upstream and out of their splashing, commanding them to be quiet, but they paid me no mind and continued to play noisily. I closed my eyes, trying to block them out, to make myself still and unmoving as a stone. But their shrieks only increased until their cries changed to frightened screams. I looked upstream and saw the little girl had fallen in. I rushed forward without thought and grabbed her, gathering her up to my chest, patting her back vigorously. She gasped and coughed against me for a moment, her limbs shaking, and I began to shake too. She could have drowned as I had in my second life, dying in a choking swirl of cold water.

I saved her, I realized. *I saved this mortal child.* And I had done it instinctively, as any other mortal would have. As though I were one of them. My head spun at the thought, with the knowledge that my body's instincts had become those of a mortal. I thought so rarely of my life as a goddess, had pushed my memories away so thoroughly in deference to Áine, thinking I could wear mortality as a disguise—but I had never expected to truly *become* one. To feel and act they did.

I pushed the girl roughly away from me and into the embrace of her siblings, who had come crowding over just as Saoirse and Áine came running, then took the girl up in their arms, holding her close as she wept in fright. The girl's teeth chattered, and her lips were tinged blue with cold. I was glad I'd saved her, of course I was, but I was angry too, that my body had acted without my leave. My punishment, which I had not thought about in so long, seemed to rise once more to the forefront of my mind and clamp chains around my wrists. I was not a god, no matter how I wished it—but I was not a mortal either, no matter how I acted. I was both and nothing, and my head and heart ached—and somehow Saoirse was *still* talking.

"Oh love." She held the girl close before scolding her, swatting her head and making the girl howl. "I've told you the current is too strong here for you. But you never listen to your mother, do you? And now you've interrupted our—"

I turned from away from them and began to stride toward the wood. I heard Áine call my name but I ignored her, quickening my pace in the hopes that she would not follow me. She didn't, and when I finally reached the cool, dark light of the wood I found I could relax enough to breathe.

"It was good," a voice said. "That you saved the child."

I jumped at Danu appearing by my side. I did not stop for her, indeed only strode faster, but she kept pace with me easily and was truly silent, making every small noise that much louder: the twigs I broke underfoot, the branches that scratched at my dress while her footsteps did nothing and her clothes remained untouched. Her graceful, quiet movements against the *noise* of my mortal body made the gorge rise in my throat, and suddenly my panic shifted sharply to tears. All I wanted was to walk alone through the woods. Why could no one let me *be* anymore? I didn't say anything, though, just continued to walk, hoping that Danu would leave if I didn't respond to her, but she stayed.

"There was a time when you wouldn't have," Danu continued patiently, voice conversational as though she had all the time in the world. Which, of course, she did.

"But not anymore," I said. "I have done as you wanted, learned their mortal instincts. I saved the child when once I would have let her drown." I gave her a bow, meaning to mock her, but slipped in the muddy ground to fall hard on my face in the mud. When I looked up, Danu was bending over me, amusement on her face, her robe spotless.

She did not move to help me even when I slipped again trying to rise to my feet. When I finally managed it, I wiped mud off my face. "I cannot *abide* spring. It is neither cold nor hot, neither hard nor soft. It is everything and nothing."

"When I found out that I was going to have a child, I was sure that they would be like me, that they would rejoice in the warm spring air." Danu extended her arms out as she crossed a rivulet of water on a vine that had stretched out obligingly. Several bluebirds had flown down onto her shoulders as she spoke, and a ring of yellow moths circled her head like a quick-moving crown. She should have looked ridiculous, but instead she was graceful and elegant; a queen surrounded by worshipful attendants. "Instead, that first spring, when you felt the warmth of sunlight on your face, you *shrieked*. Just *once*, one loud shriek that sounded like ice splintering. You hated it. Even then, I wasn't certain until . . ." She looked away, disappointment shining on her face as she remembered the happiest day of my life. "I wasn't *disappointed* in you," she said, reading my thoughts. "I was . . . surprised. You were the first child born of the gods. We had no real idea what you would be like. But when I saw you in that clearing . . . when your skin turned blue." She sighed. "I gave you winter then because I knew it would make you happy. I would do anything, Cailleach"—her eyes were glassy—"to make you happy."

"Then why won't you end my—" The words were on the tip of my tongue, but when I thought of returning home, I did not picture Tara's marble halls or even my sacred grove, but my little hut on the hill. I thought of my life as a god, going back to the days of endless pleasure, easy power—and found I didn't want it. I only wanted Áine.

I almost stumbled, as though I'd been struck. Home, now, was wherever Áine was. The realization set my heart ablaze, cleared my pounding head, and I began to run back to the hut to tell her. I was going to throw my arms around her and hold her close. I was going to tell her that I had chosen her, over the gods, over my blue skin, over *winter*. Over everything.

I didn't even notice that Danu watched me go—that I had, for once, been the one to leave.

I had wandered far and it took me some time to return to the hut: the sun had set but it had not yet grown fully dark. I was pleased to see no one around the hill and to find Áine sitting alone at the table.

"Where have you *been*, Cailleach," she demanded before I could speak, pushing her stool away so roughly it clattered to the floor.

"I-I went on a walk—" I said, startled by her anger.

"All *day?*" Áine interrupted me. "And after what happened?"

I blinked. I'd entirely forgotten the child nearly drowning. "I couldn't be around them anymore," I stuttered. "You know I hate Saoirse and her children. I had to rescue that little one from the stream when she fell in, even after I told them to go away. They were shrieking and shrieking. I couldn't bear it anymore." My words were coming out wrong, jumbled, and too fast. It wasn't what I wanted to say at all. I didn't care about any of that anymore, I cared only about *her*, about Áine, but she was looking at me with such anger that a prickle of ire rose in response. I should not have to account for all my comings and goings to anyone, not even her.

"You can't just leave!" Áine's voice grew loud. "I didn't know what had happened. I was worried you'd met some accident, run into a wolf or a bear with how far you go into those woods. Besides, you should have stayed, even if you *were* annoyed. Those children were frightened, and you didn't comfort them."

"I *saved* them," I said, keeping my voice low. "Why should I have to comfort them too? They should have listened to me, to you and Saoirse. We *told* them not to play in the stream."

"I don't understand how you can be so unfeeling, Cailleach," Áine said. "You don't even seem to care that the child nearly died. And you just left. You left me." Her voice seemed to choke at the words.

I frowned. "I didn't leave *you*. I needed some time. Just the day. That's all."

"I was *scared*." Áine's voice dropped. "I didn't know if you were hurt or needed me or if you would even come back—"

She did truly look scared, and I should have comforted her, but the guilt her expression incited in me made me upset again. I was not used to being beholden to anyone in such a way; it made me feel chained. And the truth in her words scared me—what *would* have happened if a bear or a wolf had found me? Once, nothing could have hurt me, and now everything could. It reminded me, sharply, of that torn feeling—of being neither god nor mortal—and it was with that hurt and fear that I spoke, my voice cold.

"You don't need to concern yourself with me."

Áine stared at me for a long moment before leaving the hut, slamming the door so hard that a jar of honey that had been on the edge of a shelf fell, shattering on the ground. Its contents spread across the floor, forming a sticky, golden pool covered in shards of glass. I bent to pick it up and shouted when I sliced my finger, flinging the glass at the wall and peppering the honey with drops of my own red blood. I had come to tell her how much I wanted her, needed her. How had everything gone so wrong?

I wrapped my finger in a piece of white cloth, one that Áine had just woven, heart in my throat. I was ashamed of what I'd said. I wanted to go after her, but I was afraid that I would not be able to say what I wanted to again, that my words would get jumbled up as they just had, as they so often did, and so instead I stayed and tried to go about my evening tasks, hoping she would return.

I ground wheat into flour and then cleaned and skinned a rabbit I'd caught earlier, even though I was clumsy with my cut finger. I stood over the well for a long time, trying to winch up the bucket with just one hand. After letting yet another bucket fall to the bottom, I hissed in frustration and kicked out at the stone, doing nothing more than stubbing my toe. I had gotten too comfortable with Áine, too comfortable having another pair of hands to help with the daily tasks that made up so much of mortal life.

Finally I gave up and collapsed on the little stone bench that overlooked the sea, wrapping my arms around my knees. I watched the lights for a long time, didn't realize I was crying until they began to blur. For the first time, I thought I understood what it was to be lonely. I had not wanted company as a goddess; I had been content. Even as a mortal, I had never felt this so intensely before, a *need* for someone else—a person I *belonged* to, with. I had had desires as a god, yes, but how could need exist when every desire could be met instantly? I had rarely ever even *wanted*. I ate because the taste of food was pleasant, not because I was hungry. I drank because spring water was cold, not because I was thirsty. Now, my need for Áine, the lack of her, was making something *crack* inside me.

I had long buried my head in my knees when someone touched my shoulder. I shuddered with relief; I knew by the soft graze of her fingers that it was Áine sitting beside me, touching my hair, leaning her cheek against mine. "I'm sorry," I sobbed.

"I love you, Cailleach," she replied, keeping her head pressed against mine. We looked down at the lights of the village together, and I tried to say that I loved her too, tried to tell her the truth, but I could not get the words out past the fullness in my throat, so instead I just pressed myself close to her until we both fell asleep. I woke up a few hours later, curled around her body in the soft grass. I looked up at the stars that shone above us, so many that they almost seemed to move as I watched them. I thought about what Áine had said, how she'd told me she loved me, and I was sure she did—but could that love be true when she did not truly know me? I thought of her nightmares, how she woke up screaming, afraid of demons and evil spirits. Would she love me if she knew about my mottled blue skin, the ice in my veins, my endless, immortal body?

Would she love me, knowing what I'd done? The people I'd killed?

And was it honest and fair to tell her I loved her, when I held on to such a lie?

I did not think so. And so I did not tell her that I loved her, and I did not tell her that I was what she most feared: a great power capable of darkness, wearing the skin of a mortal.

The closer Áine and I grew, the more I forgot my immortal self. Through her I learned about the villagers—not only their names and faces but *about* them, like the fact that Ardgal could not bear to kill any living thing, even though his father was the town's butcher; and that Eithne could tell how old a catch was just by a whiff of it and had not yet been cheated even by the most wily of fisherman.

I still preferred my solitude or the company of just Áine, but with her by my side, I was at least better known throughout the village. A few of the villagers even seemed to like me, like Nora, the oldest woman in the village, and Domhnall, a little boy who was always escaping his mother and running up the hill to talk to me and "help" with the bees.

In this way, several years passed, and I began to settle more and more into the grooves of village life. I had not seen Danu since our last talk in the wood, and I wondered if this was because she had not noticed the passing of time or because she just did not care anymore. Whatever the reason, I was glad.

Áine even occasionally walked through the woods with me in deep winter, though I knew she would rather be sitting by our warm fire, hands busy with a quilt she was making for some expectant mother or creating the herbs and oils she used for her midwifery. While those walks with her by my side were not quiet—Áine was incapable of silence—it was comforting to stroll hand in hand under the trees.

I had just returned from the forest one evening to find the fire out and the house dark. I was surprised: I'd expected Áine to be home by now—the croft she'd gone to had only been a little way out of town. A twinge of worry pulsed through me. It had been a long, hard winter, and I'd seen the prints that the wolves had made, closer to our hut than they usually got. I'd not heard of any in the village, but perhaps on that empty road at night . . .

I twitched around the hut nervously, lighting the fire, sweeping the floor, cutting up the mushrooms I'd found in the wood. They were Áine's favorite, with brown-grey tops that were carved into little mazes and lines. I set them on the fire to cook with a large pat of butter, turning to the door again and again in hopes I'd see her. Soon, the mushrooms hissed and crackled, becoming golden and crisp, and still she had not come.

I had just set the table, pouring glasses of wine for us both, when the door flew open and there, finally, was Áine, outlined in falling snow, face smeared with mud.

"Where've you been?" I drew out a chair for her and pulled her wet shawl from her neck. I dipped a rag in water and cleaned mud from her face—had she fallen? There was dirt smeared all the way up her dress and her eyes were red and face puffy with crying.

"What happened?" I asked gently, and she began to sob again, a thin, sad wail. I put my arms around her and pulled her close until her shoulders stopped shaking. Finally she looked up. "Sheelin, the little girl I went to help? She couldn't breathe in the cold. I gave her all I had; tried to use steam, smoke, honey, but nothing worked. I couldn't do anything for her, Cailleach. It was horrible, to see her suffer, to see her face turn pale and blue. She died in her mother's arms." Áine gasped out the last words, and tears sprang into my own eyes as I thought of the lovely little girl, shy and quiet with a shock of red hair so bright it was like looking at the sunset. I thought of her dead and cold in her mother's arms, and then thought of Siobhan, whose child had died from the winter I'd sent. The one that had killed so many, adults and children alike.

"I'm sorry." My voice trembled. "I'm so sorry." I closed my eyes as a wave of nausea swept over me, and I thought of those I'd killed that winter so long ago. Of how their families must have wept. I suddenly sprang to my feet and ran out of the hut, barely making it outdoors before vomiting in the snow. I was kneeling on the cold ground, gasping, when Áine came outside. She held back my hair, pulling it away from my face until I'd stopped vomiting, and when I turned to her, I knew I could not keep my secrets anymore. I had to tell her what I was, or she would never truly know me. Never truly love me. I did not want her to know only parts of me, such small parts compared to my long, long life before.

She must have seen something in my face, because her forehead—still streaked with mud—creased. She rested a gentle hand on my face, stroking. "What is it, Cailleach?" she whispered.

Cold seeped into my bones but I did not get up, keeping my eyes on hers. My confession poured itself out of me, as if now that I had made the decision, nothing could stop me. "Do you remember the stories that Niamh told you about that long, cold winter? The one her grandmother Siobhan lived through? Not like this." I gestured at the snow that had piled up on the roof of our house, at the white harbor. "This is nothing compared to that winter. I remember the drifts were so high that year they could bury a man. And no matter how the people waited and hoped, spring did not come. The sun could not shine its warmth through the white clouds. The rivers froze, and the sea. Even the people."

Áine nodded slowly and flakes of snow fell from her hair, glittering for a moment before drifting to the ground. "But Cailleach, that was so long ago. In my grandmother's grandmother's time. How—how can you remember it?"

I hesitated. "Did Dagda ever tell you about a goddess of winter? Of cold? A goddess whose skin turned blue as she walked through the cold world she'd created? Once, people knew her name. They called her Cailleach." I looked up at Áine. She looked so lovely, standing there in the blowing storm, hair so dark against the white of her face. "I am she. I am the goddess Cailleach."

Áine shook her head. "No." Her voice was steady, almost flat. "No, that's not true. It cannot be true. I know you. You knew Dagda. You were a child here."

"I was not a child," I said slowly. "I was the woman that he knew on the hill. The one with the little dog who he loved so much, Failinis. I had bees, but I didn't know what to do with them. Dagda helped me. He was my friend, he taught me how to collect the honey and wax . . ." I trailed off when I saw her face, then tried to continue. "I didn't know how to be a mortal. I had never been one—the other gods, they—they were once mortals. But I was not. And now I am. And I understand." I got to my feet and Áine flinched, stepping away from me. I reached toward her. "I would *never* hurt you. I was given this body by the gods as punishment, so that I would learn what it was to be one of you, what harm I had caused. I understand now, why I should not have sent the winter. I understand. And I don't want to lie to you anymore. I can't, because . . . because I love you."

A tremor crossed Áine's face, but her eyes were wide and clear. She believed me. I felt a little calmer. She believed what I was saying. I would be able to explain. I reached for her once more, but she shrank away from me.

Her next words were hard and pained.

"*You* sent the winter?" she asked. "The one that killed—so many?"

I swallowed. "I didn't realize—I didn't . . ." I tried to explain. "I had a grove. A sacred grove. It was the first place I knew the true touch of the cold. It was where Danu gave me dominion over winter, the first place I considered—considered home, safe. And they—" My voice trembled. "They destroyed it. They razed it to the ground and carved the earth and filled it with their gold and their dead. And the scent . . ." I gagged as I remembered it. "All I could smell was *them*. Their hands and bodies, their sweat and blood and greed as they—they *took* without thought. Without care. And before that, the mortals, they killed my friend, Enya. They forced her to marry against her will, to have children she didn't want, and she died—" I cut myself off, my words sounding foolish, thin. So many women married men they did not want, bore children that killed them. I could see it in Áine's eyes. How was Enya any different from them? I hadn't known then—and still, even if I had, it didn't make it *right*, what had happened to her.

But I also knew that what I had done, what I had wrought upon the mortals, *upon Siobhan* . . . that too had not been *right*. I didn't know what else to say, how to explain myself her, so I stumbled on, my words coming faster and faster. "I saw how all they knew was to *take*. They broke my heart and so I lay down on top of their mound and I brought the snow. I let it fall and fall until I could no longer smell them, no longer see what they had done. And spring—I did not let spring come." My voice faltered; I was terrified by the look on Áine's face.

"You are a *god*—" Áine's voice was hard, brittle. "And you killed—you killed thousands—because they *took* from you? From a god who had . . . everything?"

"I—I didn't understand, then. I did not mean to—" I did not know how to explain it, and I reached out once more for Áine's hand, but she took another step away from me.

"You cannot kill with intention and claim no malice, Cailleach. It is not possible." Her voice was low. "You cannot do good, true good, if you're not actually kind, and you cannot murder thousands of us—mortals"—she spat the word out as though I were not one myself, standing before her—"and claim that you acted without thought." Áine's mouth twisted. "You have no right to walk among us. No right to love." She blinked and I watched a snowflake fall from her eyelash and onto the ground. When I looked back up she was running down the hill to the village.

My heart was broken, but I was not afraid that Áine would not return when I went to bed that night. I understood her capacity for love, for forgiveness. She just needed some time. She would come back.

I should have known better.

When the door opened in the middle of the night, I was relieved.

I believed Áine had returned as she had before. I thought we could talk again. I had worried over my words; I could explain better this time, I knew it.

When I stepped out into the kitchen, I saw that my home was filled with the people of the village.

Nora. Ruaidhrí. Bride. Saoirse.

And Áine.

She stood with them with her mouth set in hatred, holding a burning torch. I did not have time to move, to scream, or even beg. Ruaidhrí, my first lover, whose hands had been so clumsy, was not clumsy when he smashed his fist into my face. I fell to the ground, dazed and bleeding. Then Bride, who had watched the sun rise with me that night we spent together, bound my feet—and Sean, who always saved fresh fish for me, tied my hands roughly behind my back—and Saoirse—Saoirse, whose child I had saved from the river, shoved a gag in my mouth. I saw the faces of people I had danced with and broken bread with and traded with—all of them, my friends and my village—I watched them turn their backs on me at the drop of a coin.

They carried me through the village and into the wood, to the clearing where the sacred oak stood. I still did not understand what they had planned until I saw the wood piled high over the stone altar that Dagda had used for animal sacrifice. I let out a sob of panic, searching their familiar faces to find Áine's in the crowd. We locked eyes, mine wide with fear, and though her face paled her unforgiving gaze did not falter as she approached the pyre.

"This woman that we have cared for and welcomed into our homes is not who we thought she was." She stared at me without remorse, even as I began to weep. "She is a demon. A wraith in a mortal's body. She has confessed to me the great crimes she has committed against us. Against all mortals. And she must be punished for those crimes."

And then she set the torch against the wooden pyre.

I thought I'd known pain before—when I'd stubbed a toe, bruised my ankle. But this—flames crawling over me, blackening my skin—was different. New. Terrible.

I screamed as I burned.

And burned.

For what felt like centuries.

And the darkness that came then wasn't sweet or cold or gentle.

It was red and hot and endless.

Endless.

the third death

When I came back into my immortal body, the pain remained. I screamed as Danu enfolded me in her arms, as the other gods clustered around me. Dagda's face was wracked with agony, and Danu was weeping hot tears onto my blue flesh. "I must ask you," she said, even as she sobbed, "what did you—"

But I would not answer her foolish question. She knew what I had learned. She had seen how I had loved Áine, and she had watched as I had been betrayed.

"Send me back! Send me back! Send me back!" I screamed in rage over and over until finally Danu pointed a finger at me and there was light, then noise, then, silence.

SUMMER

Listen.

Listen, and I will tell you a story.

The story of a girl who stood against the gods.

And from them gained her heart's desire.

As Fia grew, she no longer dreamt of feasts but of the golden goddess who said that the gods never hungered.

And though it was forbidden, Fia kept following the woodland path to Síd in Broga, hoping that she might speak with her goddess again. When several years had passed and still she had not appeared, Fia began to offer the goddess the best of what she had: the most lush berry, the golden-crisp skin of a fowl, or the softest cut of her fish—she tipped all of these into the fire with a prayer. But no matter how much she gave up or how she prayed, the goddess remained silent.

And so Fia began to ask others what they knew of the gods: What did they look like, how many were there, where had they come from? Few in her small village knew or cared, and though her brother told her every story of the gods that he knew, they were not enough to sate her.

Desperate to quell his sister's strange new hunger, her brother too began to search for stories. One day, a stranger walked into town with the most beautiful tale the boy had ever heard—that of Danu, the mother goddess—and the boy rushed home that night, ready to share it with his sister.

"She was mortal," he said with a laugh, waiting to see wonder light on his sister's face. "Once, before she was a god." The boy went on, telling her how Danu was the first of the gods, how she created the land and the seas, and about the years she had spent wandering the earth, lonely and sad, until she'd finally built her great palace. "She named it Tara. But still she looked upon her home and was sad to see it empty, so she called forth the best mortals she could find, the kindest, the wisest, the bravest, and gave them godhood."

The boy finished his story, his voice a melody, his eyes bright and eager, but Fia did not laugh or clap in delight, and the boy saw that her hunger had only grown. She lifted her chin, held her brother's gaze. "That is what I need. Godhood. Godhood, and I will never be hungry again."

the fourth life

The torch was bright as I walked into the village, death in my hands.

It was still dark, but I could see from where the moon sat in the sky that dawn was approaching. Barefoot on the rough road, I did not wince at the pain, did not pause, did not look around the village to see what changes had happened since I'd been burned. It could have been moments. It could have been generations. I did not care. They—or their ancestors—had burned me. And so they would burn too.

I swept the torch along roofs and walls, across wooden boards and vines. I could smell flowers somewhere, and I knew that Danu had sent me back in spring. That was good; there would be more to catch flame and burn.

Dawn had just begun to stretch bloody fingers across the sky when they began to scream.

I stood on the edge of the village and watched as the flames burned higher. And when I smelled cooking flesh, I smiled. I felt as though the mortal skin I had been wearing had been peeled off. I was no longer split between god and mortal. I was only god.

Full of power.

Rage.

I watched a man run out of his house, coughing on smoke, and cocked my head. Some part of me knew I had seen him before. But I could not recall his name. He looked to me like a spider—something to be crushed.

I watched as flames crept up the side of the tavern where I had first met Áine.

Áine, who had lain in my bed with me and run her fingers through my hair.

Áine, who had set her own torch against what had been my living pyre.

It had been foolish to think of myself as the same as her. As mortal. I was not. They had taught me that, shown me that my distaste of them had always been justified. They were worse than the basest of animals. Animals took to survive; *they* took because they could never be content, because they always wanted more.

I would have stayed and watched the destruction grow, would have let the fire consume the entire village and every mortal in it with satisfaction, if I hadn't seen her.

She ran toward me, hair long and black, eyes wide and blue, and I opened my arms without thought, because I loved her. I *loved* her still—only it wasn't Áine who fell into my arms. It was a child. A young girl who looked so much like Áine that I knew she must be her daughter.

The girl clung to me, coughing, choking from the smoke, and I could see where the fire had singed her hair, where soot had smudged her cheeks, her eyes a searing, cold blue in her face. In her piercing gaze I saw Nora; then Bride, her cheeks flushed pink in the morning; then Domhnall, the little lad with the cheeky smile. But it was not the thought of them that made me look to the skies and beg:

"Danu! Rain, Danu. Send rain."

It was Áine, even still.

It was how she held my hair back as I vomited into the snow, the way her eyes lit up when she ground herbs together for someone ill, the softness of her arms as we sat on the old stone bench looking out at the sea, and now—now—it was her daughter in my arms that made me beg for the end of the destruction I'd wrought.

The clear sky filled rapidly with dark clouds that unleashed rain so heavy it knocked me backward, hitting my face with so much force that I winced and pulled the child closer to me, trying to protect her from it.

I don't know why Danu listened to me then, when so many other times she had not. I didn't stay to see if the rain put out the fires entirely. I had asked for it, and that seemed enough. They had still burned me, after all. I walked back up the hill to where I knew my hut would be waiting, child in tow. I was unsure what else to do with her.

The hut looked the same as it had in my third life, still covered with roses, though they were only buds now. I looked to the forest and saw that it had receded a bit more, but not a great deal. I could not have been gone long, perhaps no more than six or seven years. The girl on my hip began to squirm, and I set her down. She stared up at me solemnly. She was young, perhaps no older than three or four, and now that we'd left the burning village, she seemed remarkably unconcerned. She had her thumb in her mouth, but as I stared at her, she pulled it out, pointing at herself. "Mór," she said, then gestured at me.

"Cailleach," I said, wondering with a jolt if Áine was still alive.

Was she frantic even now, looking for her daughter? She wouldn't remember me, of course; she would look at me and see only a stranger. The thought was both horrifying and comforting.

She would not remember me, the goddess she had burned.

She would not remember *me*, the mortal woman she had loved.

I didn't realize I was crying until the smoking village in front of me began to blur and haze. I wiped at my face then looked down at the child. I didn't want her to begin coughing again, so I opened the door to my hut and brought her inside. In all the confusion, I would say that I'd rescued the child then gone to the hut to keep her safe until the fire ended.

The hut was the same as when I'd left, my black pot swinging over the fire, jars of honey lining the shelves. I pulled one of them down and gave the girl some honeycomb. She took it from me carefully, giving me a long, almost suspicious look before biting into it. When the sweetness of it hit her tongue, she smiled, and her smile was so like Áine's—*she* was so like Áine—that it was painful to look at her. I turned away sharply and moved to stir the fire—the hut was cold in the early mornings—but the closer I got to the flames, the more I could smell the smoke like charred flesh. It was as if *I* was burning again, and I began to panic and gag. I dashed outside, lifting my head to the rain and letting it soak me until the smell finally left my nose.

The rain did not last long—by the time the sun was overhead in the sky, it had gone. I knew I should take the child back down to the village, find out if Áine was still alive, but I was not able to make myself face it. Mór had fallen asleep in my bed and slept until late afternoon, when she woke and insisted I show her the bees. The hives were still there, but when I leaned my head against them and listened to the hum, the peace I'd expected to fill my chest didn't come. Áine and I had spent our days at these hives. I could not think of them without thinking of her and her long, clever fingers gently setting an old bee back into the hive. They had loved her. *I* had loved her. And she'd had me killed.

I plucked the child from the ground, deciding that I would not be able to rest until I found out if Áine was still alive. For better or worse, I had to know what had happened to her.

Once I got to the village, I was grateful to find that no one had died in the fire. Some had been badly burned, and many of the houses would need to be rebuilt, but I had called the rain early enough.

As usual, they knew of me when I walked into town—Fianna's sister, they thought in this life. They nodded at me but were otherwise too busy helping the wounded to pay me much attention. They told me I was lucky that I lived on the hill, that I'd not lost my home as so many of them had.

Áine was dead.

When I asked after Mór's mother, they said she had died birthing Mór, that her father had been a local farmer who had joined the king's army and hadn't been seen in years.

I was devastated; I was relieved. I didn't know what to think, what to feel, as I understood I would never see her again. At least I would not have to endure her blank stare.

In this life, I saw many I'd known in my last. When I saw Domhnall, I knew I had guessed correctly that it had barely been a decade; he was only ten or so now, still a child. When he saw me, he grinned, and my breath caught. I thought Danu's magic had failed, that he remembered me—until I realized that he was smiling at *Mór*, who waved a fat hand back at him.

I would have left Áine's child in the village, but for some reason she clung to my leg, screaming when I tried to untangle her and hand her to the family who had been raising her since Áine had died. The woman shrugged. "The girl's always been an odd lass. Usually bright and happy, but when a temper gets on her she's as fierce as an angry cat." The woman was called away to help tend to a child with burns, and I stood alone with the girl once again. I decided to leave her there, directed her to stay, but I had not gone more than a few steps when I heard a soft tread behind me. I turned to see the girl following me up the hill, beaming.

"Go home." I waved a hand at her, back to the village, but the girl shook her head, frowning.

"Honey." She pointed to my hut on top of the hill. I sighed. The sun was close to setting over the sea and the light around us was pink and soft. All I wanted was to go back to my hut and fall asleep, but I did not feel equal to dealing with the disappointment of a child, so I let her follow me.

It seemed impossible—it *was* impossible—that only yesterday I had woken in the heart of winter, Áine in my bed, before she'd been called away to try to heal Sheelin. We had lain together longer than we normally would have because of how cold it was. The light from the fire had made her skin glow, making it seem molten. I had kissed her bare shoulder when I rose that morning, promising I would fix her something warm when she got home from tending to Sheelin.

Now I was standing in a warm spring breeze. Áine was dead.

And her daughter was playing in the grass in front of me.

When Danu appeared on the top of the hill, her form was still rosy with light from the setting sun. I was not surprised to see her. She didn't say anything for a long moment, just watched Mór play.

"You broke the rules," I said, and even though I could only see her profile, I could tell she was surprised that I'd spoken first. "You're not supposed to help me in this form. But you sent the rain."

Danu snorted. "You were not supposed to kill *more* of them."

"That wasn't one of the commands you set forth," I said. "Mortals kill one another all the time. You wanted me to feel *all* that comes with mortality. As far as I've seen, that often includes the spilling of blood."

"I didn't think they'd burn you." Danu's voice was soft. "I wanted to——" But she cut herself off and I saw a tear slide down her cheek. I didn't know what she was going to say. She'd wanted to help me? She'd wanted to stop the pain, the flames, the smell? In the end, what she had wanted did not matter. She had not *done* anything. As ever, she had stood by and left me subject to mortal whims.

"You should be pleased." My voice was cool. "I was punished twice for the same crime."

Danu shuddered and another tear fell down her cheek. The child must have heard her gentle sob because she came running over. Mór hesitated for a moment, then tried to reach out and grab Danu's hand. She didn't even come up to Danu's knee, but she patted her leg, making small hushing sounds. "I'm Mór," she said. "Don't cry, lady. Don't cry."

Danu's tears slowed as she bent to pick the child up. "I am Danu, child." She swept a hand over her face. The tears were instantly gone, her face calm, serene.

"You want some honey?" Mór asked. "It's good here."

"This is a good place for honey," Danu said, her face brightening with a smile.

I frowned. I did not want the girl to think that she could come here whenever she wanted. I had simply not been able to fight with her today; tomorrow she would be going right back to the village.

Danu ignored my frown and waved a hand and suddenly the garden was full of globes of spring-green light floating on the breeze like dandelion fluff. Mór squealed and ran at the globes trying to catch them, and Danu laughed, chasing after the child. I sat on the grass, letting out a long sigh, watching the girl and my mother dance after the lights as though they were falling stars.

I lay on my pallet and did not get up. I did not eat or drink.

I had taken Áine's child back to the village the next morning, then trudged up the hill alone. I knew I had chores to do—water to haul, wood to gather and chop, bees to tend—but I could not find the energy to move from my bed. I just lay there, staring at the ceiling.

I could not get Áine out of my mind.

I thought of what I could have done differently. I could have never told her about my godhood or shared the truth more gently. If she had not had those dreams, if her grandmother had not told her stories about that long winter, if, if, if . . .

I realized eventually, though, that the only thing that would have saved me was if I had not been myself. If I had only ever been a mortal woman called Cailleach.

So I lay on that pallet for days, vacillating between despair and fury.

I wanted Áine to come back.

I was glad she was dead.

I wanted to listen to her heartbeat.

I wanted to burn her as she had burned me.

I would have simply wasted away if Áine's child had not come back up the hill. I had not bothered to shut the door against the light or the dark, so she simply marched into the room. I didn't even realize she was there until there was a tug on my arm. I thought for one breathless moment that it was Áine, my Áine, ready to forgive. Ready to be forgiven. But it was Mór.

Her face was serious as she drew close to me. "I would like some honey." She said the words carefully, as though she were repeating something she'd heard.

I don't know why I got up. Why I scooped some honey from a jar and gave her a spoonful. Perhaps it was that she looked so like the woman I had loved, or that I could remember the times when I'd looked down into my stewpot and known that what was there would not fill my belly—or simply the knowledge that it was wrong to let a child go hungry if I could prevent it.

I gave her honey that day.

And the next.

And the next.

I do not know why she kept coming, but she did, and after a few days I grew tired of seeing her sitting in grime, so I wiped down the dust-covered chairs. I repaired the chink in the table so that she would not scrape her hand on it, and then I went out to the bees to gather more honey for her, and slowly, slowly, I fell into a routine.

One day I looked around the hut and realized there was nothing left to do—nothing left at all. I could no longer avoid the village if I wanted to make it through winter, so I slung a bag of candles and honey onto my back and walked down the hill.

The air was growing cooler as the sun lowered in the sky, and I took a deep breath of it before I went inside the tavern, nervous at facing the villagers again. I needn't have worried; no one paid attention to me at all. They were focused on one woman, called Aoife, who was leaning against the bar. "We can't be expected to feed her this winter too," the woman was saying. "I took her in because Áine was my friend. But I don't know that I'll have enough to feed my *own* children after the fire. Someone else'll have to do it." She looked around the room, but no one caught her eye. Everyone was tired and thin. The fire had spread to several fields, and some families were already relying on the generosity of neighbors to get through the winter. Maybe I should have felt guilt, but I didn't. They had still killed me, after all. They deserved some repercussions.

"The druids might take her," someone in the crowd said slowly.

"I'd hate to think of sending Áine's child away." The speaker was Bride this time. She looked sad, but neither did she offer to take her in.

"The druid will be coming through during winter solstice," Aoife said. "I can keep her until then . . ." Her voice trailed off.

"I will take her."

All the eyes in the room swiveled to me. I had not even realized I was the one who had spoken, and I regretted it instantly, almost took back my pledge. But then I pictured Mór from earlier in the day. She'd gotten honey in her eyebrows, and when I'd pointed this out she had giggled and smeared it all over her face. She had looked so gleeful, so happy, that I'd laughed too. A small noise, surprised and rough, but still, a laugh. And in that moment, I had not felt despair, only hope.

Hope that I could rise from my pallet every day.

Hope that the flames in my dreams would someday go out.

And some part of me believed that if our situations had been reversed, Áine would have taken in my child. She would have fed her and cared for her because she had loved me. Even as she had hated me.

I hated her.

And I loved her.

So I would do the same.

In those early days after the fire, Mór and I stayed at the hut, and I tried desperately to remember all I'd learned about taking care of mortal children from Áine and from those long-ago days with Sorcha. Mór seemed to be constantly in danger, and I was always fearful. I'd never before realized how close I was to the edge of the hill. It wasn't a cliff—a child would most likely survive a fall from it—but there was no reason to tempt fate, so I built a stone wall to keep her safe. That worked until she learned to climb the wall and sit atop it, swinging her legs back and forth and chortling to herself when I found her.

Children were a horrible mix of contradictions: if they were too cold they could fall ill, if they ate food too large they could choke. But they could also drop from a great height and then get up, laughing.

I was so busy learning these things that I did not even mark the first time Mór called me *Mama*. All I knew was that she called me, and I responded—that was all. She was mine and I was hers.

Danu was delighted with the girl but was a terrible example for her. She came often, but despite her obsession with mortals, she had no understanding of their needs. She would take Mór off to play on the sand and would forget that she needed to eat, to drink, to get out of the hot sun. Once, she even brought one of her great cats from Tara to play with the child. I'd not known about it, had been hanging laundry on the line when I'd turned and seen it stalking Mór, who'd been singing to herself while sitting in the meadow. I'd run, shouting, and frightened the beast, who retreated to Danu, whining and whimpering. Danu had not understood why I was angry, saying that the cat would never *actually* eat the child, but I'd seen the stillness in its body. The hunger in its eyes. I knew what it was to hunt for food and to hunt for pleasure; in my immortal body I had done both often.

I'd tried to forbid Danu from the hill after that, but she had merely laughed and come back the next day. And what could I do? Danu was a goddess. I was merely a mortal woman trying to keep myself and my girl—my daughter—alive.

Surprisingly, it was Domhnall, the little boy I'd known in my previous life, who helped me the most. He adored Mór, and when he wasn't helping his father on their small fishing boat, he was usually on the hill with us, playing with her and keeping her safe from Danu's disregard.

I did not only have to learn to keep my daughter from danger, I also had to learn that children, while young, were often as contrary as grown mortals. One day I handed Mór bread smeared with cheese and drizzled with honey, a treat she usually loved, but when I gave it to her, she refused to take a bite out of it.

"Eat it, Mór," I said. "It's your favorite."

"No." She turned her head away when I tried to wave it enticingly under her chin. "I hate cheese." She crossed her arms and glared at me.

"You don't," I said. "We eat it every day. And besides, it's all we have."

"I hate it!" Mór screamed suddenly, tearing the bread from my hand and throwing it at the wall. It stuck for a moment before sliding down in a white smear. I was startled more than angry, and I think Mór was too, because she looked back at me with wide eyes. We stared at each other for a long moment, and then I began to laugh. I knew I shouldn't, knew I should reprove her for throwing the bread and for screaming. But it was so foolish for a child to decide they now hated something they had eaten ravenously only the day before that it was absurdly funny. Mór began to laugh too, throwing her arms around me. "I love you, Mama." She snuggled her face into my neck.

"I love you, too." I squeezed Mór tight. "I love you, darling girl."

Mór was a charming child. She rarely screamed or threw fits like she had that day in the hut, and that spring and summer were especially wonderful. I taught her how to work with the bees, and it was a pleasure to see her round face so carefully serious as she collected a fallen bee off the ground and gently returned it to the hive. She helped me pick weeds from the garden and filled the hut with the fistfuls of flowers she gathered wherever she went.

Our first winter together was very mild, with many days of sunlight and warm breezes. It was well after the winter solstice when I woke and finally smelled snow in the air. I leapt up, running to the door and throwing it open to see a wide expanse of white. It was still snowing lightly, the flakes twirling through the air, and I clapped my hands together in glee: Mór would love it. I rushed back to our little room and tried to wake her up, gently shaking her out of the little ball she had curled into on the bed. She grumbled, twisting deeper into the blankets. "Go away, Mama," she said, when I poked her again. "I'm sleeping."

"You have to get up, Mór." I pulled her into my lap. She burrowed her face into my stomach, and normally I would have laughed and let her stay there, but I was too excited to wait so I lightly tickled her feet until she finally uncurled her body, stretching and yawning enormously. I pulled her to her feet and then to the door, where a swirl of snow danced into the house. Mór blinked for a moment, a snowflake catching on an eyelash, then shivered and slammed the door shut. She raced back to the bed and threw herself under the covers again.

"No." I pulled out the little fur-lined boots I'd made specifically for her. "We're not going back to bed, we're going on a walk."

I finally managed to wrap her warmly and have her follow me out into the woods. We walked quietly, hand in hand, and my heart swelled with happiness. My daughter, my lovely girl, was walking with me under the dark boughs, delighting in the blue and grey shadows, thrilling to the touch of snow on her face, the scent of it in the air.

Only a few moments had passed before she stopped and I turned, expecting her to be pointing at something beautiful as she always did—perhaps the tiny prints that a bird had left in the snow, the shining red berries on the nearby bush, or just the *silence*. Instead, she was scowling. "I want to go *home*, Mama."

"Don't be silly." I laughed. "We've only just started walking. Look, you can see the hill from here."

"I'm cold," she said, and I reached out to touch her face, but it was warm, and her cheeks and lips were still rosy.

"You're not cold," I said impatiently. "It's simply cold outside. There's a difference. Quiet—listen."

I cocked my head and so did she, but after a moment she frowned. "I don't hear anything," she muttered, kicking at the white powder beneath her feet.

"Exactly," I said. "That's the best thing about the winter. The quiet. The peace."

"I don't like it," Mór grumbled. "It's scary."

"It's not! It's beautiful."

"It's sad," Mór said. "The trees are cold, and the flowers are dead."

"I quite agree with Mór," Danu said, suddenly appearing from the trees.

"Danu!" Mór flung herself into her arms. "I'm cold." She shivered dramatically, as though she weren't wrapped in furs.

"I'm so sorry, my love." Danu gave Mór a kiss. "Here—perhaps this will help. Close your eyes." Mór did obediently, and between one blink and the next, the forest around us was transformed into spring. The snow had vanished, replaced by soft grass and a little running stream. The branches were covered in pale green leaves, and a wild apple tree had burst into pink bloom, the petals blowing into Mór's face. She squealed in delight and sprang from Danu's arms, chasing them across the little glade.

"I was showing her the winter." I scowled at Danu. "She liked it." Danu raised an eyebrow and I blushed. "She was *going* to like it. I was going to show her the frozen lake and how the ice crinkles up on the edge. I was going to let her catch the flakes on her tongue . . ." I trailed off, watching Mór chase after the petals. As I watched her, I was deeply hurt. I almost felt . . . betrayed. I felt as if Mór had picked Danu over me. Was this how Danu had felt when I'd loved the winter more than spring? The thought made my cheeks heat with a sudden mixture of guilt and tenderness toward

Danu, but she didn't notice because she was still bent toward my daughter.

"Make it *all* like this." Mór tugged on Danu's hand. "Take all the snow away." Danu could have, of course. With a sweep of her hand, she could have ensured it was always spring and summer for Mór, could make it so the cold never came. But after so long as a mortal I could now see how wrong that would be. The seasons *had* to roll over: spring to summer, summer to autumn, autumn to winter. Winter *must* come; it gave the plants and land a time to rest, allowed animals to sleep warm in their dens, beckoned mortals to sit around their fires and reach for one another, telling stories of the past and the days to come.

I looked at Danu and saw that she was considering it, if only to see Mór smile. "I thought we were meant to change the seasons for the good of mortality. Wasn't that why I was punished in the first place?" My voice was cold. "Besides, how will you explain this to Mór when she's older? How will you explain how you created spring with a wave of your hand?"

Danu sighed. "She won't remember this. She's barely more than a baby . . ." But her voice was halfhearted, as though she could see that the idea was a bad one. She grimaced, then disappeared as suddenly as she'd come, taking the spring with her, leaving me to deal with my distraught daughter, who had begun to howl.

"Bring it back, Mama!" Mór tugged at my hand, tears streaming down her face, stamping her feet in the snow that had appeared once more, but I just shook my head.

"I can't, darling. Only Danu—" I looked down at her wide blue eyes. How could I describe the power of a god to a child? I sighed and picked her up, taking her out of the clearing and walking with her in my arms until she calmed down and began to look around again. "Look." I set her down again in the snow. "See our prints there? We are the only ones to have tread here. And listen." I tilted my head up to the firs above us, but I did not know how to explain it to Mór. How the absence of sound made a sound all its own, crystalline and soft. I looked down at her and wished for the first time in a long time that I had my immortal body. Then I could have *shown* her. We could have held hands and skated together across ice-shining seas or swam down a mountain during an avalanche. I could have carried her through the cold, quiet places of the world until she understood what I *was*, what I had *been*. What I yearned for. But I did not have my immortal body anymore—and if I had, I realized, I would never have had her.

So all I did was look up at the dark-green firs above, hold my daughter's hand, ask her to close her eyes, and listen.

the fourth life

Three winters passed just like that; Mór never fell in love with the cold as I had, but I never stopped trying. One early spring day when Mór was about six, I was walking back to the hut with Mór and Domhnall, when I heard them talking behind me, their voices carrying on the wind.

"She was my friend. I don't know why they burned her."

I slowed down, listening intently.

"I don't remember what she looked like or what her name was, but she lived on the hill before you and Cailleach. She was the one who started keeping the bees there. And she taught me many things. That I did not have to fear them. That I should never try to make *them* afraid or angry, because once they sting you, they die."

"Was she very frightening?"

"No." Domhnall considered her question. "She was . . . quiet and kind. She liked the cold and the sound of the wolves howling at night."

"Like Mama," Mór said. "Mama loves the cold." They were silent for a moment. "Why did they burn her?" Mór sounded on the verge of tears, and I knew the story was probably too much for

Mór's tender heart, but I did not interrupt. I needed to know what Domhnall remembered. I had never asked in the village, never heard about the woman they burned, and I'd never known how to bring it up without arousing confusion or suspicion.

Domhnall lowered his voice, and I had to strain to hear him say, "I saw your mother—your first mother, Áine—come down from the hill that night. I wasn't supposed to be out, but I was playing in the snow with Eanna, and we saw her go past. She looked sick. Her eyes were red, and her skin was pale. She went into Bride's house, then into mine. I heard her talking to Mama. She said that the woman on the hill was not really a woman, but a spirit. And she had done some great evil and must not be allowed to continue living among us."

"But you said she was kind," Mór whispered, sounding shocked.

"She was," Domhnall said. "Though she didn't want people to see it. I saw her cry once over the bees, when she thought I wasn't looking. She'd found a dead queen, and she'd known the whole hive would die."

"Why do we burn spirits?"

"Your mother—Áine—said it was the only way to be sure that she couldn't hurt anyone else. It was the only way to free the spirit and send it back to where it had come. The others in the village agreed."

And so quickly, I thought. After years of knowing me. I wondered, and not for the first time, if I'd been nicer, smiled more—held their children close as Áine had—would they have been so easily swayed? Would they have found pity in their hearts, would they have come without their torches, only to plead or shun?

"I don't like her," Mór decided. "Áine wasn't my mother. Mama is. And Mama would never hurt anyone." She ran up to me, slipping her hand through mine, but I couldn't look down at her, couldn't say anything to comfort her, to protect the memory of Áine.

All I could think of was how hot the torch had been, burning in my hand.

As the years passed, my lives before became distant and foggy. With all it took to care for a child, keep her warm and healthy and fed, I simply didn't have time to sit around and think about *this* life, let alone those others, or my immortal one. Sometimes, I almost wondered if I had dreamt it—my divinity. It felt like I'd always been a mortal woman on this hill, living with her daughter, keeping bees together.

I didn't know how or when my baby had grown into an eleven-year-old.

Mór had been quiet lately, and sad, missing Domhnall. He was no longer a boy, had grown tall and strong over the past year and now worked with his father on the boat. He still came up the hill when he could, but he seemed less interested in the games that Mór wanted to play, and while he was always kind to her, she could tell that his heart was not in them anymore. Danu still came sometimes, but her arrival was always sudden and unexpected, and she would be gone again as fast as a summer storm; Mór had begun to realize that she could not be relied on. She had also started asking questions about Danu. How did she appear one moment and disappear the next? Why could she float and fly and create magical globes with her hands when no other mortal could? Danu said not to think about it, that she had told Mór to keep such things a secret and that Mór had promised, but I wished . . . I wished Mór did not have to be tangled up with immortals at all.

We were sitting in the garden one late summer evening, eating bread and honey, when Mór said, "Mama, I want a dog."

"No—" The breath caught in my throat. I cleared it and tried to sound less stern. "You play with the village dogs most days, isn't that enough? Besides, a dog would scare the chickens." I remembered the day I'd found Failinis asleep in the sun, three chickens clucking contentedly on his back. My heart was tight, as though it were being pressed under some great weight. It did not seem possible that I still missed my little dog after so many years. I wished sometimes that I could forget him, that I could make his memory vague and hazy as a dream.

"I would teach him," Mór said seriously. "He would be friends with the chickens. With the bees. *Please*, Mama." She looked up at me, her blue eyes wide, but I shook my head and told her it was time to sleep. She scowled but went inside anyway, and I slumped against the side of the hut. I hated saying no to Mór, but I wanted to protect her. What would she do when her dog eventually died? Dogs had such short lifespans, even for mortal beings. I would not let Mór know such sorrow if I could prevent it.

"I can bring the child a dog." Danu stepped out of the air. She was in her immortal form, and I raised an eyebrow at her. "We were dancing." Danu waved her hand. "Mor wanted us to all wear our immortal forms." I blinked, confused, and Danu laughed. "Morrígan." She enunciated the words slowly as though I were feebleminded. "The goddess."

"I know who she is, Danu." My voice was sharp. But I knew I

had not fooled her. I had forgotten Morrígan, had thought only of my own little girl. Morrígan, Lug, Dagda, Manannán . . . even their names were strange and hollow, half-forgotten.

Danu waved her hands. "I will bring the child a dog," she said again. "I saw one in the forest that I think she'll like. Black, with yellow eyes."

"You cannot bring Mór a wolf." My voice was firm. "She is a mortal—it would eat her."

"You loved wolves as a child." Danu laughed. "Whenever you were missing, I could usually find you playing in the snow with them."

"I was not a human child. They could not have hurt me. How can you not remember, Danu? When you were mortal, do you think your mother ever brought you a wolf?"

Danu's face darkened, but she said lightly, "Perhaps she did. I lived so, so long ago."

"If she was a *good* mother, she would not have." My voice was pointed.

Danu sighed. "You were not mortal, Cailleach. You were impossible to mother."

"Don't bring her a wolf," I said, brushing past her to go inside the hut.

Danu did not bring a wolf, but she did bring a giant white dog that was larger than Mór herself. Mór was thrilled, but I refused to let the dog stay. It had pale green eyes that reminded me too much of Danu; I did not like the way they followed me. After that, Danu brought a series of dogs, including a black one with long wiry hair, a sleek grey one with huge, sad eyes, and a white-and-black one that looked so like Failinis I took one look at it and began to weep. I shook my head and ran to the stream where I took deep breaths and splashed the icy water on my face. Mór found me there and threw her arms around me. "I'm sorry, Mama." She kissed my cheek.

I sniffed and wiped my eyes. "Did I ever tell you about my little dog?" I asked, knowing that I hadn't. I never talked about Failinis. "He looked exactly like the dog that Danu just brought." I wondered if she hadn't remembered—or if she had. "I called him Failinis. He was one of my first friends." Mór leaned her head against my shoulder as I talked about my little dog. She asked me questions as I spoke—what color had his paws been, and did he bark a lot, and had he ever stolen my dinner?—and for the first time since he'd died, I was able to think of those things gently, tenderly, and even laugh when I told her about Failinis's penchant for stealing fish.

That night as I lay in bed I allowed myself to remember him in even more detail, to remember the life we'd shared together and how good it had been, how happy we had been together. When I fell asleep that night I dreamed of my little dog again, and I woke up with a smile on my lips.

A few weeks after I told Mór about Failinis, I was standing on the docks talking to Domhnall's mother, Cara, when I saw a flick of a tail under a table that was holding fish. I watched as one of the large red fish began to slowly slide off the end. The puppy had almost managed to pull it off entirely when a fisherman saw him. He shouted and kicked at the dog, who barely dodged his boot and ran away, tail between his legs, to cower against a wooden crate. He was small and brown, with sleek fur that reminded me of a seal. I reached him just a moment before the fisherman did, a red-faced man called Fachtna who I'd never liked. I held the shaking dog against my chest, and he nuzzled into my neck as I glared at Fachtna.

"Once a dog begins to steal fish, he won't stop." Fachtna held out his large hand. "Better to let me drown him now."

"You'll not drown him," I said, thinking that I'd sooner drown Fachtna. I looked down at the dog and remembered Failinis trying to steal a fish the first time I'd brought him to the market, and though I felt a pinch of pain, mostly it was *good* to remember him. I looked down at the dog in my arms. He needed a home. "I'm taking him to Mór."

Fachtna's face changed. The villagers liked me well enough, but they adored my daughter. "Well," Fachtna grunted. "If he's for Mór, then."

I walked back up the hill still holding the puppy to my chest, and when Mór came out of the house and saw him, her eyes grew wide. Another child might have squealed or cried, but Mór just tip-toed toward us and began stroking the puppy's back. He gave a little grumble in his sleep as I slipped him carefully into Mór's arms.

"Thank you, Mama," she whispered.

Mór called the puppy Aengus, and he was as devoted to her as Failinis had been to me. They grew together, and thankfully, he remained hale and hearty, still running after Mór even into his sixth year and Mór's seventeenth.

I'd never lived so long in a mortal body, which meant I'd never had to contend with growing older as I did now. I hated it. I hated the way my body began to groan and sigh when I rose in the mornings, how the shadows around my eyes and mouth became lines that never left. The strangest thing, though, was when the monthly bleeding stopped. I had not even noticed it at first, but then I began to get hot, and even in the coldest part of winter I could not sleep with a blanket, waking with sweat-soaked clothes and a red face. I didn't understand what was happening until Cara, Domhnall's mother, told me.

We'd been friends in my previous life too, back when I'd lived with Áine. She didn't remember me, of course, but it had been easy to fall back into what we'd had, to chat about our growing children and work together. She had asked if Domhnall could work the bees with me, perhaps build even more hives, and I'd readily agreed. I knew it was a wise choice for the boy. The light in his eyes had grown dimmer with each day he returned from a day catching and gutting fish, and so, even though his father had wanted him to take over the boat, Cara had insisted that Domhnall make his own path in life.

Cara and I were walking down the hill to the village when I began to grow hot again. It didn't make sense because it was a bitterly cold day, too cold even for snow. My fingertips were numb even as my face flushed and my chest tightened with heat. I gave a little gasp and fanned at my face. I wanted to jump into the icy sea, into the little stream that ran beside the road; I would have, if I'd not been walking with Cara.

"Cailleach?" She turned toward me. "Are you alright?"

I shook my head. "I'm terribly hot. I don't know why . . ."

"Ah, the change." Her lips twitched, but I didn't know what she meant. I pulled my scarf off my head and gasped in relief as the wind blew against my bare skin.

"What change?"

Cara frowned. "When the bleeding stops. It means you can't have children anymore. Didn't your mother tell you?"

I shook my head, cheeks heating with embarrassment. It wasn't often anymore that I stumbled into bits of mortality I didn't know about. "She didn't grow old." Danu looked younger than I did now.

Cara sighed. "I'm sorry. Well. I'm surprised you haven't heard from another, but I suppose you've been so busy with Mór that you've not had much time to gossip over the years. It happens to all women. It means we can no longer have children. The heat comes and goes, but eventually it stops, and you'll no longer bleed."

But I will bleed again, eventually, I thought. *If not in this life, then in the next.* I was weary at the thought. I had *another* life ahead of me, another and another, who knew how many? *My Mór only had one,* and my heart grew sore at the thought. One, and it didn't seem fair, *wasn't* fair, but what could I do to change that except give her all that I could in this one?

Since I'd come to raise Mór, my days had moved swiftly, but I'd still never learned the mortal trick of looking toward the future. Even as Mór grew, I barely thought more than a season ahead, and only because I had to consider the bees and how to best care for them, how to ensure that Mór and I had the food and wood we'd need to survive no matter the cold. I'd never considered what it meant for Mór to be growing older.

But that spring I caught Mór kissing Domhnall behind the bee-hives.

I stumbled back when I saw them, shocked, and they broke apart, though Domhnall kept ahold of Mór's hand. A blush colored her cheeks, and she opened her lips as if to say something to me, but I had already turned away from them and marched to the wood. My head swum as I entered the cool darkness, as the sounds damp-ened around me. Mór was not a child anymore, I knew that, but I'd never really considered that she might want a lover. I had never thought about Mór leaving me, about whether she'd want to marry and have children of her own. It was a quick stab of betrayal, the way she leaned toward Domhnall, like a flower leaning toward the sun. And when I'd surprised them, she'd reached for *him*, not for me, and my heart broke a little. Though I loved Domhnall, at that moment I would have happily watched him sail away forever to keep my daughter at my side. But that was not how the world worked, I knew. They were both young and beautiful and had per-haps, I realized, always been a little in love with each other.

Mór was sitting beside the stream with Aengus when I returned from the wood. She had her legs tucked beneath her, but I pulled off my shoes and stockings and let my feet dangle in the water. It was still running with snowmelt from the mountains and so cold that my feet were soon numb.

"Do you love him?" When I asked the question, my voice sounded young. Younger than Mór's. Innocent as a god's.

Mór leaned her head on my shoulder. "I'm sorry, Mama. We were going to tell you. We just . . . the air smelled like honeysuckle and . . ." She trailed off. "He has a scar on his thumb." She lifted her own lovely hands. "He says it was where a bee stung him when he was very little. He says the woman who lived here first, who started keeping bees here, pulled out the stinger but was angry at him because he'd scared the bees on purpose and so they'd stung him. He hadn't known till then that they would die when they stung. That's why he hated working with his father. He hates to kill the fish." Mór continued to chatter on, telling me all that she loved about Domhnall, and as she spoke I wished that I'd felt the same for someone, had felt the love that she described. I had loved Áine in the way I'd known how, but it had not been like Mór's love for Domhnall, infinite, all-encompassing. How could it have been? She had known only part of me, the mortal woman. She had not known my immortal body, had never seen my skin dappled blue in the winter sunlight, had never seen me drape the forest in frost. She had not known my true self.

Well, not until the end.

I did not realize until close to the wedding that Mór and Domhnall wanted to be married under the sacred oak where they'd burned me.

I'd not been there since that day. I let Mór go under the watchful eye of Cara, but I'd never participated in the druidic ceremonies, the celebrations and vigils that were held there.

I was sitting with them in the tavern in the village when I found out. I rarely went there anymore, but Mór had asked me to come, and so I'd agreed to sit in the corner and listen to the druid-bard sing his lovely song. The melody was sad, and when it ended, I looked toward Mór, who I was sure would be weeping. Only she wasn't. She was leaning against Domhnall's shoulder and seemed to have barely paid attention to the music at all, whispering in his ear, and I had to blink away tears, missing her already even though she was not yet gone.

I was wiping my eyes and trying to rid myself of such foolish thinking when I heard someone ask Mór where they would be married. "The sacred oak, of course," she said before turning back toward the crowd, not once looking my way—but why would she? She had no idea what had happened to me there. The blood drained from my face as Domhnall looked at me. His eyes grew wide, and he came to his feet. "Cailleach?" His voice was low—he knew I hated when anyone paid attention to me—but he must have thought I was going to faint, because he made his way over. "Would you like to get some air?"

I nodded and took his arm, feeling like an old crone as he guided me through the crowd and out the door. I took a great gasping breath of the air, but it was too warm, too full of the summer scents of roses and the tall golden grain, to bring me any peace. I wished there were a snowbank I could jump into, something that would muffle my panicked breathing as I remembered the scent of burning flesh.

"Do you not approve of the oak?" Domhnall asked quietly. I looked at him in surprise. "I've never seen you there," he explained.

I'd known him for so long that sometimes I forgot he was now a man grown, wise and observant. He looked at me steadily, and for a moment I nearly told him—that *I* was the woman who had burned there. *I* was the woman who his friends, his family, had set alight. What would he say then? But, of course, I could not.

"I saw a woman burn once," I said instead. "Before I lived here. It was under a sacred oak."

I looked around the village as I spoke, not wanting to meet Domhnall's eyes. The long road had houses divided on either side, farmed fields spreading out beside them. On one end of the road was the sea, and the other end continued deeper into the heart of the country. I'd never gone down that road, never cared to see what lay at the other end. Sometimes I wondered if that was where I would have gone in this life, had I let the village burn.

"She had done something terrible," I said quietly. "So they decided she needed to be punished."

"Did you know her?" Domhnall said, and I nodded but didn't speak. He sighed and looked at my hut in the distance. "They burned a woman I knew here, once, too. She was my friend." He looked back toward the pub. "I'll ask Mór if we can get married on the hill instead. Near the bees."

Danu came the night before the wedding and stood in the garden with her eyes closed. Even I could admit it was beautiful this late in the summer, with all the flowers blooming and the leaves green— but when Danu opened her eyes, the garden changed into one fit for a god. The roses were three times their usual size, petals softer than silk. The grass under my feet was short but thick, like standing on a deep, soft carpet. There were waist-high lilies and an arch of vines that had grown braided together.

"It's too much, Danu. It's not natural."

Danu shook her head. "Nonsense. This is my grandchild. She shall have a wedding fit for Tara."

I pointed at the glowing golden lights that twirled in the air. "How will you make them all forget those?"

Danu laughed. "Darling, you've forgotten, I think, what it is to be a god. Making these villagers forget such a thing is no more difficult for me than a wave of my hand."

Her words stung, but she was right, of course. Gods could do anything. Well. Danu, at least, could.

"All they will remember is that it was beautiful," Danu continued. "They will remember Mór's wedding for generations, I think."

My heart swelled at the thought that I would be there, over those generations—that I would hear of this day again and again. I was becoming part of the history of this town, I realized.

I barely saw Mór the next day; she was so busy running in and out of the hut laughing with a group of her friends—women who, it seemed to me, had been children only yesterday. Finally, though, when the sun began to lower in the sky, Mór returned to the hut alone so that I might help her dress. She wore a blue dress that matched her eyes, and I put hammered gold bangles around her neck and wrists and twisted her hair up into a crown around her head. "You're lovely," I told her when I'd finished the braid. We could hear the noise of the crowd outside and I'd thought she'd run to go out and join them, but she didn't. Instead, she took my hand in hers. "I love you, Mama." Her eyes swam with tears. "I don't want to leave you."

I blinked away the tears that came into my own eyes. I didn't want her to leave me either, but the hut was too small. It wasn't possible for her and Domhnall to stay here with me—and besides, we'd all built them their own little house, halfway between my hill and the village. It had just been completed and still smelled of fresh-cut wood and the beeswax I'd used to polish the floors. I'd filled it with honey and candles, but my offering had been paltry. If I had still been a goddess I could have given Mór a palace, marble halls and endless warm breezes, flowers heaped over every surface. Still, it comforted me that I didn't think my Mór would have wanted such a thing; she would be happy in her small home, with her loving husband.

"You'll be near." I smoothed a hand over her hair. "You'll see me every day. I'll need you and Domhnall to help with the bees still." I knew, though, that eventually a day—then two or three—would pass without me seeing her sweet face. She would be busy keeping house, making dinner for her husband, and she would forget to walk up the hill. One day, she would have children hanging on her skirts who needed her more than I did—and she would simply not have the time to visit.

I shook my head trying to force the thought away and smiled at her. "Come." I held my hand out to her. "It's time to go."

I stood beside my daughter as she married Domhnall, Danu just behind me. I could hear her weeping, but I saved my tears for later. I did not want to miss even one moment of looking at Mór's bright face.

After the ceremony, I kissed her and Domhnall, and then I danced with them as I had not danced since Enya's time. The music was so bright, so joyful, that I could not stop moving. I danced with Cara and Ruaidhrí, Nora, even Fachtna. We ate and laughed and the hill—my hill—glowed with light.

The guests began to trickle away only when the moon was high in the sky. Mór and Domhnall kissed me goodbye, and Mór and I held each other for a long, long time, but eventually I had to let her go, and I did, smiling, refusing to make it harder for her, as she walked down the hill with her new husband, as they went into their house and shut the door. Only then did I let my smile drop, placing a cold hand against my collarbone. I felt as though my body was going to break apart, and the only way I could keep the pieces together was by pressing down hard on my own bones, trying to remind myself that I was still whole, still there, even if my girl was gone.

I looked back over my hill. Food had been dropped and crushed underfoot, and someone had knocked over half a barrel of wine, making a muddy pool. Even Danu's garden had been damaged— petals knocked off stems, roses fallen, lilies crushed. It looked as I felt, empty and lonely, and I didn't want to have to fix it. I looked around for Danu—perhaps she might just wave her hand and make it all disappear? But at some point she had gone, and I realized that I would have to do it. Alone. Alone again. I bit my cheek but did not let myself weep.

Finally, I was so weary I had no choice but to return to the darkness and solitude of my hut. I poked at the kindling to start a fire, something I'd hated doing since I'd been burned; Mór or Domhnall usually kept the flames going, but now it would be my task alone: to blow out the candles, to bank the coals, to put the heavy latch over the door. All without Mór's chatter, her soft laughter, her quiet humming.

At last, when the fire was made, I went to feed the chickens and sit on my bench, to find what peace I could. I was about to walk back into the hut and try to go to sleep when I saw a light bobbing up the road. My heart soared—Mór. Mór had come home. But when the figure turned the corner, I saw it was Cara. Her face was pale and she looked tired. When she saw me, she began to weep. "I miss my boy." She clutched at her shawl. "My husband didn't understand. I thought you would."

I nodded, tears finally filling my own eyes, and together we walked to my door. I lit some candles and we sat together drinking wine and talked. About how the sun had bounced off Mór's bangles and blinded Fachtna, about Domhnall spilling a whole cup of wine down the white shirt that Cara had just made, and Aengus sneaking a whole fish off the table and eating it in a couple of quick bites.

We talked of small, sweet things until the sun came up and we both could go to bed without weeping.

By that fall, I knew that I would not live until the next spring.

I did not know what was wrong exactly, only knew that no matter how long I slept, I woke up each day wearier than the day before, some vital part of me draining away each time I closed my eyes. I didn't have pain, but there was a tightness in my chest, and I could not seem to get a full breath no matter how deeply I breathed in.

But this time I did not want to die.

I wanted to live.

I wanted to stay on the hill, to work with Domhnall in the hives. I wanted to talk to Cara and pet Aengus. I wanted with every beat of my heart to be with Mór, my darling girl, to laugh with her and brush her hair and bind her wounds and hold her close—to be her mother for as long as I could. I wanted, oh I wanted, to *live* as I never had before.

As the days passed and my health worsened, I became desperate. I went to see a druid, but he shook his head and said there was nothing to be done. I asked wise women in the town to give me their tonics and brews, but they didn't help. Finally, I understood that I could not stop what was coming. I knew there was only one thing left to try.

I called for Danu.

It had been a silvery-grey day, the sun veiled in gauzy clouds, but it was still warm, and the air was so heavy I found it took a great deal of effort to move. Domhnall had gone home for the evening, and I'd told him I was going in soon, but instead I'd kept working—that had been a mistake. My breath was ragged as though I'd been running, and when I could not ease it, I half collapsed onto the soft grass, feeling as breathless as a rabbit caught in a trap. A few bees flew above my head, and I watched them before calling finally for my mother.

I lay there gasping for a long, long time before she answered. She helped me sit up, and at her touch, my chest relaxed and my breath came easier. The moment she removed her hand from my arm, though, I began to struggle once more.

"Danu," I rasped.

"We promised not to interfere," Danu said slowly.

"I am not asking you to interfere with mortals." My voice was pleading. "I will not even ask you to heal me. That's not why I called you. I understand the terms of your punishment. I know that I will die soon." I began to cough, my whole body shaking, a metallic taste in the back of my throat. Finally, I managed to say, "Mór." Danu's whole face softened at her name, and a small, hard hope grew in my chest. She would do it for my daughter, if not for me. "You have watched her grow up. You have seen her kindness, her love for all. She is—"

"She reminds me of Enya," Danu interrupted me. "Some few mortals have what Enya had—what Mór has. Where other mortals are embers burning low and quiet, they are like great bonfires, turning darkness into light."

I nodded, my eyes filling, and my heart surged. I had hoped Danu would see her thus.

"That is why we must do something, Danu," I said, eager. "I have lived four lives now. More than you ever did. I have seen the worst of them—but Mór is the best." I swallowed, steeling myself. "Make her a goddess, Danu. She deserves to join us in immortality. Then we will have her with us forever. Forever and ever." I coughed then, so violently that my whole body convulsed, but even as I coughed, I dared to hope. For it would not matter if I died tomorrow or if I died a thousand more times if Danu agreed. Mór would always be there at the end, waiting for me. And Danu loved her as I did. How could she refuse?

Then I looked up into Danu's face and saw how she would answer me. My heart sank in grief; I couldn't breathe. It was as if I was standing once more at the tree line, looking upon the destruction that mortals had wrought on my sacred grove—only it was not the humans that had caused this suffering. "Danu." My voice was a scrape of pain.

"I see you have learned nothing," she said, her voice flat and angry. My cheeks flushed as though I were a child.

"What do you—"

"You misunderstand, Cailleach, as you always do. I did not send you here so that you could play with death as you once played with life. Death is a part of mortality, as is loss, suffering. We should not cause mortal death just as we should not cause immortal life." Her eyes were hard. "You must stop trying to impose your will on others."

"But Mór would want—"

Danu laughed coldly. "You do not know what Mór would want. Did you ask her?"

"I am her mother; I know what is best for her."

"You are still as selfish as you ever were," Danu said. "To deny her such a choice shows that." Danu's face was twisted, ugly, and as I looked at her I wondered how long it had been since I'd seen a true emotion from her. "We do not interfere, Cailleach—how many times must I tell you? I would have thought you learned that lesson as a child."

I ground my teeth, trying to keep my tone even, trying to keep Danu from getting angrier and disappearing in a flood of light. "I understand why changing Enya's path was not possible." I wasn't sure that was true, but I would say it anyway. I would say anything, for Mór. "But you know, we both know, Mór is different. And you have done it before. With each of the mortals you gave godhood to, you interfered." As soon as I said the words, Danu's face changed, becoming smooth as glass, all emotion gone, and though I did not know why, I realized my words had been a mistake.

"She shall remain as she is," Danu said. And then she was gone as though she had never been, leaving me alone on the ground, unable to breathe, tears running down my cheeks because I knew then that there was nothing I could do. Knew that one day my daughter, my darling girl, would die. And perhaps Danu was right, perhaps I had learned nothing, because if I were still a goddess, I would have killed thousands again, I would have burnt down cities, would have held the entire world hostage in winter, until Danu acceded to my wishes to save my girl.

But I was not a goddess and I had no power. I was only a mortal woman who could not breathe.

Since that day with Danu I had not seen her or even felt a glimmer of her in the air. I had called her many times, begging, screaming, whispering, asking her over and over to grant Mór godhood. But she never responded, gave me no indication that she'd heard—and after a month of pleading, I finally stopped. I was no different than any of the thousands who called on the gods and heard nothing but silence.

On the first cold day of the year, I stood alone in my garden, looking toward the forest. The cold air had helped me breathe better, but it had not cured me. The tightness in my chest was still there, and though I was desperate to go walk under the trees, I wasn't sure that I could make it by myself. I hadn't been expecting Mór that day—she'd told me the day before that she was helping Cara salt fish before the first snow fell—so I was surprised when I saw her crest the hill.

"Why are you just standing here, Mama?" Mór's face was creased with worry. "I was going to Cara's when I saw you. I would have thought you'd be deep in the forest already on a day like today."

I tried to smile at her, but it was weak. "I was going to walk, but I am so tired."

Mór glanced at the trees then back to me. "Shall I walk with you?" she said. "I can help Cara with the fish tomorrow." She offered me her arm, and I took it gratefully. We walked slowly though the wood, and as I shuffled along, I thought about how not so long ago I had strode through this same forest, head held high. And that had only been in my mortal body. In my immortal form, I had run through the trees faster than a deer, the world a blur of blue shadows and white snow and green fir boughs. I longed for the strength of that body even as I wanted never to stop holding my daughter's arm.

"Mama," Mór said suddenly. "Mama, I'm going to come back. I'm going to take care of you, at home."

I tried to speak, tried to protest, but I began to cough. Mór wrapped her arms around me, and as I leaned into her, I knew that I would not be the selfless mother I ought to be. I would not tell her to go home to her young husband. I *wanted* Mór home. I wanted to sit with her in our warm, little hut and hear her hum, to wake in the dark and hear her soft breaths and know I was not alone. So I just nodded and squeezed her hand as we turned back to the hill.

As the days passed and the first snow fell, I became weaker; soon, I could not even rise from my bed without help. Mór never left my side, and though I was dying, those last days were lovely. Domhnall and Cara and my few other friends visited as often as they could, but at night I had just Mór. Aengus sat between us, thumping his tail as we talked, as Mór sang for me and brought me food and drink. She stoked the fire and latched the door and blew out the candles, sleeping so close to me that I could clutch her hand for comfort when I woke gasping in the dark. As the cold grew stronger, she even left the door open to let the snow drift in, as though hoping it would revive me. It became a habit to sit by the fire with her in the evenings and stare out at the gathering darkness, at the white ground and blue ice that formed a melting border at our doorway, where it met the heat of the fire.

At first, we talked of little things, about village gossip and her life with Domhnall, but as the days passed, Mór began to ask me more difficult questions. One day, she said quietly, "Why won't Danu heal you?"

I turned toward her, and her gaze was steady on mine. With anyone else I would have laughed, would have tried to evade the question, but something in her face told me that she knew that Danu was not mortal.

"She can't," I said.

"But she's—" Mór swallowed and then she said quietly, "She's a goddess. Danu is a goddess, isn't she? And—and your mother."

I closed my eyes—my daughter was so wise, but so young. "It's part of my punishment." I hadn't meant to say the words, and I saw the way Mór's eyes widen.

"What punishment?" Mór said. "I don't understand."

I was quiet for a long time. But I did not want to die and have my own daughter know so little of me and my true life—so I began to speak.

"I was a goddess, once."

I told her what it was like to run through the woods faster than a breeze. Painted a picture of the walls of Tara reflecting the sunset: pink and green and blue and fiery red. I talked of Danu's huge cats and Lug's harp and Dagda's green beard. And I held out my arm and described my dappled skin, the streaks of indigo and periwinkle and slate and every shade of blue that shifted as I walked through the shadows of a winter night.

Enya, and what had happened in my sacred grove.

Then, who they had burned under the sacred oak.

Mór shook her head at this part. "I don't— Why would she— Áine— Why would she do that to you?"

Finally, I told her about the eternal winter.

She listened quietly, her face pale, as pale as I'd ever seen it. But it was not until I reached the part where I had returned in my fourth life, walking toward the village with a burning torch in my hand, that she backed away from me in horror. "But Mama—" Her lip trembled. "Domhnall has scars on his shoulders from that night, when a falling beam hit him. Fiadh's eyes were ruined from the smoke. Fachtna has a limp. You did that? You were going to . . . to kill them? Kill us?"

Her voice was high, thin as a child's, and the look in her eyes . . . she had never been afraid of me before. It made my hands shake. "Áine betrayed me." My voice was hoarse, too fast with panic. "I was hurt— and angry, so angry that I couldn't see past it. Until I saw you." I did not say that I was sorry. Those words were paltry, inadequate, in light of all that I'd told her. In light of all that I'd done. I raised a hand to my mouth, swallowed away the pain. "I love you." My voice was raspy, and I was barely able to get the words out for the tightness in my chest. Her eyes flicked to mine, then out into the snow, and I *knew*, knew before she rushed from the hut, that she was leaving.

I closed my eyes to force back my tears. I could see the scene as clearly as if I were beside her: my girl running down the hill to her husband, her tears as she told my story, Domhnall's shock—then their knowledge, hard as a stone, that Áine had been right.

I was a woman who deserved to be burned.

They would come back up the hill again. And this time, my own daughter would set the torch against my flesh.

I knew I should flee, but I was so tired, so weak, and my heart was shattered. Because Mór, my Mór—the girl I loved most in the world—hated me, was afraid of me, and that—*that*—was worse than the pain that awaited me, worse than the scent of my own flesh alight.

My eyes were closed when the door opened, and I did not bother to look up.

But the room stayed silent.

A hand touched my arm, and I flinched, expecting to be thrown from my pallet, for my hands and legs to be tied together.

Instead, Mór crawled into the bed and wrapped her arms around me. She'd left the door open, and when the first rays of dawn fell into the hut, they lit my daughter's face, illuminating it so that she shone brighter than Danu under the brightest sun. Only then did I begin to weep.

"I will come back for you," I said softly. "Wait for me. I will come back." Then I looked at her and looked at her and looked at her. I would have looked at her until the moon crashed into the earth, until each star fell from the sky, but eventually, my breath caught, my eyelids fluttered, and darkness fell.

the fourth death

That death was the gentlest. And when I took my first deep breath in months, I knew I was again in Tara. The tightness in my chest was gone and I was back in my immortal body, quick and light and strong.

The walls of the palace were the palest yellow, the first light of dawn spreading across them. I heard the other gods gathering, felt Danu's presence at my shoulder, but I ignored them all. I wrapped my arms around my knees and closed my eyes, remembering Mór's face. Her blue eyes, the golden freckles sprinkled across the bridge of her nose, her long black hair, glossy as obsidian. Mór, my Mór, had come back, even after I'd told her what I'd done. Even after she'd learned the truth of me. So even though I wanted to rage at Danu because of her silence, her rejection, I swallowed all my anger and pride and slowly lifted my chin, looked into Danu's huge green eyes, then got on my knees before her.

"Please send me back to her. I don't care if she doesn't remember me. I just need to be with her. I need to see her again. Please," I begged. "I will ask you for nothing else. I just need to be with her. Until the end." I reached my hand out to Danu as I had not since I was a child, waiting for her, but she only looked at me with a deep and remorseless pity.

She did not reach back.

autumn

Listen.

Listen, and I will tell you a story.

The story of a girl who stood against the gods.

And from them gained her heart's desire.

—≪≫—

Once she learned that the gods had once been mortals, Fia did all she could to catch Danu's eye again.

The first year, Fia was kind. She rose early to build a fire in the cold mornings, when the air smelled of snow. She cleaned out the pigpen, and when she ruined her only good dress doing so, she did not complain. She soothed a fussy baby. She mended her brother's old boots, though he did not ask.

Danu did not come.

The next year, she was wise. She listened to every story-teller, every traveler who came to their little village. She walked to the walled fort two days' journey away and learned all she could about the kings that had divided the country among themselves. She asked the druids to teach her how to read the Ogham stones, and she carefully drew what she learned in the ashes of the fire, practicing the lines and dots over and over, until even the druids smiled.

Still, Danu did not come.

The next year, Fia was brave. She followed her brother into

the woods to hunt wolves, even though he'd told her to stay behind. She kissed Liam, the miller's son, and she jumped into
the river despite its strong current to save a drowning bird.

And still, Danu did not come.

On winter solstice, Fia went again to Síd in Broga, realizing what she had done wrong. Danu was a god. She needed
more than soft smiles and kind words, more than gentle arms
and learned lips.

She needed sacrifice.

Fia knelt at the top of the burial mound. The sun was just
rising, and it outlined the ice on the grass, making it shine as
brilliantly as jewels. Yet Fia paid no mind to the morning
around her; she simply pulled up her sleeve and held out her
forearm. "Great goddess Danu." She brought out one of her
brother's bronze knives. "I give all to you. Even my own blood."
She bit down hard on a stick, then dragged the knife down her
arm, marking the Ogham for sacrifice. She refused to close
her eyes, to turn away from the blood, even though the sight
of it made her hands shake. She watched it bead up, listened as
it hit the ground in a trickly stream—a soft, wet sound that
made her think of farmers when they killed pigs. The blood
began to run faster, splattering her dress, the ground around
her, but Fia refused to let herself be frightened. Danu required
the best among mortals, and the best of mortals did not feel
fear.

"Danu." She bowed her head to the sticky ground. "Mother,"
she whispered quietly, so quietly her lips barely moved.

the fifth life

A long, weary road.
　　A voice—my own—begging for my daughter.
Mór, I said over and over.

Mór.

I never found her.

the fifth death

I slapped Danu so hard she fell. She sprawled across the floor, and I was running toward her, and I wanted to burn her, wanted to tear out her heart as she had torn mine when she'd taken my daughter from me, but she raised a hand and I became still, immobile as a stone.

"I was *protecting you*," she hissed, voice rising. "I was protecting you from the pain you would feel when Mór did not know you! You should thank me." She drew back her hand, and I thought she was about to slap me, to flay the skin from my bones, but all she did was point her finger and send me back to the mortal world.

A world without my daughter in it.

winter

Listen.

Listen, and I will tell you a story.

The story of a girl who stood against the gods.

And from them gained her heart's desire.

Her brother found her lying on top of the burial mound. Her skin had turned blue with frost, her body hard as a stone. He blamed himself—for he was the one who had told her about the gods.

Listen.

No, cover your ears. Turn your face away. You would not be able to stand the sight of his grief, the sound of his tears. This is not a moment that should be witnessed—the night he wept over his sister and cursed the sky—the gods above and the gods below.

And then the goddess stepped from the trees.

"She is lovely," the goddess said. Her eyes were red and her skin shone silvery like the moon. "In death, you mortals could almost be mistaken for gods." Her voice was like the creak of an old tree in the wind, hollow like the dark mouth of a cave. "I am the goddess of death. And I will take her now."

At her words, the boy only clutched his sister closer to his own body. The goddess cocked her head, a curious glitter in *her eyes—a hunting bird, about to dive. The boy closed his eyes and did not let go. He would die with his sister.*

No. Another voice rang through the clearing like a bell.

Then, warmth.

A summer breeze that melted the ice, took the cold away. The boy opened his eyes and saw that the bare brush around him had burst into bloom. The ground under his body was suddenly soft with green grass, and the weight of his sister's body left his arms. A gust of white petals blew around the clearing like snow, obscuring his vision until he saw standing before him a goddess with spring-green eyes and long golden hair.

Holding her hand was a young girl, dressed in the purple red of a summer berry.

His heart dared to hope—and when he gazed at his sister, she smiled an immortal smile.

That of a girl who would never be hungry again.

the sixth life

It was hot when I opened my eyes, and the sun shone on me with vengeance. As I staggered to my feet, I saw that Danu had sent me back not in spring as she usually did, but in summer. High, hot summer. The grass around me was yellow green, as though it hadn't rained in some weeks. My skin was red like I'd lain in the sun for a long time before waking, and I was surprised at the malice in that. Malice was not something I usually associated with Danu, but I knew that she had done this on purpose, had wanted my skin to be hot and red and burning as punishment for my slap, for my fury.

I staggered to my feet and saw that I was in the meadow. When I'd lived here with Mór it had been small, but now it stretched far around me. I could see a smudge of trees in one direction and in the other, my hut. I walked toward the hut slowly; my body, which usually was strong and bright with each new life, was tired and aching, my muscles sore. I ignored the pain and moved toward my hill as quickly as I could, not wanting to let Danu know how I hurt. I would feel neither guilt nor sorrow. She had deserved my slap, and more, a thousand times more. Anger and despair curdled within me: she had not made Mór a goddess; she had let Mór die without me.

When I finally reached my hill, I went to the stream and took off my clothes, lying in the shallow depths so that it covered my body entirely, but the water in the stream, usually so cold, was warm as bathwater. Another trick of Danu's—sending me back in a summer too hot for any solace to be found. I closed my eyes and listened to the sound of the stream around me. This life, I would live as I had in my first. I would take care of no dogs and I would adopt no orphans and I would never be a mother again.

The summer was long and burning. I woke each morning soaked in sweat and went to bed the same. Everywhere I looked, I saw heat rippling from the land.

I felt Danu's eye on me every moment. She did not come down, but I could tell she was watching me, that she was as angry with me as I was with her. The vegetables that usually grew so well were small and yellowed before I even managed to pick them. The only thing that grew well, abundantly well, were her roses. They still covered the croft, and their scent was so strong that I could not escape them no matter where I went. One day I even tried to tear them down, yanking at their roots, but when I woke the next morning they were back, brighter and larger than they'd been before.

We were well past harvest when the heat finally broke, and I woke to a cool breeze on my face. By then, I had finally run out of food and was forced to go down to the village to trade for fish; then I went and sat in the corner of the tavern, watching the foam in my cup and paying no mind to anyone else until a voice rose above the crowd.

"Listen," it said. "Listen, and I will tell you a story. The story of a girl who stood against the gods, and from them gained her heart's desire."

I looked up and saw a man I didn't know sitting in the corner opposite mine. His hair was unusual, a tangle of gold and silver, and his skin was tanned as though he was always out in the sun. Beside him sat a mottled brown and yellow cat with a bushy tail and a sneering face. The man did not look at any one person in particular but seemed to sweep the whole listening crowd with his gaze as he spoke. His eyes were blue—not as Mór's had been, bright and dancing—but a grey blue the color of stone.

I looked back at my drink as he continued. I had little interest in the story of a hungry mortal child. Who among them wasn't hungry? Who among them didn't want? But then—then, he began to describe a place he called Síd in Broga, and I flung my head up, watching him closely as he described my grove—or the place where my grove had once stood.

After that, I listened as intently as anyone else as he spoke about the child, a girl called Fia. The man told the story with wide eyes, a broad, honest face, and I could see that the crowd around him believed every word. Believed that the girl had gained godhood.

I hated him for it. It could not be true. How dare this man claim that this girl was more worthy of godhood than Mór?

When he finished the tale, there was a long moment of silence, then someone began to clap, and soon the whole tavern was cheering and burbling, their voices tumbling over each other as they repeated the girl's name as though it were sacred. *Fia, the best of mortals*, they said. *Fia, the goddess.*

"Liar." I had meant to whisper the word, but it came out loud, and the storyteller looked at me from across the crowded room. He met my gaze, and his jaw tightened even though his smile did not diminish.

"Many have said the same." His voice was easy, careless. "But I was there. And I tell what I saw with my own eyes. I saw my sister become a god." The crowd gasped as he revealed that the girl was his sister, talking all at once, but he did not take his eyes off me.

I scoffed. I would not be taken in by the cheap trick of kinship. "And so you hold to your falsehoods? A liar and a fool."

"Why do you question my honesty?"

I thought of Mór. "Danu does not turn mortals into gods."

The man laughed, but I thought I saw a flicker of dark anger in his eyes. "You are the liar, then. Danu told us the stories herself. She was lonely and made the best of mortals into gods to rule at her side. Are you saying my Fia wasn't the best of us?"

"There are no *best* among mortals." Mór's face flashed into my mind. "Not anymore." I looked away from the man and back down at my drink. I was done fighting.

I drank for the rest of the night until the tavern was quiet and empty. Finally I was chivvied out the door and was about to make my lonely way up the hill when a spark flared, and the storyteller's face was outlined in red as he lit a pipe. There was something weary and sad about him now that he wasn't smiling. "You spoke of Danu as if you knew her." He blew out a breath of blue smoke. I would have walked past him, but he snaked out a hand and grabbed my wrist. His grip wasn't painful, but it was desperate. What pulled me to a halt was not his strength but that desperation, such a mirror of my own. "Do you?"

I looked into his face as I considered what to say. I had spent many long years lying—to strangers and to friends. To family, too. I could have easily lied to him as well. But when I looked at him, I saw . . . emptiness. The same emptiness that filled me every time I thought of Mór. He was grieving, like I was; I could almost taste it in the air between us—bitter and hollow and endless.

"Yes," I said. "I know Danu."

"And why do you think I lie?"

Why should I lie? Who would I be protecting? What was the point anymore? "Because she would not give immortality even to her own granddaughter."

The man blinked once. "You are Danu's granddaughter?"

"No." My voice was flat. "I am her daughter, the goddess of winter, Cailleach."

The man blew out another ring of smoke. "You do not look like a goddess."

"That is because my mother—Danu—took my godhead from me," I spat.

He blew out another ring of smoke. "That is quite a story," he said. "I almost believe you."

I laughed shortly at his insolence. "Unlike the tales you tell, this one is true."

He searched my eyes, my face. "Will you tell me the rest of it then?"

I cocked my head, considering. It would anger Danu if I told the story. Indeed, if she was watching now, she might stop me, or even kill me. But I no longer cared about Danu's anger. And if I told him, perhaps . . . perhaps he would speak Mór's name too. Perhaps he would tell her story as he told his sister's, and so others would know her, would mourn her. She would be remembered, and in that small way, never truly be gone. "If I share my story, you will tell it on the road. And you will tell it true, straight and even as a knife."

The man looked at me steadily, then nodded. "I will," he said simply, and I believed him, so I bade him follow me up the hill.

The moon had risen by the time we reached the top and it made everything look more beautiful than it was. It shone on the stream, even danced on the sea far below, and—I frowned—lit up the roses that still covered the hut. "I've never liked roses," he said.

"Neither do I."

"Then why are they covering your croft?"

"It's all part of the same tale." I opened the door, beckoning him in. Behind him, the cat, which I hadn't realized was following, whisked in too, giving me a hiss as it passed by.

"Yours?" I asked, moving out of the way of its claws and stoking the fire.

The man sighed. "Kiri. I found her on the road when she was a kitten. She doesn't like most people. Even me, sometimes. She'll go off for days and I'll think she's left me, but eventually she always finds me again."

"I had a dog once," I said, and I found it did not cause me any pain to say—as if with all my wounds open and bleeding, there were none left to feel. Or perhaps I had gone entirely numb. "Failinis. He wouldn't leave me alone for a moment. Not even when the wolves began to howl . . ." I trailed off, looking down at my braided hands, feeling as though all my lives were tangled up together. How could I ever hope to begin my story?

"Perhaps, before you start your story, we should learn each other's names," the man said. "I'm Fionn."

"I have told you my name already," I said. "Cailleach." And with that, I knew how to begin. "I was once a goddess. This body"—I

stretched out my fingers, my hands red and rough from work—
"never used to hold even the barest mark. I did not know pain, I
never bled. I could do—*did* do—anything I wished. I could hold
starlight in my cupped palm and let it trickle down my wrists. I
could weave the light of the moon into cloth and wear it as a gown.
I did not know about pain, death. Loss." I closed my eyes. "Then
Danu brought me among the mortals. I met Enya."

I told him about her, my friend. Holding hands, lying on the ice
together. Laughing, singing, howling. Her father's betrayal . . . her
death.

Then I shared with him something that no one else knew.

What I had done after Enya had died.

I'd gone down to the stream where we used to play together
and, though it had been high summer, I dove to the deepest part of
the water, filled my skirts with stones. I let myself sink down and
down into it. I wanted to go where Enya had gone, but I knew that
as a goddess I could not follow her.

Instead, I closed my eyes, and I slept.

When next I woke, all I saw was blue.

Not the sky, but the water. Ice.

It crusted on my eyelashes, in between my fingers and toes. A
hard cocoon of it encased me, and even when I woke, I stayed there
a long, long time. The world under the ice was silent. I could not
hear the screams of birds or the wind through the trees. I could
not hear the sound of the other gods chattering together in Tara,
and I could not smell the mortals.

"I don't know how long I was under that ice," I said. "But eventually I left and began to walk the world again."

I described my years wandering the earth, how Danu had created the druids, the feast she had commanded me to attend. Then I

told him about my sacred grove, about how the mortals had destroyed it, had built the mound he called Síd in Broga.

"I lay on top of the mound, and I let the snow fall around me until I could no longer smell them," I said.

Then I told him about my punishment. About my lives. My deaths. I talked until my voice grew hoarse, until finally I had nothing left to tell. Until I'd even given him my daughter's story, her name.

"Mór." His rich voice made her name ring through the hut. Then he looked directly at me. "I will say her name. I will say it over and over until the whole land sings it. I swear I will keep telling her story, as I will keep telling my sister's." His eyes never left my face as his fingers grazed my cheek. They were long and graceful. "I am sorry," he said softly. "That the gods are so cruel. Even to their own."

I swallowed, his fingers tracing a line of fire down my throat. I had not realized how much I ached to be touched. But— "Your sister," I began. "That is not her true story. Is it?"

He stopped. He was silent for a moment, dropping his gaze to his hands before looking up once more to meet mine. "I think we've had enough stories for the night." His voice was quiet.

I leaned my cheek into his palm and acquiesced. Forcing the grief back down my throat, I closed the distance between us.

I had felt Danu's eyes on me that whole summer, but once I met Fionn, I forgot about her entirely until one day near winter.

I'd been asleep, my head on Fionn's chest, when I was jolted awake by the smell of rotting roses. It was just before dawn, and Danu was standing in my little room, blinding me with her golden light. Fionn shifted and swore as he too sat up, rubbing at his eyes.

"Danu? Why are you here? Couldn't you at least *knock* before—"

Danu raised an eyebrow. "This is *my* house. I created it. I'm the one who keeps it from falling down on your head." She sounded mild, but not as angry as I'd expected after the violence of our last altercation. It was like her, though, to flit from one emotion to the next.

She might have forgotten, or let go, but I had not. "Leave," I snapped, pointing toward the door, but she ignored me, sitting down on the edge of the bed.

"Look!" She pointed up to the roof. "I know you don't like the roses so I removed them."

"They're . . . foul." I looked up at the ceiling where the flowers were putrefying.

"Well I didn't think you'd want me to just *whisk* them away. It will confuse the mortals less, if they thought some blight had just gotten to them." Danu began to hum, seeming well pleased with herself.

I fell back on my pillow. Why was she here? "It's nearly winter, the roses were already dead," I finally said, and Danu threw up her hands.

"I was trying to do something kind for you, daughter."

"You can do nothing *kind* for me, Danu, not anymore." I thought of my daughter's young, perfect face. Fionn, who'd been quiet the whole time, wrapped an arm around my waist.

Danu's face crumpled, but I did not accept her sadness, her tears. She had chosen this path. This path for both of us. All I wanted was for her to go.

"Perhaps I should see what you've done," I said, hoping if I took her outdoors, she would leave us alone.

It was an unusually warm morning for how late it was in the year. My bare feet weren't even cold as I walked out to look at my house. The green vines that had covered the roof like a little cap had turned black and slimy. Some of the vines had fallen to the ground, looking almost like carrion. The air smelled of salt and decay.

"How is *this* kind?" I waved a hand at the destruction Danu had wrought.

"I thought—" Danu's throat caught, as though she couldn't get the words out. She looked so beautiful, standing there in the rising sun, even though her eyes were bright with tears, and I hated her for it, for her loveliness, when my lovely daughter was dead and buried in the ground. "I wanted—to make amends."

For Mór? The anger rose within me again. "You can never make amends."

"You don't understand," she reached her hands out to me, pleading. "She would not have *remembered* you. It would have been too much, Cailleach. For you to have been with her, but for her not to know you. To have her reject you as her mother."

"You do not know what would have been too much for me," I hissed, the words low in my throat. "I wanted to be with her no matter the cost. You do not understand how much pain a mortal can handle."

"I'm *your* mother, Cailleach. I *know* you. Down to your very marrow." Danu's eyes were wide, almost wild. "I've known every moment of your life. From the second you began to grow in my belly to this very moment. Every time you have felt pain, so have I. Each death you have died, I have died with you. For each tear you've wept, I've cried an ocean more. And I tell you, having Mór look at you with blankness on her face would have destroyed you."

I shook my head in disgust and turned to leave her, but she grabbed my wrist.

"Did you never think about what your punishment entailed? How could she forget you, and not me? She did not know me, Cailleach. She did not look at me and know comfort or love. She saw only a goddess. Someone to fear." Tears slid down her cheeks, but I had no sympathy for her. She had still taken my choice away from me. I would have wanted it, even through the pain. I would have had her look at me blankly a thousand times if I could have been with her.

"I held her hand," Danu continued. "Domhnall had died just weeks before, and I knew . . . I knew she would not last without him. I held her hand and I told her that she was safe. That where she was going, she would see Domhnall again. But I lied, I don't know if—" Her lip trembled. She didn't know if it was true. She knew nothing of death. And she never would.

"Please leave," I said quietly.

I could not talk about Mór any longer. I did not want to picture her dying, I did not want to think about her being frightened even with Danu by her side, and I did not want to wonder if she'd called out for me, or thought that she would see me again, at the end.

Fionn was full of contradictions. When he was not telling a story, he rarely spoke. He wanted to sit in the tavern late into the night but did not want to talk to the villagers who often gathered around him. He smiled often, but no matter how broad his smile stretched, there was a heavy weight in his eyes, a deep sorrow that I recognized but could not get him to name.

Nearly every night that winter, Fionn slept in my hut, but he did not come and live with me as Áine had. In some ways, being with Áine had been easier. She had been so cheerful, so full of common sense. We had never actually discussed her coming to live with me; after Dagda's death, she simply didn't leave, and that had satisfied both of us. With Fionn, though, things were different. Sometimes he just . . . drifted away. He would be in the same room with me, looking at me, sometimes even talking, when I would suddenly realize that *he* was not truly there anymore. I tried to understand what was happening, to ask him what was wrong, but he always said that everything was fine and he was just weary or thinking up a new story. But I knew something was amiss.

When spring came, he began to pace about the hut, as restless as the green buds uncurling on the trees. I had been showing him how I introduced new swarms to my beehives when he carelessly swatted at a bee that had landed on him while he looked out over the harbor. "Fionn," I said sharply. "You just killed that bee."

Rather than apologize, Fionn just said, "It's time for me to go."

I started, staring at him. "Go? Go where?"

"I came to Daingean Uí Chúis just for a season," he said. "But I am a seanchaidhe. I walk the road and tell stories. Sometimes I stay in one place for a time, but . . ." He spread his hands and waved them in the air. "It has been too long. Daingean Uí Chúis is lovely. And you are lovely. But I cannot stay."

The thought of him leaving made my eyes fill with tears, and those tears made me angry—I had planned on having no attachments in this life, no one to lose, to grieve. Why had I allowed him into my life? When had he become so important to me? "Then leave." I turned from him. "I'm not keeping you tied to my apron string. You can go this very moment if you wish."

"Cailleach." He tried to lift my chin toward him, but I stepped out of his grasp and began to viciously tear weeds from my garden. He sighed, then ran his fingers through his hair. "On the day we met, you called me a liar," he said softly. "You were right, of course. But I would like to tell you the truth now. The truth about what happened to her. To Fia."

Fionn's Tale

Fionn took a deep breath, and then the words began to tumble out of him as though he'd been waiting a long time. "The first part of the story is true. Fia was my sister, my twin. And she *was* hungry. I did find berries one day, and I thought only of her hunger when I told her about them. I did not know all those berries would cost me. Fia decided that the only thing that would cure her hunger—our hunger, was godhood—and she set out to be kind, good, wise. All the things that Danu prized."

All the things Danu claims *to prize*, I thought bitterly. Mór had all of them, every single one, and Danu had not given her godhood.

"But nothing she did worked," Fionn continued. "Danu did not turn her eye to her again. So one year, on winter solstice, Fia went back to Síd in Broga. She brought one of my sharp bronze knives and she . . . she dragged the knife down her arm, marking the Ogham for sacrifice." Fionn shuddered, then took a sharp breath. "Fia had always hated the sight of blood, but she watched it anyway and refused to let herself be afraid. She bowed her head and called to Danu, begged for the godhood her heart so desired."

I sucked in a breath, suddenly sure that Danu had just left her there, had let her bleed and bleed—

"Danu came."

I breathed out again.

"But she was angry, her eyes glittering, and even before she spoke, Fia knew to be afraid."

"'Mortals do not become gods,' the goddess proclaimed to her. 'Not anymore.' She placed her hand on Fia's cheek, but the gesture was not tender, her hand hot as a poker fresh from the fire. 'I am tired of hearing your voice, child. Do not call on me again.'" Fionn let out a long sigh. "When Fia returned later that night, she was distraught and told me the whole story. And we agreed"—Fionn's hands were fisted together—"we agreed that she would give it up. That it was too dangerous to continue her quest for godhood. I even said that I would travel the roads with her, that I would become a seanchaidhe as she wished, if only . . ." He trailed off, and I wanted to reach out and hold him. But his body was stiff, as though it were costing him all he had to tell this story, and I thought that if I touched him, he might fall apart.

"She pushed me to go east, and I agreed. With every step she seemed to become lighter, more joyous, and I was convinced it had worked—I had won her smile back. We arrived at a tavern after days of walking, and as I went to ask for lodging, I overheard her speaking to someone, asking where she might find the place that Danu was rumored to have been born when she was a mortal herself. It was then I realized that she'd tricked me, that her quest for godhood was not over, but in fact had begun anew." Fionn put a hand over his face. "It sounds so foolish now, how could I not see the truth? But I was young, and I loved her with all my heart. I wanted to believe that I had brought her back from the darkness.

"'Why isn't this enough?' I demanded when I confronted her, voice an ache in my throat. I gestured at the fields stretching green and gold around us, at the twinkling lights of the little village we could see in the distance.

"'It *can't* be enough,' Fia said. 'Fionn, don't you understand? It can't be.'

"'I will make certain you never want for anything. I promise.' I held out my hand and looked at her, sure that she would take it. My sister. My twin. My heart.

"Fia backed away. 'You cannot make that promise.' She shook her head. 'Only a god can. And you are not a god.'"

I could picture her so clearly, though Fionn had never described her, could picture her thin, sharp face, her golden hair clouding around her like a halo.

"'Neither are you,' I pled with her.

"'But I will be.' Fia lifted her chin as she told me this. 'With or without you, Fionn. I will become a god. And I will make sure'— she swept her arm as though she were encompassing all the world in her gesture—'I will make sure no one is ever hungry again.'"

Fionn sniffed, wiped at his eyes. "I refused to go with her. Said it was too dangerous, and we parted ways." He reached his hands toward me, as though pleading with me to understand. "I thought she would come back eventually, and so when I went to Síd in Broga on one cold winter's day, I did so only to feel close to her again. I did not expect to find her body lying there, among the other treasure and sacrifices that the jealous gods demanded."

the sixth life

"She had carved 'sacrifice' on her own chest," Fionn said after a long, long time. "But this time . . ."

"This time, Danu did not come." I wiped a tear from Fionn's cheek with my own shaking hand. "I'm so sorry," I whispered. "Perhaps if I had not sent that winter . . . perhaps there never would have been such hunger, even generations later. Perhaps Fia would not have been so endlessly hungry. Perhaps all of this could have been prevented."

Fionn wrapped his arms around me, hushing me. "I know what it is, Cailleach, to do something you regret. To move through the world even as endless, crushing guilt piles on you like stones."

We were quiet for a long moment. Then I asked him, "Are you not frightened of Danu? Do you not worry that she will grow angry at the lie of Fia's godhood?"

Fionn shrugged. "I do not fear death. What more could Danu do to me? Besides, all storytellers lie. We weave together pieces of stories we hear on the road, and we add to them: the laugh of a red-haired woman, an old man's croaking voice, the way the lad on the road sang softly to his cow. All stories are lies, and all stories are

truth. And Fia . . . this is all I can give her. It is not godhood. But it
is a kind of immortality."

Fionn left later that day. He kissed me, promising to return the next
winter, and I watched as his form grew smaller and smaller until he
disappeared on the horizon. I scoured a pot, filled a dish with honey
and water to give to my bees, swept the floor, and kneaded the
dough I'd set up earlier, all without a thought for the work. I was
thinking instead of Fionn and Fia. Had she kept traveling the roads
and found nothing, then returned to Síd in Broga? Or had Fionn's
rejection sent her fleeing immediately back to the place she felt
most connected to the gods? Had she thought, even at the very
end, that Danu would still come?

I lay on my pallet that night but could not sleep. Every time I
closed my eyes, I could see her as clearly as I had during Fionn's
story. I could see her huge, desperate eyes. *Hungry eyes* . . . But how
could I know what she looked like? I had never seen her. Never
met her before. I had not been near Síd in Broga since . . . since . . .

Since my fifth life . . .

My eyes flew open, and I got up, feeling that I was finally tugging on the right thread in a tapestry, the thread that would finally
unravel the whole thing. I paced the house endlessly before going
outside. I was in my thin shift and shivering, but I didn't care, because as I looked out over the hills stretching eastward, I began to
remember . . .

I had walked the roads, half-mad, calling my daughter's name. I
had been desperate to find her, to find my Mór, and when I did not

find her in Daingean Uí Chúis I had finally taken the road out of town. I had walked only where my feet took me, until finally, they brought me east, toward my sacred grove—the place that mortals now called Síd in Broga. I do not know why my thoughts had turned toward it, perhaps in my madness I believed that returning to the place I had once loved above all else would bring her to me. It hadn't, of course, had been nothing more than the burial mound I'd once found there, and I had left it, cursing the ground, until I finally stumbled into a tavern in a nearby town to drink myself into oblivion.

A tavern, where I had met Fia.

Now I was sure.

But what had I said to her? I could not remember.

Over the next days, as winter drew closer, I could think of nothing else. A tightness wound around my chest. What if *I* was the villain in Fionn's story? What if the girl had told me her tale, and in my madness, I had hurt her for trying to claim what Mór had not received? What if I had taken a knife in my hand and brought it down against the girl's chest? What if all those times he had held me close, he had been holding his sister's murderer?

The not-knowing was unbearable. So one day, after the cold had drawn in, after I had gathered my honey and made my candles, I pulled my cloak around myself and set off on the road east, toward Síd in Broga and the answers I sought.

The road was long and cold, but I was able to make my way there well enough by following the stars. After all, Síd in Broga was close to Tara, and I knew the stars above its sky as well as I knew Danu's own face.

I couldn't see Tara, of course, not anymore—that was reserved for the gods—but I could *feel* when I drew close to it as any mortal would because of how wary my body grew, how tightly coiled. Hair rose on the back of my neck and my heart raced like that of a rabbit that knows it is about to be spotted by a hawk. I was surprised by my body's reaction, had supposed that when I came close to Tara I would feel excitement, perhaps even joy, at the thought of being near the place I had once called home. But even though I remembered how lovely Tara was, how it looked when the walls shone with the sunset, the ease of feasts that appeared with a wave of the hand, and beds piled high with fat, soft cushions, I could not bring myself to think of it with anything but fear. There sat Danu, with her power to shape the word; Morrígan, with her sharp weapons and sharper smile; Manannán, with their power to bring up storms from the depths and swallow mortals whole. They—Danu, Dagda, Morrígan, Manannán, Lug—were the gods, the Tuatha Dé Danann. I was only a woman and had been one so long that my own immortal days felt nearly lost to memory. I could have stood there and tried to fight the teeth-rattling terror that gripped me, but instead I turned resolutely away. What did it matter if I feared the gods now, or if they saw I did? I was not here for them; I was here for Fionn and Fia.

I walked even as night fell and the stars rose. While the ground around Tara might have frightened me, the woods I roamed were so familiar and comforting that I closed my eyes, letting my mind fill with the sounds and scents I had loved for so long. I could smell pine and fir and a cold wind that betokened snow, and I could hear squirrels running and mice scampering, even a wolf howling, long and high.

Then snow began to fall and the wood grew quiet, until all I could hear were my own crackling steps. Though I was cold and growing colder, I kept going, stalwart, until I saw Síd in Broga rise ahead of me, covered in a blanket of white.

I climbed the slope slowly until I stood atop it, looking out at the cleared land. It had been an eternity since I'd stood here, and still it seemed as though it had been no more than a heartbeat. Somewhere deep inside me was that endless grief, but it was different now, mixed up with other aches: the loss of Failinis, Áine's betrayal, and my Mór. Mór and Fia and Enya, bright, brave girls who were all dead now.

Like them, I would be brave.

I bowed my head and closed my eyes and pictured Fia's face. I knelt where she must have, pressed my hands against the ground gone cold, and pictured her wide hungry eyes. I braced myself to remember—and then, with a reeling gasp, I did.

The night came back in flashes.

I was sitting in the tavern, mad and grieving. I had not found Mór at Síd in Broga and I'd known then that it was pointless to look for her. She was dead and buried and her children were dead and buried and I would never see her sweet face again, and I was desolate, inconsolable, furious—and I wanted to scream at Danu, but she no longer listened to me. And so, when the bard in the tavern that night told a story about Danu, extolling her virtues, her kindness, and love for mortals, I snarled, "You want to know the truth of the gods?"

No one listened to me, of course. They could tell I was mad.

And then, dark and hungry eyes.

Fia, who had come in the door in search of food for her long journey ahead.

She heard me, and she said, "Yes. I want to know. I'm Fia. Tell me."

I remember trying to study her, being unable to focus on her face, just

those eyes and that ring of golden hair. I remember demanding more ale.
I remember saying, "You've heard the stories all mortals have. About
Danu. The great mother goddess." My voice was cold and biting. "From
her tears, the seas were filled, and from her blood, the land was given
crops and flowers and all manner of trees. She shaped the hills and val-
leys after her perfect breasts, after her rounded hips. But still she was
lonely. Still she searched for more like her. Other gods. But she could not
find them. She was alone. So she created a family. Other gods, created
from mortals she brought forth: Dagda and Morrígan, Manannán, Lug."

"Cailleach." Fia leaned toward me, and I gave a hard, angry laugh.

"No," I said. "No, she did not create Cailleach. She gave birth to
her. Cailleach was the only god who had never experienced mortality.
The only god who did not understand death, pain." My teeth were grit-
ted. "Perhaps if she had created me as she did the others all that hap-
pened would not—"

"You?"

I took a long drink from my glass, beer spilling down my neck as I
nodded. "I was Danu's child. Her own daughter. And then one day I
had a daughter, and when I asked her, begged her, to give her own
grandchild godhood, Danu said no. She was angry that I'd asked for
such a thing. Angry. And I do not understand why she would be angry
that I asked for immortality for my own child." I was shaking my head
vigorously. "She said no, and I do not understand, I do not under-
stand!" I slammed my hands on the table and my drink spilled, but I
paid it no mind. "You know what I think?" I seethed. "I think she can't.
I think she's a liar. I think she's not as powerful as she claims, and she is
terrified of what would happen if mortals found out, if the other gods
found out. Because why should they worship her, then?"

I was raving. I was desperate, and I blamed Danu. I did not
truly think what I said was true. But the girl believed me. I had

seen it in the way her eyes widened, in the paleness of her skin and her trembling hands as she turned and fled.

And now, though I had not seen it myself, I could picture what had happened to Fia next.

She must have gone back to Síd in Broga, where it had all started. She must have knelt and traced the floor where she had once spilled her own blood, and then she carved the marks in her chest while she called Danu's name.

The goddess had appeared before her, voice ringing with anger. "I told you not to call on me again."

the sixth life

When I called Danu's name now, I knew that she would come, just as Fia had known.

She stepped out of the whirling snow, and when she saw where we were, she paled. She had thought that I had called her to my house on the hill. She obviously had not been watching me, had not seen me make the journey to Síd in Broga.

"Why are you——" she said, but I cut her off.

"Did you kill her? Did you kill that mortal girl, Fia?"

Danu pursed her lips. She was in her usual mortal form, but when I asked the question, I saw a glimpse of the goddess she was: long, golden hair, eyes so green and sharp that a glance could tear my skin to ribbons. "No."

I stared at her in disbelief; the lie was glaring. "Why would you kill a young girl? One you gave a feast to? One you talked to?"

"*I* didn't kill her." Danu looked directly at me. "You did."

I gaped at her. "How can you possibly put her death on me?"

"You told her secrets. Secrets not meant for their ears. As soon as you told the girl, her life was in *your* hands."

"What secret?" I cried. "I was . . . crazed! I barely remember

what I said. To be a secret, I would have needed to know it was—"
And I realized, then, what she had admitted. What she had meant.
I swallowed. "It was a *lie*."

I thought of the tapestry Dagda had woven depicting all the stories I'd heard, all the stories the mortals had been told.

The ones that *Danu* had told us.

About how she had found some secret magic that had given her
godhood. About how she had used that secret magic to turn other
mortals into gods like she was. It was her greatest feat. It was one
of the stories the mortals loved the most. I stared at her, and I realized the truth with total, gripping clarity. "You don't *know* how the
gods came to be," I said slowly.

Danu did not say anything, not yet. She only looked at me. And
there was anger in her eyes, dark and deep, but I saw something
else too—*relief*. And as I watched, her body seemed to release, to
loosen. And then she began. "You've heard how the great goddess
Danu brought spring to the world. How she cared for the mortals
under her charge. You've heard how lonely she was." Danu's eyes
filled with tears. "Let me tell you the rest."

After Danu built her palace in Tara, she showed it to the mortals. Not all of them, only a few men and women, the best: kind,
curious, brave storytellers and believers. The women she would
send away with gifts: flowers and furs and richly dyed cloth. The
men she would ask to stay. For a day, a week, a year. Eventually,
though, all of them grew tired of the splendor of her halls. Eventually, they all wanted to return to their mortal lives and comforts.
Their families. Danu did not object; she knew what it was to be
lonely—and besides, she was sure that one day, one of those men
would leave her with the one thing she wanted most: a child. She
never lost hope. Even as the years passed and the men she'd once

been with grew grey and withered, she believed that each new mortal would be the one.

Yet even though her name spread across the world, even though the voices of mortals were always with her, she was still a god alone. Apart. And Danu began to wonder if perhaps gods did not have children in the way that mortals did. Perhaps she was meant to create gods from mortals, as she herself had been created.

So she turned again to mortals. First, she sought out the gentlest, those who would pause their labors to lift a baby bird back into a nest, who avoided treading on green shoots in spring and called her name not for themselves but for others. She called them to Tara. She convinced herself these mortals would become her children, her godkin.

The first was a soft, elderly man called Cairbre who had no family of his own but rocked the babes in his village as tenderly as any mother, weeping when they wept. The second was a tall woman called Gráinne whose face was always set and stern but who shared her pot with any who were hungry, friends and enemies alike. The last was a woman called Bláth, who was short and slight and had a round face covered in golden freckles. She was gentle with all, with children and madmen and bees and the flowers, and so the goddess loved her best.

She told each of them why she'd called them, and they smiled—even Gráinne—so brightly it was as though they'd been touched by the setting sun. *Yes*, they said. *Yes, make us like you. Make us gods.*

So, Danu reached a hand toward Cairbre, palm open, and beckoned. She thought that, as with the rest of what she did, she only had to *want* it. *Come*, she invited. *Come, and be made new.*

He stepped forward, basking in her light. He was still smiling, even as his skin began to turn grey, even as he took another step, when his body began to disintegrate. He reached for Danu, his out-stretched hand meeting hers, and at that slight graze the mortal Cairbre blew away in the breeze. Danu gasped and turned toward the other two. Their eyes were still filled with awe even as their mouths stretched open in screams. Danu rushed toward them, arms out. "No," she cried. "No, please, do not run. Cairbre must not have been worthy. But you are, my friends. You are." Gráinne stumbled back, but Bláth, lovely Bláth, stood her ground, her eyes wide, but trusting as a child's. She looked at Danu thus until her skin, too, paled to dust and fell away.

Danu spent that night and many after it weeping. What had she done wrong? She had gathered the gentlest mortals, those most like her.

But perhaps she had not understood, exactly, what made a person worthy.

So she would try again. She would learn. She would find better mortals, the best.

And she did.

She found the kindest, those who fed the poor their own dinner and refused to lift a sword against another.

She found the bravest, those who jumped into battle ready to defend their king, their kin—those who stared down a snarling wolf about to attack a child.

She found the curious, those who wanted to unlock the inner workings of the world, who bound up wounds and worked long hours to create potions that would heal those around them.

She found the believers, those who spent their hours praying to the stars, to the moon, to her.

She found the storytellers, those who looked at a cloud and saw a bird, a flower, a tree, those who gathered the village around them and told them about great and terrible deeds that had been done before.

But no matter which mortals she gathered, no matter which ones she reached toward, they all met the same fate. Their flesh could not contain the power of her godhood. She tried to hold them, to save them by pressing them against her own immortal flesh, but they crumbled to dust in her arms.

Each and every one.

Until Tara was covered in a film of grey ash.

"Finally, she stopped trying." Danu took in a deep, shuddering breath. She held her hands up to me, as if in penance. "The other gods, they thought I created them. But they just came to Tara one day. Remembering, as I did, some kind of mortality. They were confused. Afraid. I did not want them to fear me; I did not want to be left alone again. And they were *thanking* me. So I told them . . . I told them only what they seemed to think themselves. That *I* had brought them to Tara. That I had given them godhood. It was a small lie. I didn't think it would matter. I just—it was good to be needed, to be turned to, to be loved, again. And then"—Danu looked down—"too much time had passed, for the truth."

I didn't think it would matter. Of course she had not. I'd always known—nothing mattered to Danu, not truly, unless it somehow served her. Unless *she* mattered. I thought of the bodies, so many of them, turned to ash; it was clear she did not mourn them. They would only have *mattered* if she'd succeeded. As it was, they were only playthings. Experiments gone wrong. Less than her, insects, nothing more.

"Why did you kill the girl?" I finally asked.

Danu's eyes were wild. "She was trying to hunt down the old

stories. She was desperate to become a god. And when you told her . . . no matter why or what you believed . . . well. She could have discovered the limits of my powers. My greatest secret. So I couldn't let her live."

"But you punished me." My teeth were gritted, though my voice remained steady. "You sent me to live among them because I killed them, because you wanted me to learn a lesson—but you have done worse, for eons. Tara is built on their bodies. Even now, Fia had to pay for your lies. How could you punish me? And you were mortal once, you *did* know better. You are nothing more than—"

Danu's voice crashed against mine, a wave battering at the shore. "I was *chosen*. I was righteous among them. I was kind, good. They—whoever it was who chose me—knew I would protect mortals."

Sharp fury crackled along my spine, and finally the rage in me snapped. "You don't remember!" I shouted. "You have no idea how you became immortal. How you became a god. You could have drunk from a stream and been transformed. You could have been attacked by a wild animal or fallen down a dark well, or—"

"How *dare* you question me!" Danu's eyes began to glow with anger. "I loved my neighbors. I cared for the poor. I gave all. And I was given all as a reward."

"You don't remember your own mother's name," I scoffed. "You do not know why you were chosen and not others. It could have been a mistake. All of you could have been a mistake. I am the only one among you who was *born* a god. All of you were *made*."

Danu laughed, a wrenching, horrifying sound. "Oh, Cailleach, my love. You were *made* too. You might have a goddess for a mother, but your father was as mortal as any."

I froze, my hands trembling. "What did you say?" The world was spinning under my feet. I had a father? A *mortal*?

"He stayed with me only one night, leaving me with a child growing in my belly. I do not know why it worked with him, and not with the others." She placed her hand on her stomach, her face both tender and angry. "I thought for a while that you might be a mortal too. That you might experience the life that I never did. One that ended in death." She looked around at the bare mound we stood on. "It was here that your skin first turned blue. Here that I realized that you were one of us, a god who would never die, never know true pain or fear—and I could not explain your presence, your powers, any more than I could the others."

I could not breathe. "Why would you not tell me that I had a mortal father?" My voice rasped. "What if—what if I'd wanted to meet him?"

Danu met my gaze with her own, sharp and defiant. "Why do you think I brought you to Mooghaun?"

"But I didn't know any men there, only Sorcha and Enya and—and—" *Cormac.* Danu looked away from me, and suddenly I knew with a sickening twist in my stomach. "Cormac was my father?" I whispered. "But Sorcha—you were friends—"

Danu waved her hand. "Don't be foolish. He was a man. He only wanted what all men wanted. And Sorcha never knew."

"But you told me that he was good, that he was the best among mortals—and he was with you—all while he had a wife living. And then he married off Enya when he knew that she didn't—and Enya. Enya." I whispered the words. "Enya was my sister."

Danu looked at me then with pity. "She was a mortal. She wasn't your sister. Not truly."

I began to cry, the broken, choking sob of a child. "I begged you to stop the marriage, to take the babe away. But you refused, you said we could not *interfere* with mortal lives. You let her die. She was my *sister*. You could have swayed Cormac. You knew I loved her, and still you let her die. Do you not even have so little power as that? To stop the death of a mortal? Are you truly so weak?"

Vines exploded around me, yanking and twisting me so that I hung suspended in the sky like a star, the wind howling in my ears, hail slashing at my face. Danu had torn away her mortal skin in a flash of light. The goddess before me could have drowned the world in a deep green pool with flick of her hand, an idle thought. In the face of her naked power, I could do nothing. The vines tightened around my throat, and I began to choke. "I am the world!" Danu's voice was the howl of the winds, the fall of an avalanche, an echo from the depths of the earth. "I created the waters and the lands, and I give the mortals food and rest and succor. I have the power to end and to *begin,* and I ask for nothing in return."

"Worship," I managed to choke out. "You ask for worship."

"They *want* to worship." Danu's voice was high, pleading. "They want to believe that I am all-powerful. And what is the harm in that? And it gives me power, it ensures that I can continue to give. I have given them something to live for, to strive for." Her hands dropped to her sides and the vines at my throat loosened.

"Their worship is for *you,*" I said, my voice hoarse. "For *you,* so that you can feel as though you are *chosen.* Even though you aren't. Even though none of you are. You twist their desires, their needs, so that they are always on the brink—of starvation, plague, war, hardship. You *need* them starving so that they turn to you. Why? Isn't the power you have enough? The wind comes at your bidding, and the sun, and the flowers. The lights in the sky dance at your wish. You can call feasts from the air and bring butterflies to your shoulder in the midst of a blizzard. You live a life of endless pleasure. Why is that not enough?"

As Danu looked at me, her face changed. Half became the broad, red-cheeked woman I recognized as my mother, the one who had sent light through the air for Mór to chase. The other half was the goddess—endless, immutable—the one who had killed a girl who caught her in a lie.

"The gods do not explain themselves to mortals," she said finally, voice ringing through the air before I was thrown to the ground, left alone in the cold winter night.

the sixth life

I stayed there sprawled in the snow like I had so long ago, and I thought about power.

As a god, I would not have been able to die. I would have lain there and let the snow pile up until it choked the world around me. What did it matter if the world ended in my grief and pain? I would have lived. I had not cared; I had *wanted* them to die.

Danu could have saved Enya. Perhaps not from death, I understood that now—but at least from having to live a life she did not want. Yet Danu had not done it. Just as she had not stopped the famine that had brought Fia to this mound. Each time she'd had the choice—to tell the truth or save herself—and each time, she'd chosen herself. I grimaced, disgusted at the thought, but knew I had done the same as a goddess.

It was an endless, selfish power we gods had—power that we used on a whim, granting or refusing prayers according to our own desires. What had it done for humankind to know the gods lived? Only given them false hope.

I did not want the power, the immortality, anymore. I did not want the ice in my fingertips or the breath of all the cold winds on my lips. I did not want to look down and see my skin turn blue. I wanted only to return home, to my croft on the hill—to bring my bees honey water, eat bread that I had made with my own hands, and lie in bed with Fionn and listen to his heart beat. I wanted no more of godhood: I could see now, the cost would not be worth it.

And *perhaps*—I had a sudden rush of hope, as though the sun had just shone on the dark recesses of my mind—perhaps I did not *have* to ever get it back.

My skin tingled with relief as the realization pierced me deeper and harder than ice. I would live this life with its mortal pains— pains I felt even now, in the coldness of my hands, my numb ears and frozen toes, my shivering body. I would let time pass too slow and too fast; I would never have enough of it. But I would toil with my hands and find meaning and home and love.

I was mortal, and I would bargain with Danu, ask her to let me remain so. In exchange—and the thought came with only the barest pinch—I would keep her damning lies. And if I died as a mortal, she would not have to fear that I would give away her secret; the worship she so desired could go on and on and on. I could die and I could join those I loved. Failinis, Dagda, Siobhan, Enya.

Mór.

I began to cry at the thought, at the relief of it, because at the end of this life, no matter how long or short it was, I would hold her again.

the sixth life

When I finally saw the road that led back to Daingean Uí Chúis, the little village on the shore of the sea, I wept. It was *my* village, my home. And I would not leave it again.

The storm had come here too, and it took me a long time to pick my way through the ice and drifts back up the hill to my hut. How many times in my six lives I had walked up this hill? How often had I hated seeing the hut sitting there, round and stone and filled with the objects that made up my mortality: the old black cauldron, the jars of honey, the straw-filled pallet.

The snow slowed, becoming lazy and gentle, and before long I could see my hut. Blue smoke blew out of its chimney, light shone from its windows. I slowed. Who was there? Then the door opened, and I saw, outlined against the golden light, Fionn. Fionn, back again.

And my heart leaped with joy and I ran toward him, letting him wrap his arms around me and swing me into the air until we were both laughing and crying.

I lay with him in bed long into the night, not wanting to sleep, only to look at him.

"Where did you go?" he whispered, long after I thought he'd fallen asleep. "I came back, and the hut was dark and dusty. It looked like you had been gone for weeks."

I looked away from him, pressed my face into the pillow. I wanted to tell him what I had learned about Fia, but I was afraid of what Danu would do if I did. The anger that I'd held against Danu for so long had dissipated with my choice to remain mortal. She had not done what I'd asked, but being certain now that I would see Mór—would see all those I loved—again at the end had eased the hard knot in my heart. I could not predict Danu's own feelings, though. She had seemed half-mad there on the mound. Angry and desperate and pleading all at once.

I decided it would be better to wait. Danu would forget eventually, as she always did, and then I could tell Fionn the truth.

"Do not ask me. Not yet." I could tell he wanted to press me, could see it in the taut lines of his body, but he said nothing, and my heart seemed to expand at his silence. He trusted me to tell him what I could, when I could. I was so moved, I grasped his hand, turned his face to mine. "I love you."

It was the first time I'd said I loved him, but it didn't feel strange. In some ways I felt as though I'd always known him. Always loved him.

He twined a strand of my silver hair around his finger. "Would you have loved me when you were a god?"

"No," I responded quickly. Fionn laughed and I did too, blushing a little. "I am sorry. Sometimes I still forget that mortals do not always want the truth to the questions they ask." I sighed. "I only meant that I did not love *anyone*. I was not *with* anyone, before I became a mortal. As a god . . . I was enough. Sufficient. Unto myself."

"Then I am glad that I did not meet you as a god." Fionn traced a finger down the side of my face. "I'm glad that you are a mortal woman."

"I am too." The truth of it almost sent me reeling. I thought back to when I had cursed the gods for making me thus. "If your sister had found a way to become a god, would you have done it? Would you have exchanged your life, your death, for godhood?"

"No." Fionn pushed himself up on one elbow and looked at my face. "No, I would not." He ran his thumb along my lips again. His skin tasted of dust from the road. "I do not want to go on forever. I do not want to forget the strength in my arms as I cut down a tree, the smell of the fresh-cut wood, the little pains of hands covered in splinters and cuts. I think life as a god would become dull." He kissed my knuckles and gave me a small smile. "It is strange to say to such things to an *actual* immortal being. But perhaps if I had been born a god, I would think the same as you."

"No," I said. "No, eventually you would realize you are right."

Fionn continued to walk the roads in spring and summer and came back to me each fall. I worked with my bees, and I got a new dog, a playful puppy I called Blue.

Danu did not visit, and I did not call for her.

I was happy.

I stopped counting the years, but many passed, and with each one, I wished only to continue this life for as long as I could.

Fionn returned before Samhain most years, but I was not alarmed when he missed one. The roads were sometimes dangerous, and I knew that he would be making his way toward me as fast as he could. But one year, after several weeks had passed, I began to grow nervous, always looking toward the road, keeping the door open so that I might hear any movement. I even missed Kiri, who I sometimes thought would outlive us all.

I woke one day to a warm breeze on my face even though it was late in the season, after harvest. The warmth of the day discomfited me, and I was anxious as I went about my work. It was odd to have a day that was like summer, but without any insects humming or green grass blazing over the hill, and it filled me with a sense of foreboding. To ease my anxiety, I tried to think of Mór instead, how she had loved days like these, called them a gift to help ease us into the colder season.

I was still picturing her that evening and made her favorite stew. My hands were flying, chopping onions and carrots as I remembered the first time I'd made it for her, when she was just five—how she'd eaten a whole bowl, then sat back, stroking her rounded stomach as though she were an old man, telling me that her body was "all warm, Mama!" I had laughed and tickled her and—

"Cailleach, my love."

I spun around, and as I turned, I gouged the knife deeply into the meaty part of my palm, between my thumb and finger. "Fionn!" I was so relieved to see him that my knees went weak.

He was smiling when I turned around, but then his face fell. "Ah, Cailleach, what have you done to yourself?" He pulled my hand to his and looked at the deep gash there.

"It's your fault," I said, though the relief at seeing him made me smile. "You startled me! But it's no matter." I hurriedly took a spare cloth and wrapped it around my hand, turning to him. "You're back."

He put his arms around me, and I leaned into him, inhaling the scents of the road that he always brought back with him: smoke and grass from the fields he sometimes slept in, and a deep, earthy smell, like just-turned soil after rain. I would have stayed there longer had Kiri not jumped up onto Fionn's shoulder and given me a suspicious look. Fionn laughed and shooed her away before releasing me, looking around the hut for a long moment. He bent over the cooking pot and inhaled. "It's good to be home."

In the weeks that passed after Fionn's return, we were so busy getting ready for winter—gathering the last of the honey and wax, harvesting our garden and filling up holes in the hut's roof—that I did not pay much attention to the gash on my hand. I knew it was not getting better, noticed red streaks spreading out from it and up my arm, but I didn't have time to waste worrying about it. I could see, in the way the squirrels were hiding away nuts and how the mice were building their nests, that the winter would be bad.

When we went to bed one night, Fionn kissed my cheek then pulled back. "You're hot as a fire," he said. "Are you ill?"

"I'm fine," I said. "It's just a small thing."

I do not remember much of the next days except tossing and turning on my pallet, swimming in and out of dark dreams where I burned and burned and burned. Someone forced a bitter brew down my throat, and I choked on it, but they held me firm until I swallowed.

Still, I was *so* hot.

Finally, one night I woke to find cool air on my face. I managed to open my eyes and I saw a sky full of stars. I sighed in true pleasure, realizing that I lay on the pallet outside, and that Fionn was stretched out beside me. There were tears running down his cheeks.

"Fionn," I said hoarsely, and he jumped. He raised himself up onto his elbow and smoothed a hand over my hair.

"I didn't know what else to do." His voice shook. "You were so hot. I thought you would burn away if you were inside another moment."

"I forgot that you can die from something as small as a cut on the hand." I said this lightly, with a weak smile—but I didn't actually *believe* I was dying. I wasn't old. And I needed more time—I hadn't yet asked Danu to let me remain mortal. I'd meant to, of course, long ago, but I'd been afraid to call her at first, in case she was still angry, and then . . . then I supposed I'd forgotten. Life had been busy; I'd been needed, by the land and the villagers and Fionn. But I couldn't hold off any longer. This illness had been a lesson. I felt the fragility of my mortal body as I had not in some time. I knew it was time to tell Fionn the truth. And then I would call on Danu. Tell her that I did not want to return to godhood. Tomorrow, I promised myself. Tomorrow.

I coughed. "Do you remember, years ago? You came home to an empty house and asked where I'd gone."

He frowned, gently sweeping his hand across my brow. "Yes, Cailleach, but why do you think of it now? It can wait. You should rest, you—"

"No, Fionn." I closed my eyes, took a deep breath. "It must be now." I gathered myself. "I went back to Síd in Broga. After you left that first time. I went back because . . . because I remembered her, Fionn. I remembered Fia." I looked into his eyes, into his face which I loved so. "She sounded so familiar, when you spoke of her, but I didn't realize until you had gone—I'd met her in my fifth life. When I went looking for Mór. It was just chance, I was in the tavern in some town to the east, mourning, drunk, and she came looking for food and heard me raving about the gods. I told her . . . I told her that I thought Danu had lied." I told him the rest of the story as best I could, about how I'd confronted Danu on the burial mound, why she'd killed Fia. "I am so sorry." I was weeping by the time I finished the story. "I am so sorry that I met her. I didn't know what I was saying, didn't understand what I was doing. The fate that I had pushed her toward. But Fionn, you have to know—it was not your fault. She just . . . she was too brave. She stood against the gods. And she forgot to be afraid."

Fionn did not respond at first but wept, his eyes still on the stars. I worried that he would not turn himself to me, but when I reached a tentative hand to him, he took it. He did not reproach me, and he did not leave me. He only held me close, letting the cool night air flow around us as we cried for what we had done. For the sisters we had loved and the sisters we had lost.

the sixth death

When I woke next, I felt different. I was no longer hot, and for a moment I was relieved, thinking the fever had finally broken.

But I was cold, too cold and . . . I sat up in shock and fear, looking down at my blue skin.

I was sitting on one of Tara's cold marble floors. And I was immortal once again.

I bit my lip to keep myself from crying out, my mind swirling. This would not be the end of my time with Fionn. I would not let it be. My eyes narrowed as I heard a gale of laughter coming from the other room. They were here and had not even noticed that I had died. But no matter. I closed my blue hands into fists. I knew Danu's secrets. It was time to wield them.

When I'd first been given a mortal body, it had been confusing, clumsy, and weak, and now I felt the same way in this immortal one. As I walked through the palace, my skin shifted once more to different shades of blue with each shadow, but as I watched it transform, my gorge rose, as though I were witnessing something unnatural. The power in my body made me uneasy. It had been a long time since I'd walked the world as a god, and my stride was so powerful that when I looked back, I could see imprints of my feet in the marble. I thought of how I would tell Fionn about that, how I would describe it for him; I was sure I would return to him—I would make it so.

I was still thinking of Fionn when I reached the dining room. They were all there, eating a feast. Or perhaps it was a normal meal; I could no longer tell what they would consider abundance. I looked on everything with mortal eyes now.

At first they didn't even notice me enter the room. Then Lug looked up. He swore, dropping the small bird he'd been holding, which bounced on the floor but didn't leave greasy prints on the marble, didn't even leave an imprint of its ruby sauce.

Danu waved her hand, gesturing for one of her great cats to pick up the bird, and then her eyes met mine. Her mouth opened in an absurd O and there was an explosion of sound as they all rose to their feet and began shouting.

"How did you get here?"

"You can't kill yourself. It's impossible."

Danu waved her hand once more, and silence fell over all of them. They looked so foolish, standing there. Their bodies were simultaneously powerful and indolent, and though they had all been eating, you would not have been able to tell. Their lips did not hold a shine of grease and their fingers were clean, though they had just been dipping them into a sauce as red as blood. There were no crumbs on their table or in their beards. They looked so . . . false. As though they were playing at eating, at living. I could not help but laugh.

"How are you here?" Danu cut through my mocking. "What did you do?"

"I died, Danu." I bit the words out.

"But how?" Danu demanded. "Did you fall? Did you . . . meet a wolf in the wood?" I laughed again, and the sound was so bitter, so harsh, echoing through the hall, that Morrígan flinched and Dagda covered his ears. "But you weren't . . . you weren't ill," Danu said. "I looked in on you the other night and you were just . . . asleep, with that man in your bed." Her eyes were wide, bewildered.

I held up my hand, my perfect, whole hand. "I cut myself," I said. "I was cooking and Fionn surprised me."

Lug laughed. "A mortal cannot die from a cut. They are so clumsy they would be falling over dead every hour, every moment."

I stared at him. "They *do* die every moment."

Lug opened his mouth but then closed it again at the look on my face.

"I'm sorry," Danu finally said. "I know—"

I raised my chin. I did not want her sorrow. "I must speak with you alone, Danu."

The other gods began to protest but Danu looked at me with fear and anger in her eyes. "Leave," she said finally. "I would speak with my daughter alone."

I only spoke when they had left and the hall was empty, and I chose my words carefully.

"I wanted to thank you."

Danu's hands clenched. This was not, I knew, what she expected me to say.

"I understand why you gave me mortality," I continued. "I understand now what I never could have before—that mortals are *more* than the gods. That they experience more in a single day than we do in a lifetime. I'm—grateful to you, for this gift. For the lives that I have lived."

Something softened in Danu then, something eased, and a person who did not know her might have seen it as benevolence. I saw it for what it was: self-satisfaction. A goddess receiving what she thought was her due. This was good. I needed her to feel thus.

"Cailleach, I'm so glad to hear—"

"And"—I spoke over her—"I do not want to return here, to this unbounded decadence." The walls of the throne room were glowing with color, the feast of fat things spread out on the long table. "I want to remain a mortal, and I want to die as one."

Danu looked at the table and then back at me, her eyes wary but curious as though she truly wanted to know. "Why would you wish such a thing?" Her voice was soft as the wind through a golden field of grain. "You would never again see your skin change color." She stretched out her hand and cast shadows that brought out the blue. "You would never again walk the world or sleep in a snowbank or swim in icy seas. Why would you give up all your power?"

"I want to see my family again." My voice was almost a whisper. Danu opened her mouth to speak, but I raised my hand. I had one more request. "I want to go back to Fionn," I said. "I want to wake up in his arms and I want him to remember me."

"We promised not to interfere." Danu frowned.

"Danu." I took a step toward her, my eyes intent on hers. "I know your secret. And you know what will happen if I speak it."

At that, her eyes widened, then narrowed. "Are you threatening me, daughter?" Her voice was a hiss.

"It is not a threat." Even in the face of her ire, I stood calm. "It is just the truth. There are limits to all things. Even to your power. Even to you."

"How dare—"

"I will not fight with you again, Danu. I am here to bargain." I took a breath. "I want Fionn. I want him to remember me."

I saw the fight in her face, the frustration with the game I played with her—*my* game, for once. The rising hope in her eyes, the desire to simply sweep her hand and return to her feast, to her gods, to those who believed in the fullness of her power. And after a long moment of looking at me, fear and curiosity and anger still tangled up in her expression, she took the easy, gentle path. As I'd known she would.

She pointed a finger at me. "Return."

the seventh life

"Cailleach!"

Fionn was shouting my name when I opened my eyes. "You weren't breathing," he gasped, "you weren't breathing."

Then he pulled me close to him and the stars were above us and I was alive again, alive and in my own mortal body, and he knew me. Fionn knew me. He, a mortal man, and I, a mortal woman.

My next life. And my last.

My seventh life was long and sweet.

Fionn continued to travel the road each year, returning to me before the snow fell. I continued to keep bees and gather honey and turn golden wax into golden candles. I made friends with the villagers and held their children on my knee and watched them walk and then run and then dance, but I had none of my own. I'd had Mór, and at the end of this life, I would I hold her again.

And, for the first time, I grew not just older but truly old. My back began to ache and my eyes to cloud, my face filled with lines. Fionn's hair and beard became grey, his strong hands shook when he held a knife, and eventually he stopped walking the road. It relieved him to rest, to lay down his voice and begin working with wood, spending the last years of his life carving little animals for the children of the village.

I was so busy with our lovely life that I did not notice at first when Fionn began to cough.

One day, I found him sitting on the bench that overlooked the sea. He put his arm around my waist, leaned his head into me. "Cailleach, my love. I am dying."

My eyes blurred with a rush of tears. He had not lied to me since that day he'd told me the truth about Fia. And yet I could not, would not, believe him now. Nor could I look him in the eye. "Don't speak such nonsense."

He pulled me into his lap, and I wound my arms around him. "I will miss you, my love."

"No." My voice shook, the tears spilling from my eyes. "No, please. Don't leave me."

Fionn pressed his lips against my brow gently. "You know, more than any, that nothing can stop death." He twined his hands with mine. "You gave me back my life, Cailleach. And I hope I have given you one in return."

I buried my face in his chest and cried for a long, long time, and he let me. Held me close, kissing my hair, my temples, my eyes.

I lifted my head to look at him. "You might go before me, but I will come too, as soon as I can." I held my age-spotted hands in front of me. "I made a decision when I last stood before Danu."

Fionn frowned, removing his arm from around my waist to meet my gaze. "What do you mean? You will not die. Not really.

Eventually Danu's punishment will end, and you will become what you were—are. A goddess."

"I am not a goddess any longer, and I never will be again." My voice tremored with eagerness, with the excitement of finally telling him, of him knowing we would see each other again. "I am mortal. I realized when I confronted Danu about Fia that I could not go back to that world of indolence and power. I will not go back."

"Danu won't let you—"

"I bargained with her—I would keep her secret, I told her. If she let me die a true death. She agreed."

Fionn stood, pushing away from me. His back was bent now, and he leaned on a long wooden staff he had carved himself as he looked out onto the sea far below. "You are a coward," he said.

I reeled back as though he'd slapped me. "What?" I did not know what else to say. Fionn had never spoken to me so harshly before, and when he turned, I saw spots of color in his face.

"Cailleach, you have received what none of them did—not Enya or Mór or Fia. The chance to become a god. And not just any god—but one who understands what it is to be mortal. To live and die, and to watch those you love live and die. You are the only one who will not forget, who loves us for what we are. Who will speak for us."

"But if I become immortal again, I will never see those I love." My voice trembled. "I will never see Failinis or Enya, Mór, you."

"Cailleach, my love." He came back to me, placed his hands on my wet cheeks; I had not realized I had begun, once more, to cry. He leaned his forehead against mine. "By becoming a god again, you would honor all of them. You could do what Danu has never done, comfort and guide and protect. Give, rather than take."

"I will forget," I whispered. "You do not understand what it is to be a god. It is endless eternity. It is how Danu became the way she is. She forgot her mortality. So will I, eventually."

"You won't," Fionn said simply. My heart ached at his easy trust, his faith. "You have lived as she never lived, died as she never died. And you had us. Your friends, your family. You will remember."

"You would curse me like this? You would have me never be able to see you again, never touch you, know your embrace?"

"You will. One day." He spoke with utter conviction. He smiled gently. "My love, Danu has not *always* been. She will not *always* be. And neither will you. Eventually the Tuatha Dé Danann will pass. Eventually, you will die. And then, then we will be together again."

Fionn died two days later, clasped in my arms.

the seventh life

After Fionn's death, I was alone as I had not been in many years. I did not know what to do, so I went about life as normally as I could, keeping my bees, tending my garden, trading for fish in the village, taking the time I needed to mourn him—all the while thinking about his final words. His belief that I would remember mortals even if I became a god again. His faith that I would take care of them. Guide them. Love them.

And his certainty that one day, even the gods would end.

I thought of Danu too. I had spent much of my seventh life determined not to remember her, but now I pictured her as she had been, new-made and alone. I did not know if her other stories were true, if Danu had made the world as she claimed, but I did believe her when she spoke of her loneliness. I felt that solitude when I woke alone in my croft on the hill, all the people I had loved, gone now, taken by death before me.

Still, I was not sure what choice I would make.

One night I was on my pallet, lost in thought, thinking again of Fionn and what he had told me, when I began to drift. It was late, the fire flickering, and I blinked and suddenly there was Siobhan, the first mortal who had ever shown me kindness, standing over my bed. The words came to my lips: "I'm sorry, Siobhan, so sorry about Brigid."

Siobhan's face was hard but not unkind. "I know you are," she said. "But your sorrow will not bring her back. I thought of her every day until I died. My wee girl."

"I lost my own child; I know what it is to—"

"No." Siobhan cut me off. "Your child *lived*. You saw her walk and run and play. She married and had children and grew old. I never saw that." Tears ran down my face, but I did not contradict her. She was right. Mór had died—as all mortals do—but first, she'd had a life. Because of me, Brigid never had a chance to know such joy.

For so long I had blamed mortals for their greed, but it was I who had taken from them. "I did not understand."

"And do you now?"

I woke with tears on my cheeks.

Somehow, I knew death would come that day.

I climbed from my pallet, made porridge in my old black pot, slowly poured in the honey I had harvested with my own hands. Then I went out to my hives. This year I had not destroyed them, so I could still hear their gentle humming.

I placed the hives into a cart and brought them through the wood until I reached the little clearing where I had stumbled upon Failinis. The thought of him made me smile. Rescuing Failinis had been my first selfless act as a mortal. I bent to touch the ground where I had found him, then rested my hives against the trees. Failinis had loved the bees. He had never snapped at them or frightened them, would just follow them with his eyes, gently bump them with his nose. I hoped my bees would enjoy creating new hives in this clearing, turning it into a place full of flowers.

Thinking about Failinis gave me courage enough to lie down, to look up at the sky growing dark. I held up my hands, and in the evening light they looked blue again. I closed my eyes and let myself remember.

That first day, when I fell in the mud and it splattered wet on my cheek. Siobhan's eyes on me as she told me about the child I'd killed. A dog whimpering, struggling in the underbrush, then licking my hand, his body warm against my chest. Áine kissing me, brushing my long silver hair with her gentle hands, and then those same hands holding a burning torch against my throat, and me screaming and screaming. Then, Mór crying in fear. My daughter in my arms, and me holding her tightly, vowing to never give her up, and dancing at her wedding. My girl leaving me—then coming home, holding my hand. "I love you, Mama, I love you," she was saying. The world grey as I wandered it, looking for my daughter, and then finding Fionn—the miracle of Fionn—strong and solid in my arms, telling me a story, smelling of smoke and earth. He was saying my name.

"Cailleach," he said.

"Cailleach." Their voices were a chorus in my head.

"Cailleach." Enya reached her hand out, just as she had all those centuries ago. My first friend. My sister.

I lay there for a long, long time, remembering. So that I would not forget.

Snow began to fall.

And I called her name.

the seventh life

"You are dying." Danu's voice was soft.

I nodded.

She loomed over me for a long moment, then, to my surprise, she lay down beside me and took my hand.

"I will stay with you. Until the end."

I closed my eyes for a moment, thinking about their faces. Then I turned my head and looked at my mother. "I understand now, why you did it." It was not quite forgiveness—I could not forgive the death, destruction, the pain—but I could offer her understanding, at least. "You didn't want to be alone."

Danu's lip trembled. "I did not want to hurt them." Her voice was hoarse. "But if they discovered my secret . . ."

"You want to be needed. You want them to call on you and praise you and speak to you, to remind you that you are wanted." Her eyes were huge, brimming with tears, and in that moment, she seemed like a child to me. A child who did not have a mother and who had been frightened in the dark and so had come up with a story to protect herself. "It is dangerous," I said slowly. "To be a god afraid."

Her breath was a gasp. "You were not there, in the world that was. Before the other gods. Endless quiet. And only me."

"You are no longer alone, Danu," I said. "And this cannot go on."

We lay in silence.

"I was not born a god, as you were. You are the only one among us who wasn't fashioned by some unseen . . . creator, or force. Or accident." A tear fell down her cheek. "The more they call our names, the more I know we are not forgotten. If they keep calling on us, surely we will be allowed to stay."

"I do not want to stay." My voice trembled with the force of my desire. "I want to hold my daughter again. Don't you, Danu? Don't you want to hold Mór again?"

"What if it all ends?" Danu's voice was so quiet I would not have heard it if she hadn't been right beside me. "If they . . . they do not call on us. What if we fade?"

"Perhaps one day we will. Perhaps not. But do you truly want to continue as it has been? Bearing this cost? Do you think that is right?"

Danu's eyes were wide, frightened, but she did not answer me. Finally, I said, "I do not think you should have control over all the turnings of the world." I stood, and she followed me. "Give winter back to me."

She looked at me, uncertain. "But you said you didn't want it. You said you wanted to die as a mortal, to be—to be with your family."

The ache in my throat was sharp. Snow fell on our shoulders, settling on mine, but melting the moment it touched Danu's golden head. I swallowed the hurt again as I had so long ago in a clearing very like this one. "You will forget your sadness, eventually. You will do all you can to protect your secret." Danu opened her mouth but didn't protest. "And even I . . ." I looked for a moment into the woods. "If I take back winter I will forget too. The days are so long as a god. So unending. If I take back winter . . ." I looked into her spring-green eyes. "I would need the power over spring too, so that I could never send an unending winter again, so that I cannot lose myself. I would become two. Cailleach, the crone of winter. Brigid, the goddess of spring."

"Spring," Danu whispered. "In spring they love me with their all. In spring I feel . . . I feel as though I was given godhood because I truly *was* good. The best among them."

"Perhaps that is why you should give it up."

A tear fell down Danu's cheek, then landed on the cold ground. Where it fell, a violet blossomed.

Finally, she looked back up at me. "To make this so, I would have to take from your winter self. From *you*, Cailleach. You won't be able to endlessly walk the deep blue places of the world. You won't be able to stand against an avalanche of snow or sleep in a lake encased in ice. It would not be the same."

"I know." I took her hand. "But if I do this—if you do this— perhaps eventually, we will atone. Perhaps, when this world does end, we will be able to greet those we loved with pride. Knowing that we did all we could for them. And for the other mortals under our care."

Danu stared into my green eyes, so like her own. She traced the contours of my face. She did not say that she loved me or that she was sorry or that she wished she had been different. Instead, she reached out a hand.

I reached back.

spring

The druid is alone on the road.

As he walks, he looks for spring.

He searches for green shoots of grass and small white flowers shaped like tears. He listens for birdsong and sniffs the air hoping that the smell of snow will be replaced with that of dark earth—of growing things. It has been a long, cold winter. His robe, once golden, has not been washed in weeks and is so covered in dust and mud that it looks brown.

He peers deep into a bramble, thinking he glimpsed a purple flower, and so he does not see her when she first appears on the road.

He falls to his knees.

His head is bowed. He is afraid to look at her golden face, but she gently tips his chin up until he is looking into her eyes.

Green eyes.

"You are faithful," the goddess says quietly. "You have been faithful for so long."

"Yes, my lady," the druid says, dropping his eyes again. He wants to bend, to kiss the hem of her robes, to curl up like a mouse against the hot power that he *feels* in her fingertips—but he does not move.

The goddess trails a finger down his cheek. "I have come to tell you . . ." She gazes away, and the druid begins to shake because she looks . . . sad. What could cause a goddess such as she sorrow?

The goddess turns her face back to his. "You were looking for spring." Her smile is sad still. "It might be later than expected but . . . it will come no matter what, druid. Spring will always come. This I promise you."

The goddess leaves her hand on his face, but tilts her chin up, squares her shoulders in a gesture so *common* that the druid is surprised, because in that moment she looks like a mere mortal, a woman, finding her courage. "I have come to tell you to spread the word to your brothers. Your sisters. To the mortals. You do not have to worship us any longer."

The druid does not understand. He is old for a mortal, but he is still a man. He does not remember that there ever was a time without worship.

"Once, long ago," the goddess says, "your kind did not build altars or call our names in prayer. You did not give us the best you had or spill blood for us. We lived separately. Mortals with mortals and gods with gods. We can live this way again. You—mortals— no longer have to make us offerings for us to offer you protection. You no longer have to fear us."

"We are not afraid, my lady," the druid says, though this is not entirely true. They do fear the gods. They fear that they will not listen, and also that they will listen too closely. Hear too much.

The goddess drops her hand from his chin. He is bereft.

"We love you, my lady." The druid kisses the hard-packed dirt of the road, too frightened now to touch even her hem. "You are our mother."

The druid wishes he had not looked up, because the goddess begins to weep, and the sight is so heartbreaking that if he had a sharp stone in his hand, he would gouge out his own eyes so he might see it no longer.

"I was a mother once," the goddess says softly. "To a little girl called Mór. I wish—" The goddess cuts herself off and suddenly she is no longer crying. "No matter." Her voice is smooth as ice. "Worship as you will, but know that it is no longer required. Eventually . . . you will stop."

"Never," the druid cries. "We will never stop, Danu!" The goddess smiles, and the druid's body fills with warmth as though he has just drunk a barrel of whiskey.

"Danu," and she says the name gently. "Danu is no longer the goddess of spring. I am, and I will remain while you still have need of me. I will remain until the day you do not. Until the day you, or your children, or their children, forget. Then we will end. I will end." She closes her eyes. "And I will get to hold her, once more."

The druid blinks, and he is alone again on the road.

At his feet, a cluster of white flowers grows.

Brigid

My name changes each spring.

The biting, winter taste of it—Cailleach—becoming softer and gentler, easier for their tongues. They call me Brigid—the name Siobhan gave her daughter.

When spring comes, I am no longer a crone, shriveled and rimmed with blue, because each year, my bones crack on the day spring returns. My limbs are torn open as buds force their way from under my blue-dappled skin, where they have been waiting, waiting, waiting, to return.

ACKNOWLEDGMENTS

This is the hardest book I've ever written. Thankfully, I had two people in my corner who not only made it easier but made the book what it is today. First, my editor, Nidhi Pugalia. Thank you for pushing me, for making this book better than okay. I could literally not have done this without you.

My brilliant agent, Jim McCarthy, was with me every step of the way with encouragement and reassurance, and did not blink when I told him that I was yet again working on something new— thankfully that idea *did* eventually work out, turning into *The Winter Goddess*. Thanks for everything, Jim.

I begged my team to get Jim Tierney to work on the cover— and I'm so glad I did. I feel so lucky that he has a design vision, because in this I am sadly and terribly lacking.

Molly Aitken is one of our most prodigious talents writing today, yet she took the time to read and praise my novel. It means the world to me, and everyone needs to go read her books, which are far superior to mine. Thank you for your friendship, Molly.

Without my team at Viking Penguin, this book would not exist.

Thanks to Sara Carminati and Jennifer Tait, my copyeditor and proofreader; Chelsea Cohen, my production editor; Raven Ross and Mary Stone, my marketing team; Becca Stevenson and Rebecca Marsh, my publicity team; as well as Nick Michal, Matt Giarratano, Andrea Schulz, Kate Stark, and Brian Tart for making this book shine.

My family is large and ambitious and yet they always have time to support me no matter what. Some of them might not *read* all my books . . . but I'm sure they'll get to them "eventually." Even so, they are my favorite people in the world.

My in-laws actually read my books. So, you know. They might be better than my actual family.

Love and thanks to Katie, Alex, Jarin, and Inna.

Pippin makes me play hide-and-seek with him, which makes me smile and laugh even on the worst days. Thank you, Snap.

Tyler showed me how to love winter. Without him, this book would not have been possible. Thankfully, with him, everything seems possible.